PINING FOR YOU

JASPER FALLS

LYDIA MICHAELS

BAILEY BROWN PUBLISHING

PINING FOR YOU

A Jasper Falls Novel

Special Holiday Edition
With Bonus Recipe

PINING FOR YOU

Jasper Falls Book One

Written by Lydia Michaels

ISBN Print: 978-1-7371244-5-0
ISBN eBook: 978-1-7371244-4-3

Published by Bailey Brown Publishing
Cover Design by Lydia Michaels
Edited by Theresa Kohler; Oxford Comma Editing
Copy Edit by Loren Brake

© Lydia Michaels Books 2021

For Lauren Campbell, because you've been with me from the start.

1

Five Weeks until Christmas

Children screamed as a pattering of footfalls rattled the rafters hard enough to shake the dust on the windowsills. Skylar's gaze latched onto a trembling fleck of dirt as it descended from the open wood cupboards where the serving dishes sat. The dust drifted like snow right into Great Aunt Colleen's coffee.

That wasn't the only thing hiding in Aunt Col's mug. Chances were, that porcelain cup held an Irish coffee strong enough to strip the paint off a car.

Skylar breathed in the mayhem and grinned.

Homeyness, especially around the holidays, hid in the chaos. They weren't the sort to put on a Good Housekeeping centerfold worthy Christmas. Their family was more along the lines of vintage tacky meets fire hazard.

Skylar adored how everything smelled like heat baked boxes from the attic, and how melted decorations still made the cut each year. Her favorite holiday accent was the lollypop ghost bundled in bathroom tissue that somehow replaced the baby Jesus that went missing more than a decade ago. That, and the toy trucks the kids usually added to the nativity, made the perfect McCullough display.

Wax stained boxes waited at the foot of the stairs in the foyer, each one hiding away treasures and trinkets that seemed to release the season's magic. She'd helped Gran bring them down from the attic earlier, but it would take a week to set all the decorations out. For the whole month of December, the big house would resemble a winter wonderland.

Family would gather. Aunts would bake with the kids. Uncles would steal cookies set aside for neighbors and friends. The teens would raid the liquor cabinet, and someone would always get caught. Aunt Sheilagh would pull a massive prank on Uncle Kelly, thereby setting into motion more revenge pranks until one got out of hand and someone got hurt. Pop would grumble that there were too many people in the house, and Gran would threaten to call Santa every time the kids horsed around too close to the Christmas tree. It was the absolute perfect shit show, a pure hurricane of chaos that breathed nostalgic memories into each crazy year.

Thirty or forty tiny legs stampeded down the old wooden stairs—typical of every Sunday dinner—and the shrill voices of several mothers ordered the kids to "*calm down,*" "*stop behaving like animals,*" "*go outside,*" and one stern threat to "*settle down before someone loses an eye!*"

More crumbs settled like soot into Aunt Col's coffee. Gran was about as domestic as they came, but dusting wasn't her forte. In an old house like the big house, she often claimed she left the dust so flowers might grow. In reality, the dusty sills were a result of Gran's age, a primitive log cabin built for storybooks, and the growing arthritis in her hands.

The stampede of little ones raced through the kitchen

and out the back door sending a gust of cool November air through the house. Deep baritone voices droned from the wrap around porch. As usual, Skylar's uncles had some sort of "man toy" occupying their attention.

Thanksgiving was next Thursday, and this year, the uncles were planning to deep fry a turkey in addition to the two the aunts were already roasting. They were a big family made up of McCulloughs, Clooneys, and Mosconis, and that was only her mom's side.

Skylar's dad was a Marcelli, and they had their own crazy traditions, as well. As much as she loved the noise and chaos of both her Irish and Italian relatives, she appreciated that her mom and dad kept their individual families apart on most holidays. Otherwise, it would be culture overload—and they might shatter the sound barrier from the sheer volume of their gossip alone.

The Marcellis got Easter, and the McCulloughs got Thanksgiving. Christmas was split—her Italian side getting her family for Christmas Eve, when they celebrated the Feast of the Seven Fishes, and her Irish side getting her family on Christmas Day, when each person consumed no less than four thousand calories and sipped Gran's homemade Irish cream until they were fall down drunk.

Gran and the aunts always prepared multiple main courses for holidays. Uncle Finn had big plans for this Thanksgiving, plans that involved a vat of oil, blow torches, and one beloved bird named Augustus.

In the battle of bird versus man, Skylar's money was on the bird. There was no way her Uncle could eat an animal after he named it—no matter how much of a master hunter he claimed to be.

When the deep fryer arrived this morning, every male relative became a culinary expert on preparing poultry, arguing which way the bird should be prepared and how long it should cook—as if any of them had ever prepared a full meal in their lives.

Finn set up the deep fryer on the back porch of the big house to do a "test run." But everyone knew it was just a way of showing off his new toy. Egos flexed and voices carried like thunder from the porch as they debated over who should get the job of dropping poor Augustus next Thursday. It was a classic clash of McCullough-Clooney-Marcelli know-it-all-syndrome.

Men were often scarce in their family when it came time for chores like doing the dishes or setting the table, but whip out a power tool like a leaf blower or deep fryer, and they fought to take over.

"Maureen, your coffee tastes like shite!" Aunt Col grimaced as she chewed on the sooty brew in her cup.

"How the hell would you know? You likely burned your tastebuds clean off with the amount of whiskey you dumped in your cup," Gran snapped, always defensive whenever anyone criticized something that came out of her kitchen.

"It's bitter and gritty. Tastes like it's old. I'll need to floss when I'm done."

"The only thing old and bitter in my kitchen, is you. Drink it and shut the hell up."

"I'll make a fresh pot," Skylar offered, accepting Aunt Col's mug and dumping its contents down the drain of the old farm sink. Her lashes fluttered as the fumes of alcohol hit her eyes.

"You shouldn't be drinkin' coffee this time of day, anyway," Aunt Rosemarie chimed in. "It's not good for your blood pressure. Didn't the doctor warn you about having too much caffeine, Colleen?"

"I'm sure my blood pressure would go down if you got off my arse about it," Aunt Col grumbled.

Skylar set the filter full of grounds under the drip and started a fresh pot to brew. Her aunts' incessant bickering was more of a love language than any sort of irritation. Skylar had grown up around it and hardly noticed anymore. Just as Gran argued with her sisters, her mom quarreled with Aunt Sheilagh and all her other siblings. Big families meant big mouths.

Drying Aunt Col's mug with one of her grandmother's worn tea towels, Skylar drifted closer to the door to get a peek at the huddle of uncles. A wall of broad, flannel clad backs blocked her view of the deep fryer. She chuckled at the lower level of boys, dressed just like their daddies in denim and plaid, standing hip high and trying to shoulder their way into the cluster.

They huddled around a tall metal pot, discussing cutlery, sipping beer, and arguing which type of oil would fry the turkey best.

"Peanut oil has the highest flash point," Uncle Braydon argued, earning a confused scowl from Uncle Kelly.

"How the hell do you know that?" Uncle Kelly didn't know much about grilling or other carnivore kinds of cooking on account of his wife being a vegetarian.

Braydon shrugged. "I heard it somewhere?"

"Where?"

Uncle Finn smirked, using his beer can to point at his brother. "Bray's been watching the cooking network!"

"So?" Braydon shrugged defensively. "They have good stuff on there."

Kelly slung an arm around his brother's shoulders. "What's the matter, Bray? Is Becca's cooking not doing it for you?"

"I heard that!" Aunt Becca snapped from behind Skylar in the kitchen. "My cooking's fine, Kelly."

Skylar returned to the sink to grab another dish to dry. It was no secret that all the McCullough women, including Kate, Skylar's mother, strove to reach the domestic rank of her grandmother's culinary skills.

The subtle decline of Gran's kitchen space spoke of age wearing her down more than anything else. To outsiders, Maureen McCullough could give the Energizer Bunny a run for its money. But to those closest to her, the changes in her energy were clear.

As the eldest granddaughter, Skylar always felt a special connection with Gran. She liked to think Gran felt it, too. It was no chore to spend Sundays together, helping her prep meals for their enormous family, especially since she'd been doing it since the days when she needed a step stool to simply reach the sink.

"Skylar, be a dear and get the big serving bowl out from the lower cabinet for me. My knees aren't what they once were. I don't have time to get stuck on the floor today."

"Sure, Gran."

When Skylar passed the backdoor again, the men were arguing over how to field dress a deer. They had been drinking since eleven a.m., on account of it being Sunday, a religious day. Her family worshipped four deities—Jesus, football, food, and beer. Missing mass was a mortal sin, only second to missing Gran's Sunday dinner.

"Where's Uncle Colin?" she asked, passing Gran the bowl she requested.

"Oh, he stayed after church to collect for the food pantry. Thanksgiving's one of their biggest drives of the year."

"I forgot he was doing that." Skylar had big news she wanted to share and she didn't want Colin to miss her announcement. "Will he be here for dinner?"

"He better be."

She smirked. Even Uncle Colin, who had nearly become a priest before marrying her Aunt Samantha, and dedicated most of his free time to helping others, didn't have a pass to miss a Sunday dinner.

Steam billowed from a collection of pots on the stove and the house smelled divine. With almost everyone present, the heat indoors climbed to sweltering, despite the autumn chill. Aunt Rosemarie, who had been in a perpetual hot flash since last century, opened all the windows in the kitchen to let some air in, along with the shouting male voices outside.

Some of the rowdier uncles were already getting that crazed, combative look in their eyes that usually led to a wrestling match on the front lawn. Skylar could tell by watching their body language, who was gunning for a battle and who was hoping to escape the day unscathed.

Staring out the window behind the sink, Skylar scanned the yard where the kids played. Her gaze snagged on her dad, standing alone by the cars, notes spread out over the hood of their family's SUV, rocks acting as paperweights so they didn't blow away as he hunched over his scribblings searching for answers he'd been desperate to find.

"Mom, did anyone tell Daddy it's Sunday and he's supposed to have the day off?"

Her mom joined her at the counter, her stare following Skylar's. She sighed. "He's just so worried about his deadline. If they don't get that grant funding, he'll be crushed."

It wasn't news to discover her parents had struggles. Skylar suffered no illusions that life got easier as people grew older, mostly because her parents never sheltered her by hiding how hard they both worked. But her dad needed a break.

The man worked non-stop. Even when he was present, he wasn't fully with them. His mind was always on work—more now than ever before.

Setting down the damp tea towel, Skylar grabbed a cookie off a cooling tray and pushed out the back door. She skirted the testosterone fest on the porch and worked her way through the Jenga-jammed cars in the driveway. Vehicles were puzzled together like tight Tetris blocks, and the disorder made her twitch.

Her dad was too engrossed in his work to hear her approach. "I brought you a cookie," she announced, a few feet away.

He looked up, brow pinched, and a look of disorientation in his eyes as if he forgot he was standing in a driveway at a family dinner.

She set the cookie and napkin on the hood of the car, her eyes sparing only an impersonal glance at the columns of medical coding covering his notes.

"Thank you, pumpkin."

She rested her hip against a headlight and crossed her arms over her chest. "I thought you took off today."

He sighed and scooped up the cookie. "I'm just trying to figure out some last minute changes before we push the proposal through." He took a bite of the cookie and paused, shutting his eyes to truly savor the homemade perfection. "Did Gran make these?"

"Yup."

"You can tell. She sneaks walnuts into them no matter how much Aunt Col bitches that no one likes nuts."

No one liked Aunt Col's cookies.

The front door slammed and a car started on the other side of the house where she couldn't see. The vehicles were so jammed together, it could have been anyone borrowing a car to run into town for an errand. In a family this big, no one had any real claim to private property or privacy, so if car keys were left lying about, grand theft auto was practically invited.

Skylar glanced at the pages of scribbled notes spread across the hood of the car. Her dad gave up working in the lumberyard to follow his dreams of becoming an epidemiologist, but few people in their family truly understood the work he did, so she imagined it got lonely at times. She wished she understood his work more so that they might have more things to talk about.

He spent nearly a hundred hours a week isolated in his lab, doing research and writing grant proposals with his team. She hardly saw him anymore, and the older she got, the less he seemed able to bond with her. Her heart longed for the simplicity of the days when he used to push her on the tire swing and call her his little pumpkin.

"Why don't you come hang out with everyone, Dad? Sometimes walking away from a project for a little bit puts things into perspective. Maybe you'll see the answers you're looking for when you come back—refreshed."

He grinned and pulled her close, pressing a kiss to the top of her hair. "When you say things like that, you sound too grown up to be my little girl."

"I am a grownup, remember?"

"Never," he teased. "To me, you'll always be four years old, with rosy cheeks and pig tails. My little pumpkin."

She patted his arm. "Well, this *four-year-old's* going to grab a beer." She pushed a doting kiss onto the dark stubble of his cheek. "Don't stay out here too long."

"A few more minutes and I'll be in."

She nodded, knowing a few minutes would turn into another hour and then some. He'd stay focused on his work until he lost daylight or was called inside for dinner, whichever came first.

Things were getting rambunctious around the deep fryer, so she skipped stealing a beer from the cooler on the porch, not wanting to get roped into some pissing contest about whose truck, buck, or gun was bigger and better. Her uncles might all be grown men, but when they got together, they had a habit of regressing to competitive little boys.

Just as Skylar returned to the kitchen, Aunt Col was refreshing her coffee with the whiskey Gran kept hidden under the sink next to the Windex. "Hit me up, Aunt Col."

Colleen nodded, removed another mug, and doused the

bottom with three fingers of Tullamore Dew before topping it with coffee.

"Cheers." Aunt Col clanked her mug to Skylar's and returned to the stove.

Skylar lightened her coffee with a dash of cream, but her eyes still watered at the first potent sip. Someone fell off the porch and she winced at the clatter, followed immediately by a burst of masculine laughter. Such compassionate uncles she had.

In a few minutes the wives would start yelling at the men in the same voices they used to scold the children. And the uncles would obediently disperse to help set the tables like chastised little boys, because no matter how primitive and caveman-*esque* the McCullough men behaved, they knew how their bread got buttered, and the McCullough women always called the shots in the end.

Gran bustled through the cellar door with wild green eyes, shoving a bushel of potatoes into Skylar's arms. "Oh, thank Christ you're back, love. Your mother left because we ran out of diapers and James got into the chocolates with Pop. Well, you know how he is with dairy. He's covered in shite. I mean the stuff shot right out his arse and up his back. Your grandfather's nowhere to be found, of course. Vinnie's upstairs with your brother now, trying to get him in the tub, but you know how boys are—bitching and moaning about the slightest inconvenience. I mean really, how dare we ask them to pitch in with the kids? Anyway, I have to go check on them. You peel these potatoes and—whatever you do—don't let any of your uncles take the blowtorch out of the kitchen. I hid it under the sink next to the whiskey and Windex."

Gran said all of this without taking a single breath, while also backing out of the old farm kitchen, drying her hands on her battered apron, and stealing a sip of Colleen's coffee.

Skylar blinked, her arms trembling under the weight of so many potatoes. "O—okay."

The other aunts worked like military chefs supplying a feed line.

Aunt Sheilagh glanced over her shoulder from where she chopped celery at the counter and snickered. "Nothing like another super sane Sunday dinner at the asylum. Drinking yet?"

Skylar lugged the potatoes toward the table and dropped the bushel onto the floor. "Aunt Col fixed my coffee."

"Oh, damn, you're committed."

Skylar shrugged and began peeling. "Do you really think Finn's going to cook Augustus?"

Sheilagh snorted. "Not a chance. My brother's way too soft to kill that bird. It might as well be a pet by now. Twenty bucks says his whole family orders off the vegetarian menu this Thursday."

Skylar shook her head and hid a chuckle. "He should have never named it." Uncle Finn had five kids who spent the summer feeding and loving Augustus. "Do you think he knows?"

"That he's an idiot?" Sheilagh filled the large pot with water for the potatoes. "Probably. I've been telling him for years."

"I meant the bird. Do you think Augustus knows his days are numbered?"

"Work while you gossip, love." Aunt Rosemarie patted the idle peeler in Skylar's hand. "It's how we make the side dishes so juicy."

Sheilagh hauled the pot of water to the table so Skylar could soak the peeled potatoes. "Finnegan won't be killing any turkey this year. He'd devastate the kids. Hell, Gianna made the damn thing a pilgrim hat!"

Skylar laughed. "Are they frying something today?"

"Lord, help us." Aunt Rosemarie joined her with another peeler. "Let's just hope no one gets rushed to the emergency room. I don't feel like driving on the interstate. It's Sunday, all the kooks are out."

"Let's hope they don't burn the house down," Aunt Sheilagh grumbled.

A loud explosion rattled the house and Skylar flinched, her shoulders shooting up to her ears as her eyes went wide with concern.

Gran's voice echoed from upstairs as a storm of profanity rained from the rafters and all the kids came barreling into the kitchen from the den to see what caused the commotion.

"What was that?" several little voices demanded.

"Sweet Mary and Joseph, I told those bloody bastards not to use that thing on my porch!" Gran stormed into the kitchen and snatched a wooden spoon off the counter. It was her weapon of choice when commanding an army of idiots. "I'm going to beat someone's arse if I find one scorched inch on my house! Vinnie, get your brother out of the tub. Sheilagh, check the roast."

A cloud of smoke billowed into the kitchen from the porch and Gran coughed, batting the smog away with an irritated swing of her hand. "For Christ's sake, Finnegan! I told you something like this would happen. Is anyone hurt?"

Coughs diluted into laughter. "We're okay, Mum. Just a little taken by surprise."

Gran swung the spoon, clipping Uncle Finn in the shoulder, but the shot was muffled by a thick layer of flannel. "This is why we can't have nice things!"

Skylar herded the kids away from the commotion. "Okay, munchkins, everyone get to the dining room if you want to see the surprise I have in my bag."

The children raced into the dining room like a stampede of caribou and she followed, snagging her purse on the way.

"Do I need to get my car keys?" Aunt Col yelled. "I swear to God, is it too much to ask for us to have one peaceful Sunday dinner where no one gets hurt? Bloody Christ, it's like a zoo exhibit around here. You're nothin' but a bunch of wild animals."

Skylar wiped her watering eyes, glad to get away from the smoke.

Uncle Pat poked his head inside the kitchen and yelled, "No injuries!"

"Yet," Aunt Col mumbled into her mug.

"Skylar, where's the surprise?" Gianna asked and the rest of the kids followed suit calling for her attention and crowding her waist like a litter of puppies looking to get fed.

"You have to be sitting to get a surprise." Luckily, she always carried a secret stash of candy.

The table filled with little bodies as Skylar dug through her purse. She dispensed individually wrapped pieces of dark chocolate as the aunts loudly lectured the uncles for what was yet another stupid act they'd be retelling for years. Apparently, deep fryers worked great for wild game and fries, but not apple pies.

Gran marched through the dining room to the hall closet on a mission to find more rags. "A bunch of imbecilic jackasses, I raised." She returned a few seconds later with a stack of dishcloths. "How they even dress themselves in the morning is beyond me. My poor holiday wreath I just bought at the church craft show is melting off the damn door, blown to bits with pie filling—" She paused and scanned the room of chewing pudgy cheeks. "Sweet, Jesus, what the hell happened to Maeve? Did she get the shits, too?"

Skylar laughed at her little cousin, who wore a mask of melted Godiva. "It's chocolate, Gran. Just one piece to keep them occupied while the uncles clean up the mess out back."

Gran tsked. “Before supper, Skylar? I don’t know why I even bother makin’ rules if no one’s going to follow them.” She bustled out of the dining room to deal with the disaster on the porch.

Skylar used a napkin to clean Maeve’s face, but paper wasn’t cutting it. “Okay, everyone line up and don’t touch *anything*. We’re taking a field trip to the bathroom.”

Skylar marched the kids to the powder room in the hall and supervised as they washed their hands and faces. Only one hand towel was injured in the making of this disaster, but she believed the stains would wash out.

Her mother eventually returned with a box of diapers for James, who was long past the age of potty training, but that’s what happened in a family of six kids when everyone else was busy.

“Oh, good, Katherine, you’re back.” Gran appeared. “We still don’t have the corn shucked.”

Sometimes it seemed like Gran had some sort of maternal tracking system on all her kids. Skylar’s mom shrank a little and she took pity on her.

Always a beautiful woman, her mom still had lustrous auburn hair with deep highlights that appeared more ruby than copper with age. She never needed makeup, and it had been years since Skylar saw her in anything other than cotton or flannel, but hidden beneath those maternal rags lived a bombshell of a woman. And on the nights when her father looked up from his work and remembered his wife, Skylar often caught him staring at her in awe, as if he still couldn’t believe how he’d landed such a babe.

It had been months, maybe even more than a year, since her parents went out on a date, She wished they would make some time for themselves away from family, but there was always so much going on. Lately, stress hid in the creases around her mother’s eyes, eyes which always seemed too glassy as if she was about to cry or had just finished crying.

But no matter how overwhelmed she might seem, she still had that fiery McCullough temper all the female relatives owned. "I just walked through the goddamn door, Mum. Give me a second."

"Don't get mouthy with me, Katherine. Dinner's almost ready and I've already used the spoon once today. I'm sick and tired of you kids sassing back when I tell you to do something."

Frazzled, her mother shoved the box of diapers in Skylar's arms. "Take these up to the nursery and put one on your brother. Then tell Vincenzo to give me a hand with the corn." Grumbling under her breath, her mother followed Gran into the kitchen.

Skylar never minded helping, especially lately, since her dad had been working so much. But she hated seeing her mom so tired.

Skylar stilled, mid-way up the staircase. She'd seen her mother act like this before—exhausted, rundown, at the end of her emotional wits.

As if conjured by her thoughts, her mother reappeared in the hall and paused at the sight of Skylar lingering on the steps. "I thought I told you to go—"

"You're pregnant."

Her mother's eyes bulged. "*What?*"

"You're pregnant, aren't you?" Jesus, she knew McCulloughs were into big families, but at some point it began to seem a little irresponsible. "Mom, how could you let this hap—"

"Oh, give me a break, Skylar. I barely have the energy to dress myself let alone have another baby. And your father sleeps at the lab more than he sleeps at home, lately. Get real and get those diapers up to your brother."

"Have you taken a test?"

"No, and I'm not going to. I know my body. I'm not pregnant."

"But without a test—"

"For the love of God, Skylar, I know you worship your father, but the man is, in fact, human. Unless I'm working on the second coming of Jesus, there is no way in all of God's holy land that I'm pregnant! Are you satisfied?"

Satisfied, and a bit chastised, she huffed. "Fine." Maybe her mom's foul mood was the result of needing to get laid. She marched up the steps to find James.

With Frankie away at Penn State and her dad's busy schedule, they were short two men. Skylar didn't have an abundance of time, but she helped out when she could.

However, lately, she'd been working on focusing a little more on herself. If Skylar were able to actually get ahead on her plans, she might be a greater help to her overpopulated family as a whole. But prisoners of Alcatraz had an easier time escaping than the females in her family.

Classes at the local community college ate up a great deal of her schedule. Finals were around the corner, so she sometimes crammed at the library until it closed. With so many relatives always buzzing about, quiet places to study were extremely hard to find.

She'd been a student at the community college for more than two years, but her time there was finally coming to an end. By the New Year, she'd be in possession of one associate's degree and half way to her bachelor's. Things were about to get very expensive.

When Skylar didn't have her nose stuffed in a book, she was racing around town delivering pizzas. With the holidays approaching, and a ton of relatives on her gift list, she'd been picking up as many hours as possible at her grandfather's Italian restaurant.

Money equaled freedom. The more financially stable she became, the easier it would be to finish her degree.

Yet, somehow, the direct focus on herself with little thought of others always filled her with guilt, as if she should be thinking of her family first. Maybe she should dial it back to help out more at home.

Her stomach pinched at the thought. How would that work when everything inside of her wanted to move forward with her dreams of becoming a teacher?

She wanted to help her family, but she also needed to think about herself. Hopefully, her dad would get approved for the grant and things would go back to normal soon, because no matter how strong her mother was, she was never quite as happy as she seemed when her dad stuck by her side.

When Skylar found Vinnie, he seemed put out at having to watch his brother for all of twenty minutes. "Mom wants you to give her a hand shucking the corn."

He scoffed as if this was an extreme hardship. Skylar was certain he had other crucially important thirteen-year-old things to do.

"Go help her, Vinnie. And don't complain."

"Why can't you help her—"

Before he could finish the sentence, she sent him a scathing glare that said she helped plenty and he better get his butt down stairs and shuck some corn.

"Fine," he grumbled, closing out whatever game he played on his phone.

She shook her head and scooped James off the floor. "Where's Hannah?"

Vinnie shoved his feet into his shoes and stood. "Who knows? Probably sexting Jason."

"Ew. Don't say that about our sister."

"She drools over every random that contacts her. Her phone's a cellular biohazard."

"Vinnie, stop it! You would punch anyone else for disrespecting your sister, so don't you talk about her like that."

He shrugged and went down stairs. She carried James to the daybed against the wall. "Does your belly feel better?"

"My truck!" He pointed to the toy truck on the carpet.

Skylar retrieved the toy and handed it to him, earning a great big smile. "If only everyone's problems could be solved so easily."

James needed the most care, but he still held the rank of the easiest sibling at the moment. Her younger sister, Hannah, was at that age where the world felt like it was caving in, and the slightest inconvenience earned a massive, dramatic meltdown. It also didn't help that Hannah had never been the sort to suffer in silence.

Frankie was the football star, following in their dad and Uncle Luke's footsteps, so the family nearly threw their backs out with applause every time he displayed a basic skill. Hannah was the attention seeker with terrible instincts and a nose for finding trouble. Vinnie was the quintessential middle child who spoke in a language written of resentments. James was the baby, completely dependent on others and the most innocent of all.

And Skylar... She was the most dependable, the one who needed the least care, and was, therefore, the easiest to overlook. As the second oldest grandchild in the family, she'd been a babysitter for every child that came after her—and there were *a lot* of children.

Thank God she liked kids.

James blew raspberries into the air and sucked on his toy truck. His eyes grew heavy, but it was too late in the day for a nap.

Skylar tried to wake him up with a silly song. "The wheels on the truck go..."

He smiled. "It's bus!"

"It could be a truck. Sing with me. The wheels on the truck go..."

"Wound and wound!"

"Round and round. The wheels on the truck go round and round, all through the town."

As they sang, the sleepy glaze in his eyes faded.

Her mom worked in the office up at the lumberyard with most of the uncles during the week. But with one parent reliant on grants and the other stuck in an office at the family business, there wasn't a lot of extra spending money, especially with three college age kids. No wonder her mom looked so stressed out.

In a family the size of theirs, there were always a million little things that needed to get done. And never enough time to focus on one single issue alone.

No matter how exhausting a big family could be, Skylar couldn't imagine it any other way. Her family was nuts, wild, always busy, and always bitching about something, but they were the absolute best of the best.

Gran took care of all the grandkids during the day, but there were so many little ones under the age of five, even her invincible grandmother seemed overwhelmed lately. Sometimes Skylar wondered if their family's record breaking number of offspring was the result of poor family planning or just simply life. Maybe adulting was tough no matter how many kids a person had.

In an attempt to lighten the load, Skylar attended the community college. She'd proven she could be fiscally responsible and make sacrifices for others, but after two years and finally finishing her associate's degree in Childhood Education, it was time to move on. She wanted her chance to attend a big college—and she planned to do it without costing her parents more money or stress.

"Give me your foot." Skylar slipped a sock over James's toes and wrangled his legs into a pair of denim overalls.

"You're too cute for your own good." She lifted him and kissed his cheek. "One day you'll be just as bad as the rest of them with those irresistible McCullough eyes."

He squealed and laughed when she blew a kiss into the crease of his neck. Her heart burst with warm love and she hugged him tight.

As much as she wanted to travel and have the college experience, being home with her family wasn't a bad alternative. She loved her siblings and her little cousins. Before long, they'd all be grown. If she left Jasper Falls, she'd miss watching them grow.

The letter in her back pocket seemed to grow in weight as she weighed her options and struggled with indecisiveness. She'd researched financial aid and built a good foundation, but what if her leaving cost others too much? Aside from the minor expenses loans wouldn't cover, what if her family needed her here?

As she considered this ongoing dilemma, she also wondered if her brother Frankie hesitated in the face of opportunities the way she did. Maybe that was why he got to go to the big college, because he didn't second guess himself or feel guilty about focusing on his own future and putting everyone else's needs second to his own.

"I'll just have to feel Mom and Dad out," she confided in James. "I'll tell them my news and see how they take it." The trick was getting them alone in the same room for a few minutes without any chance of disruptions or distractions. "Sound good?"

"Simba." James lifted his stuffed lion and roared.

Her return smile was bitter sweet. Not only would she miss her cousins if she accepted the offer to transfer to Shippensburg University—a *real* college with a football team, branded sweatshirts, and the whole shebang—she'd miss watching James grow.

She grazed her fingers over the letter in her back pocket. She'd been carrying it around for a week, looking for the right opportunity to share her news. Maybe she should just tell them at dinner. She could tell the whole family. Perhaps that would be better—even more exciting.

"Let's go find Mommy."

Forgetting his stuffed lion and truck, he ran off to find their mom. Fearless and undaunted by any future challenges that might crop up in his way. She needed to be more like her brothers, both big and small.

She made up her mind. As soon as everyone was seated and settled for supper, she'd announce her good news. And it was *good* news.

So why did she feel like she would somehow be letting everyone down?

❄

The kitchen smelled amazing when Skylar returned downstairs. The deep fryer drama on the porch seemed to conclude, and now the men loitered around their wives like hungry hounds begging for scraps. The women chased them off with instructions to set the table as they transferred steaming side dishes from metal pots to serving bowls while the kids once again washed-up at the sink.

"We have no dessert now, thanks to all of you," Aunt Sheilagh griped at her brothers.

Uncle Luke threw a dishtowel at her face. "Like Mum ever has just *one* pie."

He was right. Gran always kept an arsenal of desserts hidden away for emergencies.

Skylar was so anxious to share her big news, the words wanted to burst out of her. She waited for the perfect opportunity, a moment—just a split second really—when everyone shut up so she could steal the spotlight. It didn't come.

Halfway through the meal—no hint of the usual chaos

quieting—an argument started over who would win the games next Thursday and who was ahead in the fantasy football pools.

"I got five to seven odds on the spread next week," Uncle Kelly announced.

Uncle Luke perked up. "What's Vincenzo paying?"

"He said it was up to five hundred when I talked to him on Friday."

"Five hundred dollars?" Gran's brows lifted. "That's an awful lot of money to bet on one game."

Vincenzo, Skylar's Italian grandfather on the Marcelli side, grew up in Philadelphia and liked to pretend he had mafia connections, which he did not. But he wore the gaudy gold jewelry and the mob style tracksuits as if he were a method actor preparing for the role of a lifetime.

Deeply committed to his self-fabricated delusions of power, he even tried to run for mayor once. But he didn't quite have the pull of Hoffa and he lost by a pretty extreme landslide. Suffice it to say, no one was allowed to speak the current mayor's name in her grandfather's presence if they wanted to eat at his restaurant. And no one in Jasper Falls cooked like her grandfather—including Gran—so *everyone* wanted a seat at his table.

If Skylar ever broke the news about Shippensburg to her McCullough relatives, she had to do it all over again on the Marcelli side. She dreaded breaking the news to her grandpa Marcelli, as he had a few misogynistic tendencies in regard to the females of their family. All three of her dad's sisters still worked and lived at home and he always told Skylar she had her priorities right whenever she showed up for a shift at the restaurant.

Skylar liked working there, but it wasn't what she wanted for a career. And her decision to stay in Jasper Falls had more to do with finance than any sort of loyalty to her family's business.

Once, her mom told her how desperately she'd wanted to leave town after high school. That hadn't worked out for her, and she claimed she had no regrets, but deep down Skylar thought she might harbor a few.

Skylar loved her town and was in no rush to leave, but some part of her believed she needed distance from her family in order to find her independence. She just hoped they would understand.

"Bray, how come you're not in the football pool?" Luke asked, glancing over the spread that passed around the table.

Skylar's dad chuckled. "He owes my dad from the last game."

Gran gasped. "Is that true, Braydon? Are you in the hole with Vincenzo like some degenerate?"

"Shut up, Ant." Uncle Braydon shot her father a look. "No, Mum. I just haven't had the chance to get it over to him."

Skylar wondered if other families openly discussed illegal gambling as if it were nothing to be ashamed of.

Uncle Kelly chuckled. "You're afraid of Vincenzo. Just admit it."

"No," Braydon argued, only there was a slight tremble to his tone. "What's he going to do, ban me from the restaurant?"

"Careful, Uncle Bray," Skylar teased. "My grandpa thinks he has a special connection to *The Man Upstairs.* He might put the *maloik* on you."

Her uncle shot her a scowl. "Kate, control your smartass daughter."

Her mother shrugged. "She's right. Hope he doesn't put the evil eye on you."

"That's enough of that talk, Katherine," Gran said. "We've got enough problems. We don't need to invite pagan superstitions into the mix. Besides, for a man so connected to God, I've never seen him step foot in church."

Skylar's dad laughed. "Vincenzo worships The Big Guy in his own way when he washes his car on Sunday."

No further explanation was needed, as everyone who knew her grandfather, knew that the ritual of the Sunday car wash might as well be a religious compulsion. And because Grandpa Marcelli often claimed cleanliness was next to godliness, he said it excused him from mass.

That was just the tip of the iceberg in terms of her grandpa Marcelli's backwards thinking. The man was a lovable menace who believed respect was deeply rooted in fear.

He yelled at and threatened anyone who set foot on his pristine front lawn, which was one of his most prized possessions after growing up in the city. He deeply believed a man could never eat enough processed meat, struggled to understand why any woman would want to work outside of the home or family business, and only prayed for three things—health, winning lotto tickets, and that the Philadelphia Eagles made it to the Superbowl.

"Well," Gran continued, "I think it's inappropriate to bet on Thanksgiving. It's a holiday. Holidays are meant for family and church."

Braydon cocked his head, his brow furrowing in confusion under his golden curls. "Ah, yes, Thanksgiving, the holiest day of all the holidays mentioned in the bible."

Aunt Sheilagh snorted. "I believe it's also the birth of Jesus's turkey."

"Jesus had a turkey?" Gianna asked from the kiddie table.

Maeve's eyes widened in awe. "Like Augustus?"

"Great," Uncle Finn grumbled. "Now, look what you started."

Aunt Sheilagh shrugged. "You're the one who wants to slaughter a holy bird on Jesus's turkey's birthday."

Gran scowled. "Don't joke about Jesus. It's Sunday."

"Yeah," Uncle Kelly laughed. "Jesus jokes are specifically limited to Mondays."

Before he could get the full sentence out, Gran reached over and swatted him in the back of the head. "You, stuff it." She pointed her fork at the rest of her kids. "And the rest of you, I want no more talk about gambling at the dinner table. There are young, impressionable children listening."

Kelly heaped more potatoes onto his plate. "It's the second biggest game of the year, Mum. Everyone's betting on it."

Gran buttered a roll and shrugged. "I like the parade."

Luke chuckled. "You can bet on which float makes it to Macy's first."

"Don't be a smartass, Luke." She bit into the dinner roll. "Maybe I'll place my own bet with Vincenzo, then I'll take all your money and go to Macy's myself. We'll see who's smart then."

"You don't even know who's playin', Mum."

She scoffed. "Like that matters. Vincenzo will tell me."

"God help us all if we add degenerate to her resume," Skylar's mom muttered. "Ant, tell your father not to accept any money from my mother."

"Katherine, I don't need you micromanaging the way I spend my money," Gran snapped.

"Can I be excused?" several children fidgeted with boredom, and the aunts did a quick inspection of plates before letting them go play.

"You're not going to gamble with my father-in-law, Mum. If you lose, he'll expect to get paid and you'll make a *thing* out of it."

"She's right Maureen," Pop chimed in. "This isn't like playing cards for quarters with your sisters."

"Oh, as if we still play for quarters, Frank. Where the hell do you think I got the money for that new riding mower you love."

Uncle Paulie and Uncle Liam both stilled and scowled at the great-aunts who appeared riveted on cutting their food.

"What the hell's she talkin' about Colleen?" Uncle Paulie snapped. "How much money are you three bettin' on cards?"

Without flinching, Aunt Colleen angled her knife at Uncle Paulie and popped a Brussel sprout in her mouth. "I don't know who you think you're questioning in that tone. Don't you go concerning yourself with our wagers. I don't bother myself with the paycheck pools you hold every week at the lumberyard. Besides, it was Rosemarie that lost the week Maureen bought the mower."

Uncle Liam scowled at his wife. "You lost enough money to buy a *riding mower*, woman?"

"Hush, Liam. Your supper's getting cold."

Gran smirked. "I think I'll swing by Vincenzo's tomorrow when I'm in town."

Before anyone could object, one of the kids knocked over a full glass of milk and everyone scrambled to contain the mess. Two other cups tipped over in the clean-up process and several pieces of silverware dropped onto the floor.

As dinner carried on, voices grew louder, and soon, everyone not shoving food into their mouths, was shouting. The hairsplitting decibel was typical, though no one was actually angry. That was just how they communicated. Her family could break the sound barrier at a family meal.

She glanced at her sister, hoping to find an ally. Just a glimpse of eye contact was all she needed and she could mouth the word, *I have big news...*

Hannah's head angled toward her lap, her eyes focused on the phone in her hands. She'd passed the entire meal hardly touching her food, her fingers glued to the device as she rapidly texted someone.

Skylar loved her family. She adored how obscenely obsessive they could be about each other. But sometimes she wished everything could freeze and she could dip her toe into the glow of the spotlight and steal everyone's attention for a few seconds.

A baby started to cry and her Aunt Mallory jumped to her feet, cursing that the squeals made her milk come in. The men used the distracting chaos to slip out of the dining room into the den only to be ordered back by their angry wives to clear the tables.

The next thing Skylar knew, dinner was over and she missed her opportunity to make her announcement. The words, *I got a grant,* dissolved on her tongue, before ever finding a chance to escape.

Her fingers once again traced over the folded envelope in her back pocket and she smiled. Regardless of others ignoring or acknowledging her success, the small grant was a big deal. Maybe that was all that mattered.

She cleared her plate, rinsed a few dishes in the sink to do her part, and slipped outside. Remnants of apple pie dripped off the porch railing and Gran's autumn wreath was scorched, the gold synthetic leaves melted and deformed. She moved downwind from the scent of melted plastic.

Lowering to the porch steps, she removed the acceptance letter from her pocket, affectionately running her thumbs over the university's return address.

Two hours was a long drive from Jasper Falls. It was doable, but not very realistic if she also wanted to continue working at the pizzeria.

Ultimately, she wanted to take more than one class, but the grant only covered one three credit course during the upcoming winter session. It didn't cover meals or housing or any of the other expenses like books.

Maybe she was making a bigger deal out of it than she should. A winter session was a far cry from a regular semester. She folded the envelope in half, wondering if this was just some recruitment scheme to get new students enrolled.

"Hey." Her gloomy expression split with a smile as Uncle Colin appeared, car keys in his hand as if he was hoping to sneak in unnoticed.

"You missed dinner."

"I know." He glanced over his shoulder to the house. With the windows open, all the brash voices carried in a familiar but not very tempting show of pandemonium. "Any fights break out?"

She shrugged. "Nothing out of the norm."

He lowered to the step beside her. "What do you have there?"

Of all her uncles, Colin was probably her favorite. He was the youth minister at their church and very active at the high school. He'd helped her make the decision about going into early childhood education.

She closed her hand around the envelope, covering the university branding. "It's nothing."

"Doesn't look like nothing."

She fumbled with the letter, unfolding the envelope, and exposing the return address for him to read.

"Shippensburg?"

"Yeah. They offered me a grant to take a class during their winter session." Pride rippled deep inside of her as she said the words out loud.

"That's great, Skylar. Are you gonna accept it?"

She shrugged. Everyone had been so busy lately, she doubted half of them realized she was finishing her associate's from the community college in less than ten days. Typically, students graduated the program in the spring, but she needed an extra semester to make up for the time she lost working at the family restaurant. She didn't want to make a fuss.

Besides, it wasn't as if she were getting her bachelor's. She could hold off on all the pomp and circumstance until she finished her full degree. Hopefully, things would be a little less chaotic at home by then. If not, she might have to wait until she earned her master's to squeeze her way into the spotlight. But that's how it was with big families.

"I want to, but I don't know if I can afford it. Shippensburg's a hike—too far to commute and I don't have housing." The more she thought over the barebones offer the more she accepted it was likely a recruitment gimmick.

"Did they say you have to attend in person? I know a lot of students who attend college virtually."

She shrugged again. Virtual wasn't necessarily the college experience she was hoping for. "I guess that's an option. It's only one class. Anything more, and I'd have to pay out of pocket and get student loans, so I'd have to keep working."

It wasn't like she was making a killing delivering pizzas and waiting tables at Vincenzo's, but it helped. And being that the restaurant was family owned, she had flexible hours and plenty of time to study in the back when things got slow.

"Have you asked your parents for help?"

She shot him a doubtful glance. "Dad's been so stressed out with his research. Mom keeps saying he'll make the deadline, but I don't know. If he doesn't get this grant, another epidemiologist will, and he'll be out all the time and money he's spent. Plus, they're already paying for Frankie's school and Hannah wants to go out of state."

Colin frowned. "Not a single part of that answer had to do with my question, Sky."

She sighed. "I don't want to be a burden."

He bumped her shoulder with his. "Hey, you're their

daughter—*not* a burden. You should tell them. Families are great at coming up with solutions when they put their heads together."

"Yeah, when they're together. Everyone has so much going on lately. I don't want to add more stress to their plate."

She didn't know what her parents had in terms of savings, but she sensed it was running low. Voices traveled in a house with a family the size of theirs and only four bedrooms.

"What about financial aid?" he asked, seeming to follow her thoughts.

"That would be a must, whether they help me or not. I can't expect them to support me." She was twenty-one and perfectly capable of taking care of herself. College debt was normal.

"How much time do you have to decide?"

She needed to give them an answer by the end of the week. "Classes start in December."

"Well, if it's any consolation, I think you should do it. Keep going after that dream and eventually you'll get there."

Her dream was to one day own and operate her own preschool, since Jasper Falls didn't have one. Technically, once she earned her associate's, she'd have the necessary credentials, but she wanted a more comprehensive background in education—she wanted the state recognized certification and bachelor's degree.

"It's just one class," she reminded him.

"Credits don't expire. It all adds up. And eventually, you'll run out of excuses, Skylar. Don't take too long to make up your mind, or you might also run out of time." He stood and placed an affectionate hand on her shoulder. "This is a step in the correct direction."

"You're right. I don't know why I play things down like this. It's like I'm afraid to do something if it's just for me."

"There's nothing wrong with doing something solely for yourself."

He had a point. She knew it was a good point. But that didn't relieve the guilt she felt, as if taking her focus off everyone else long enough to focus a little on herself might somehow disrupt the balance of the entire family.

But, God, she wanted to do this for herself. She wanted to feel the selfish indulgence of going after exactly what she wanted with no consideration for how her choice might affect others. Just once.

Drawing in a deep breath, her hands tightened around the letter. "I think I'll take the offer. I can take the winter class online, like you said."

"Good. I think that's the right choice. And you can always look at schools closer to home in the future if it's the distance that scares you."

She wasn't afraid of leaving Jasper Falls. She was afraid of letting down her family. Her parents depended on her help. It wasn't a hardship for her to stick around, especially since she pitched in and mostly supported herself, but it might be a hardship for them if she left.

"I think I'm better off commuting to college anyway—wherever I end up going."

"You've got plenty of time to make and change your mind. Trust me. If anyone knows about changing paths, it's me." Colin stepped fully onto the porch and pocketed his keys, but paused to look her in the eye. "And tell your parents, Sky. They'll be proud of you."

"I will. Thanks, Uncle Colin."

"Any time."

2

THE SHIFT from Thanksgiving to the Christmas season rolled into Jasper Falls with the subtlety of a ballistic sneeze. For weeks, everything had been pumpkin spiced and blazing autumnal aesthetics, but the second the turkey was served—Augustus was alive and well—fall colors faded to silver and gold, and the town glistened with tinsel, twinkle lights, and holly.

The first snow hadn't arrived yet, but the blue sky wore a gray, gossamer blanket of clouds and the air tasted metallic with cold. Red noses and shivering faces filled the overcast streets of Jasper Falls. In a town where winters were long and snow often reached shoulders, the population bustled about like bears preparing to hibernate through a long winter.

Painted store windows were dressed in greens and reds while locals wired streetlamps and truck grills with evergreen wreathes. The scent of crackling leaves was gone, and cinnamon, mulberry, and balsam reigned the new three kings.

Skylar took her foot off the brake, slowly maneuvering through the bustling foot traffic crossing Main Street with their arms weighted by packages and some men dragging tightly wrapped pine trees. Shoppers were busy finding those early post-Thanksgiving sales.

Breathing in the scent of oregano and garlic steaming from the brick oven pizza warming the seat to her right, she smiled and turned up the radio. The Waitresses belted out the upbeat lyrics to "Christmas Wrapping", and she sang along, making up the words she didn't know and always messing up that one line about the cranberries.

Skylar loved this time of year. She loved the excuse to be a little extra. The festive winter accessories—*because a girl could never own too many scarves*—brought her a deep, inexplicable joy that validated Christmas was in fact her favorite season.

She adored every little detail—the caroling, the baking, the compulsive, almost predatory, shopping and sale hunting, the scent of pine needles, the kisses under the mistletoe, the life-sized nativity, the cozy fires, the bulky socks, the layers upon layers of clothing, the hot cocoa, and oh, how she loved the magical mornings of a freshly fallen snow. But most of all, she loved watching the children.

Christmas carols played as candles glinted in windows. Goodwill and charity abounded all around. The holiday season was such a magical time of year. It enriched her spirit and painted the world with a picturesque lens.

As she glanced at the hay-stuffed manger in front of the church, she smiled. Pair that with Santa's rosy cheeks and a spiced glass of eggnog, and she was in heaven.

She couldn't wait to see all her younger cousins sit on Santa's lap this year and—

"What the hell?" Her brow creased as a tiny little body stood on a park bench, stretching to reach a red balloon tangled in a bare tree. Where were her parents? And where was her coat?

Skylar slowed her car and scanned the area for a

possible chaperone to the small girl but didn't see any adults nearby. Hitting her turn signal, she carefully pulled over and rolled down her window.

"Careful," she called and the little girl flinched, a guilty look taking over her curious expression. Skylar hadn't meant to startle her. "Is your mommy or daddy around?"

The child wrung her hands nervously. "I'm not a'posed to talk to strangers."

She grinned. Smart kid. "My name's Skylar. Is that your balloon?"

She nodded and shivered.

"Would you like me to help you get it down?"

As if it just occurred to the child that she was alone, she looked around and her eyes welled with tears.

"Oh, don't cry." Skylar shut off the car and climbed out. "I'll help you." Stepping onto the bench, she caught the string of the balloon and pulled it down. "How about we tie this to your wrist so you don't lose it again."

"Okay." The girl's little fingers were freezing.

"I'm a little warm." Unraveling her scarf, she held it out to the child. "Can you hold this for me?"

The girl nodded and Skylar wrapped the wool around her narrow shoulders, tying it like a shawl. Her full cheeks wore a rosy blush and a smudge of whatever she'd had for lunch stuck in the corner of her full lips. As she chattered her teeth, the scent of peanut butter and jelly tickled Skylar's nose.

"Now, where did you leave your mommy?"

The girl scrunched up her face in the most adorable fashion. Her dark brown eyes moved like pools of chocolate, and her red nose sniffled against the cold. Her hair looked like it hadn't been brushed in days, but her mismatched clothing was nice, pressed, and top of the line.

"My mom doesn't live here."

"Oh. How about your dad?"

"He's at the bank talking to people. He always talks."

Skylar stood from where she'd been crouching and stared down the block. Sure enough, there was a huddle of people outside of the bank. "What do you say we walk back that way and try to find him?"

"Okay."

She held out a hand and five tiny, chilled fingers curled around hers. She'd traveled quite a way from the bank, and no one seemed to have noticed she'd gone missing.

"Do you see your dad?"

The girl nodded. "He's wearing a red tie."

"Mayor Buchanan is your father?"

"That's not his name."

"It's not?"

"No, it's Daddy."

Such precociousness earned a smirk. "Well, let's go say hello to Daddy."

Three men and two women surrounded the mayor on the sidewalk, each one speaking of interests in the town. He appeared concerned but bored. Only when he spotted Skylar approaching with his daughter and her red balloon, did his expression come alive.

"Addison?" He glanced around as if just noticing she'd wandered off. "Where were you?"

"My b'loon got away, but Skylar helped me find it."

The group of constituents acknowledged the child, but continued voicing their concerns. The mayor stepped aside and crouched low, doing a quick inspection of his daughter's person.

Under the cowlick of a perfectly manicured head of thick hair, his brow furrowed and his fingers traced the fringe of Skylar's scarf she'd wrapped around the girl. "Where's your jacket?"

The citizens paused but seemed eager to get an answer. However, the mayor's distraction seemed to halt any promises of future change.

Mr. Simms, a rotund man in a worn, quilted flannel frowned, obviously wanting to continue communicating his personal needs to the mayor. "So, should I contact your office?"

Mayor Buchanan removed a silk square from his pocket and wiped the child's nose. "Yes, call the office and my assistant will help you, Mr. Simms." Brushing a hand over his daughter's hair, he said, "What have I told you about wandering off?"

"But my b'loon—"

"We can always get you another balloon. There's only one of you." Taking her hand in a secure grip, he stood and faced Skylar. "Thank you for returning her."

The constituents dispersed and the mayor no longer appeared as cool and collected as he had a moment ago. Dragging a hand through his neatly combed hair, he mussed his part, looking very much like he could use a drink.

"It's really no problem."

"I'm usually more aware. And Addison is usually at home with her nanny, but she... Well, it's a long story. Suffice it to say, I'm without childcare at the moment, something about long hours and—never mind. You don't want to hear the autobiography of a single dad."

She smiled, having enough relatives to know what a challenge child-rearing could be. "It's okay. I get it."

"Do you have kids?"

"Me? No. But I have lots of siblings and little cousins. Last I counted, I believe there were more than twenty." And that was just on her mom's side. Eventually, her Marcelli aunts on her dad's side would get married and have kids, too.

"*Twenty?*" His green eyes widened. "Siblings?"

"No, cousins. Only five of them are my siblings. But if you count second cousins, it's more like forty."

"I assume you're the oldest."

"Second, actually. My brother, Frankie, is a year older. We're Irish twins."

"Irish twins?" With his straight nose and strong jaw, he looked especially handsome when he frowned, sort of like authority gone cock-eyed.

"Born within a year of each other. It's a common problem in my family."

It was a little embarrassing during her teenager years when her mom waddled around pregnant, and Skylar's friends assumed her parents spent all their free time humping like bunnies. But she supposed it was better than having parents that fought and broke up in divorce. Despite the rampant dysfunction of her family, most of her relatives were insanely in love with their spouses.

"That's a lot of kids."

She smiled and shrugged. "I come from two big families."

"No wonder you're good with children."

"I hope so. It's what I went to school for."

Sharp interest flashed in his jade eyes. "You're a teacher?"

"Almost. I just earned my associate's degree in early childhood." Technically, finals were still being graded, but she was confident she passed.

"Really? And what are you doing now?"

"Daddy, I gotta tinkle." Addison tugged at her father's arm and he started walking.

Being that they were in the midst of a conversation, Skylar walked with them. "Right now, I'm registered to start a class online at Shippensburg and working at my grandfather's restaurant."

"In town?"

She pointed down the road to Vincenzo's. "The pizza shop."

"You're a Marcelli?"

She nodded. "And my mom's a McCullough."

Oddly, he didn't seem concerned with the McCullough side of her family, which most people took great interest in, since they made up a good portion of the town's population.

His frown pinched his brow and his eyes moved as if he were solving a math problem in his head. "Your grandfather ran against me in the election."

"I remember."

The mayor didn't appear apologetic or boastful as he said, "He ran a good campaign."

"Not as good as you, though." She gave him a cheeky smile.

"No." He smirked, his stare lingering on her face as he studied her for a moment.

His attention made her very aware of her appearance and she felt the urge to escape such scrutiny, but also a slight urge to pose under his inspection. "I should probably get—"

"How attached are you to working for him?"

The balloon connected to Addison's wrist bopped him in the head, scuffing against his neatly styled hair, and he casually swept it away.

It was her turn to frown. "At the restaurant?" She shrugged. "It's a job."

"Would you be interested in something more related to your field?"

Her steps slowed. One busy single dad plus one curious under-clothed child equaled negative one nanny. "That depends." What was he asking?

"On?"

They reached Town Hall and stopped walking. Skylar hesitated. "What exactly are you offering?"

"I could ask you the same." Addison tugged on his arm and he glanced down but didn't let go. "I'm desperate. She needs someone to watch over her while I'm at work. What do you need to know to consider the position?"

"The pay and why your last nanny quit."

Addison broke away from his grip and tugged open the door. Without breaking eye contact, he tracked his daughter's steps and called over his shoulder, "Go right to my office, Addison."

"Okay, Daddy."

The little girl disappeared with her balloon and his aura shifted into something more serious and slightly intimidating. Despite seeming distracted before, now that Skylar had his full focus she understood this man was the resolute sort, single-minded and determined and not used to being told no.

"I can promise the pay will be substantially more than you're making at a pizza place. And the last nanny left because I work a lot of late hours. I need someone there all the time, not to work but to be available—a governess. It's a campaign year, so my schedule will only get busier. I don't want to worry if I'm held up at a fundraiser or running late after a board meeting. I need someone there to look after Addison, prepare meals, enrich her mind, and handle the usual daily responsibilities she requires to be well cared for. And it has to be someone dependable because I can't afford the time it takes to keep replacing nannies every few weeks."

"You want a live in?" And why was the turnover so high? Did it really have to do with the hours he kept or could that sweet little girl possibly be hiding a demon inside?

"For now, I think that's best." He eyed her carefully. "Interested?"

"You don't even know me."

"Teachers need background checks, so I can assume you're not a criminal. You're educated in the right department, and my daughter seemed to trust you. Plus, I'm desperate. It's not fair to drag Addison into my stuffy office day after day when she should be playing and exploring like a regular kid."

He glanced up the road where the mayor's mansion towered. The historic, Georgian style house gleamed against the overcast sky. "I'm rarely home and there is an entire wing of the house that goes unused most days. I promise you would have plenty of space and there are more than enough rooms you could convert for studying. I assume you're virtual."

Her head was spinning. "Yes. For now."

Skylar considered the lack of privacy at her home. She'd been sharing a bedroom with Hannah since they were babies. There was never a bathroom available when she needed one and hot water was on a rotation schedule. Plus, if the pay was actually as substantial as he made it sound, she might be able to afford more classes. They would be online, of course, because the job would be here, but still...

"How much are we actually talking?"

"Name your price."

Did she have a price? She was currently bringing home about three hundred dollars a week. If she took the job, he'd be paying for her living expenses. That would be one less mouth for her mom and dad to feed, one less lightbulb on at night, one less shower a day. Should she deduct those expenses from her rate?

God, she sucked at negotiating for herself.

Unsure how to price such a job, she threw the ball back in his court. "Why don't you tell me what you're comfortable spending?"

"I'm willing to offer thirty thousand, but that's negotiable."

Her eyes bulged. "Thirty thousand *dollars*?"

"That's a fairly low childcare salary, I believe."

She wasn't used to having credentials, which she supposed she now had. *Huh, being an adult was pretty cool.*

"Y—yes, that's a decent starting salary." She'd be a fool to turn him down. Was this seriously happening to her? She cleared her throat and tried to act professional. "How long would the position last?"

"Addison just turned four. She can't start kindergarten for two years due to her birthday being in late fall. She'll need a governess until then."

Skylar smiled at the term governess, as it filled her head with visions of Julie Andrews twirling down a hill in the Alps and making clothing from curtains. Then her thoughts sidetracked to Jane Eyre and she catalogued how handsome her new boss was.

Stop that!

She glanced away to hide her blush. "I'll have to let my grandfather know."

"Of course."

"And I'll need some time to pack and—"

"Whatever you need. If you require a moving company, I can arrange that. Like I said, I'm desperate."

She considered her half of the bedroom and the few items she owned. She really only needed to pack clothes and a few personal items. Maybe a couple books from her shelf. "I don't think I'll need a truck. I don't have much."

A woman in her thirties with blonde hair pushed open the door and popped her head out. "Rhett, you have a meeting with the union reps in five minutes, and Addison wants to know if she can have a snack." She briefly glanced at Skylar, giving her a tight-lipped smile that didn't reach her eyes, and skipping any hello.

Mayor Buchanan sighed, appearing frazzled once more. "I'll be right there." His focus returned to Skylar, but he still spoke to the woman at the door. "The file on the refinery proposal is in my briefcase. Make three copies of the letter from the foreman and brew a fresh pot of coffee. Addison can have a banana." He seemed to have a knack for focusing on multiple problems at once. "When can you start?"

Realizing he'd turned the conversation back to her, Skylar mentally stumbled through her schedule. "Tomorrow?"

"Perfect. Erin will go over the details with you."

The woman—supposedly Erin—waited, holding open the door to Town Hall, and the mayor stepped over the threshold. "Thank you, Ms. Marcelli."

When he said her name, the word seemed to whisper right up her spine in the form of a chill. "My pleasure."

His eyes held hers for an additional second and she felt the strangest sensation in her stomach, but it disappeared the moment his tone returned to business. "I'll, of course, need your background checks and all the normal payroll stuff. We can go over everything tomorrow. Be at my home before eight."

She nodded, her attention pulling back to the familiar mayor's mansion at the end of Main Street, just before the church. "Okay."

The woman finally retreated and he paused, holding the weight of the door. "And I guess I should ask your first name, Ms. Marcelli."

"It's Skylar."

His hard jaw softened as relief touched his face and he smiled. The slight curve of those full lips transformed his already beautiful face into downright breathtaking. "Nice to meet you, Skylar. I'm Rhett Buchanan."

The chill she'd felt chased away by something warm. "I know."

He wasn't even speaking, yet he somehow dripped charm. She wondered how much of his personality had been polished for a life of politics and how much was actually authentic. Overall, he seemed like a nice man.

Her grandfather would not be happy about this.

3

"WHO WAS THAT?" Erin handed him a cup of coffee and took his coat.

Addison raced over to inform him that her balloon had popped when she closed it in the bathroom door. "Can we get another one, Daddy?"

"Sure." He took the file of copies from Erin and headed into his office. "That was Addison's new nanny."

"She's a McCullough."

He sat behind his desk, where a list of messages waited. "Actually, she's a Marcelli."

"But she's related to the McCulloughs. You can see it in her blue eyes."

He hadn't noticed the color of her eyes, because he'd been too distracted by the beauty mark on her cheek and the way her dark hair caught in the wind. She smelled like Christmas cookies, soft hints of cinnamon mixed with sweet vanilla.

"I didn't get into her genealogy. Do you have an issue with the McCulloughs?"

"No. I used to date one." His personal assistant shrugged. "They're fine, if you don't mind a little crazy."

The word *crazy* got his attention. "What are you saying?"

She swept a hand under her blonde hair, curling it around the back of her neck and dragging it down the front of her blouse. "They're just a little...off. They all live up on that mountain off the grid. They're sort of...lawless."

"Well, if she wants to work for me, she'll follow the laws. I already told her I require a background check."

His stomach dropped. Had he made a mistake? She seemed like a decent woman—kind, patient with Addy, in possession of the proper credentials. He was running out of options, and a run-of-the-mill babysitter wasn't going to cut it.

"I'll keep an eye on her." She handed him a printout of the day's agenda. "Don't forget the foreman's name is *Ron.* Last time you accidentally called him Don. And the other rep is named Brian. He's the one with the wife who needed help filing for an LLC."

"Right. What was the LLC for?"

"Jewelry, I think. But I could be wrong. Maybe a gift shop. It's opening after the New Year."

"Got it." He should have never had that fourth cup of coffee. "Don."

"Ron!" She shook her head. "You need a day off."

He laughed. "Tell that to the town."

"Fix your tie..." Before he could lift a finger, her hands were on him. She fussed with the knot, and all he could smell was the candied scent of her lip gloss.

His mind flashed to Skylar Marcelli's lips. They were natural, no sticky gloss, no color. Just soft little pillows cushioning that sweet little mouth—

"There." Erin patted his chest.

Disturbed by the trajectory of his thoughts, he cleared his throat. "Thank you." He needed to get laid.

The secretary, Jan, appeared at the doorway. "Rhett, your ten o'clock is here."

"Send them back."

Erin left and Rhett stood to greet the union reps. After shaking hands, they took their seats. He warmed up with some small talk. "How's your wife's store coming along, Brian?"

"Great. She's real excited for the grand opening. We hope you'll be able to stop by."

"I look forward to it. It's good to see another small business come to Jasper Falls."

The meeting commenced, and Rhett listened carefully for ways he could help the union in an effort to secure their vote in the upcoming year. He loved being a politician, but experience taught him there was always a trade-off. Sometimes he wished he could run on his beliefs alone, but that wasn't how the world worked, at least not the American government.

He scratched their backs and they scratched his. And while everyone noticed the changes taking place in their little town since he'd revealed the revitalization project, not everyone was pleased with the modifications. But there were always critics.

Some bitched about the constant construction. Others complained that the tourists made too much noise. And several were opposed to simple modernizing in the form of necessary traffic lights where there were none before.

Change was never easy, but the small town folks of Jasper Falls sometimes seemed offended by even the mere hint of it—even when the result meant simpler, happier, more financially stable outcomes for everyone.

With the addition of new commercial establishments came tourists. And with the right budgeting came additional money for infrastructure. Better roads meant less flats, easier winters, and safer drives. But God forbid the town shut down a main stretch of road for a day to make the modifications.

Their small economy was booming with the start of new restaurants and shops, but every time the coffers opened, the residents of Jasper Falls shared their opinions about where the money should be spent.

Opinions were as common as assholes. Everyone had one. And being mayor meant Rhett got an up close and personal whiff of each one. Some were harmless, but others really stunk.

He couldn't renovate the park without justifying why they were not repainting the curbs. If one street got new landscaping, he needed to replenish all of the public gardens.

Some days, dealing with the unending complaints from the townsfolk was worse than fielding the one hundred *how come* questions he got from his four-year-old daughter. Speaking of...

He hadn't emerged from his office since his meeting ended. The sky had darkened and the phones had stopped ringing hours ago. He closed out his emails and straightened his desk then went to find Addy.

Her tiny, sleeping body curled up on an upholstered chair in the waiting area, a tartan scarf draped over her arms like a blanket. Jan's desk was tidy and her chair empty. All traces of constituents gone.

He turned to find Erin holding a freshly rinsed coffee pot. "You're still here?"

She drifted past him, returning the kettle to its home and readied the grounds for the next morning. Her stocking feet were bare against the carpet. "You work late, I work late."

His concern returned to his daughter. "Did she eat dinner?"

"Jan made her a cup of noodles."

A sense of failure crowded him. His daughter deserved

better then dehydrated noodles cooked in an office microwave.

Brushing a tangle of curls back from her face, he whispered, “Addison. It’s time to go home, sweetheart.”

Her eyes opened, and she bestowed a smile he didn’t deserve. “Daddy.” Wreathing her arms around him, he scooped her off the chair.

His body came to attention as the soft, wool scarf brushed against his face and he breathed in the delicious scent of cinnamon and vanilla. The subtle hint of perfume held a womanly appeal, completely contradictory to his daughter’s youthful scent, and his mind jerked to images of Skylar Marcelli.

Addison hooked her legs around his hip and he rubbed the wool between his forefinger and thumb. “Where did you get this?” He already knew, but he needed confirmation.

“Skylar gave it to me.”

“Do you like Ms. Marcelli?”

He wasn’t sure why using her surname felt safer than her first. Perhaps it was the knowledge that he was out of nannies and needed this arrangement to work. No room for missteps.

Addison crunched her face. “Who’s that?”

“The woman you met today. That’s her name.”

“Nuh-uh. It’s Skylar.”

“Marcelli’s her last name.” They were getting off track. “Did you like her?”

She nodded. “She rescued my b’loon.”

“Would you like to see her again?” She wouldn’t have a choice, but he was curious.

“Okay. I can give her back her scarf.”

“First we’ll have it cleaned.”

They waited as Erin gathered her coat and belongings, then locked up the office. “I’ll see you in the morning.”

She glanced back, her gaze lingering on Addison as she sighed. "Goodnight, Rhett."

"See you tomorrow, Erin."

❄

Rhett had all intentions of adding the scarf to his dry cleaning that evening, but somehow the soft accessory skipped the pile of wrinkled shirts and jackets. He refolded the material and breathed in Skylar Marcelli's recognizable fragrance, shutting his eyes and wondering why he found the fading scent so comforting.

It reminded him of department stores around the holidays or bakeries on Sunday mornings. There was something nostalgic but borrowed in the scent, something he knew didn't belong in his memories, but captured a sense of longing he'd suppressed years ago. Maybe it smelled like a teacher.

Setting the folded scarf aside, he let his curiosity move to more pressing concerns. By the end of each week, he always felt like his world was on the verge of collapse. And since losing his last nanny, things had only gotten more hectic. Hiring Skylar Marcelli seemed like a good call.

Despite not knowing her, he couldn't escape the gut instinct that she would be good for his daughter and that meant she would be good for their situation. He loved being a father. Addison was his entire world. The challenge rested in not just being her parent, but figuring out how to be a good parent, a role-model and dependable source of security, something he didn't have while growing up.

He needed another term as mayor to continue all the changes he envisioned. If he got reelected, he stood a chance of building a community perfect for his daughter, a place where she would be safe and always know a sense of home.

Growing up in a situation with pronounced limits, he developed an obsession with knocking down barriers. If someone said something was impossible, he proved them wrong.

The biggest obstacle of his past had always been his background. People saw a boy dressed in hand-me-down rags with unkempt hair and assumed privilege would always be lacking in his life.

Maybe it was, because nothing had ever come easily to him. Every luxury he claimed as a man came from hard work, sleepless nights, and cut-throat determination. He proved that sometimes success comes from grit as much as it arrived from privilege. But goddamn, he was tired.

He'd always pushed himself to the brink of collapse, always thinking he had nothing left to give. Then Addison was born.

Having a daughter meant acting out of love not resentment. Being a father required him to tap into something pure he wasn't sure he possessed. It couldn't be genetic because his mother wasn't the loving sort, and his dad left before he ever had the chance to meet him.

Most days Rhett faked parental confidence, but eventually, as his daughter grew and revealed this incredible little person with thoughts and opinions and an astounding ability to love, he discovered that caring for his child, loving her, putting her first, and assuring she never wanted for anything, well, that was the easiest job he'd ever had. Challenging, sure. Exhausting to the point of lunacy, especially when she was an insomniac infant. But taking care of her was also so easy.

And it made him wonder, if being kind and patient for his flesh and blood came so naturally to him, why had his own parents struggled with the task? Perhaps it was him.

No matter how hard he'd pushed himself, Addison

brought him purpose and he pressed himself twice as hard to secure her a safe and happy life. He still struggled to decide stupid things like scented or unscented fabric softener and he felt like a true criminal whenever he accidentally got shampoo in her eyes, but most days he was able to guess the best choices. And every day she smiled up at him as if he himself had hung the moon and stars.

No one had ever looked at him that way before. Parenting was supposed to be selfless, but he selfishly did it for her adoration. Even on the days he screwed up and left her sleeping on an office chair with nothing but wax noodles and peanut butter and jelly in her belly, she still made him feel like he was doing the best job in the world.

He wanted to give her a better world. He started small, as the mayor of a little, hole-in-the-wall town, but aspired for bigger things. Perhaps he'd run for state representative, and move into bigger branches of government, earn higher pay, and fund the best education money could buy for his brilliant daughter.

But larger government jobs couldn't be run strictly from his small town, and he'd have to travel. Addison would be older by then, but still young. Childcare was a necessity, and he struggled to determine if his ambitions were purely for her benefit or if the sacrifice she paid for his success might somehow cost them in the end.

Being a father created an endless tug of war between providing financial stability and a paternal presence. While men and women successfully acted as single parents all the time, playing the role of both mom and dad, he couldn't help wishing Addison had both presences in her life. Hiring governesses seemed the closest substitute for the element of female nurturing he didn't have a clue how to provide.

Jasper Falls had been a backwoods town five years ago. Hell, the town hadn't even had its own name. It had been numbered as merely a district in Center County, Pennsylvania.

When he moved to Center County, he saw potential. Everything about this place screamed dusty, small-town charm. It was just hidden under the stench of buck-lure and diesel fuel.

It was after midnight when he finally made it to the kitchen and constructed a sandwich. He wasted no time on condiments or lettuce, too distracted by his open laptop on the counter. The office had just launched the new website design for the upcoming campaign, and he wanted to review it carefully before anyone else.

Sitting at the table, hair still damp from a shower and bare feet pressed to the cold floor, he slouched in his lounge pants and skimmed the site.

Women were his key demographic. He appealed to any fanciful natures and sold an image of old world, country charm. His analytics told him they were also the residents that spent the most time reading his website, so they really amped up the storybook appeal.

The male residents grumbled about unwanted changes but ultimately listened to their wives, but Rhett still had to work to appease everyone. Gaming laws and fishing tournaments could go a long way on winning their favor, so he also had to play those roles as well.

Once they rebranded District 23 into the enchanting town of Jasper Falls, citizens began to trust his vision and believe that such a fantasy might actually have a shot of becoming a reality. But the locals never let him forget they were the sort who put great credence in a man's word, didn't take kindly to strangers coming in and changing too much, and that this was a place that believed Sundays were for God, football, and homemade cobbler.

Staring dispassionately at his sandwich as the cold meat flopped lifelessly over the plain, white bread, he tried to imagine it was warm, country cobbler. He tossed the half-eaten sandwich onto the napkin and returned to his work.

Did Skylar bake? She smelled like cookies. Had she ever made cobbler? Why was he thinking about her at one in the morning?

Shaking his head, he pondered Erin's earlier comment about the McCulloughs being *crazy*. The older generation founded the lumberyard, which employed almost eighty percent of Jasper Falls. They didn't strike him as foolish. It struck him as smart. But he supposed big mountains came with big secrets, and anything could happen that far off the grid.

The screen switched to Facebook and he typed in the last name. Hundreds of McCulloughs populated the search engine. Then he deleted the name and replaced it with Marcelli.

Three women he recognized as Vincenzo's daughters appeared and then he saw Skylar, smiling against a field of sunflowers. It seemed criminal for any woman to be that pretty. She probably had some punk boyfriend who didn't have a clue how out of his league she was.

Since she would be taking care of his daughter, he took a few minutes to search her profile. Somehow he ended up on her Instagram.

Damn, she had a great smile. Dark brown hair and deep olive skin and the bluest eyes he'd ever seen, swirled with radiant shocks of gold and evergreen. He couldn't find her age, but guessed she was in her early twenties.

Hoped—because if she wasn't, that made him the filthiest letch around.

"You're such a creeper," he mumbled, scrolling further down the grid of her pictures.

It was research. His own personal background check. She was his new employee, and it seemed logical to get a feel for the woman who would be spending her days with his daughter. He was doing this for Addison.

He rolled his eyes, trying not to slip on his own bullshit.

There was nothing startling about her social media. Compared to some, hers seemed rather tame.

He paused and smiled when he spotted a cute picture of her in a wool cap, holding a cup of coffee from the café in two hands covered in copper gloves.

Her caption read, "*Dear gourd! Orange you happy it's fall, ya'll? If you don't like autumn puns, you better leaf now, because I'm about to get as cliché as pun-king pie under a harvest moon sky!*"

He chuckled, reading through a dozen clever autumn hashtags. His favorite was *maybe she's born with it, maybe it's maple leaf.*

His mouth tightened around a smile. She was funny. He read her cleverness as a sign of intelligence.

She had a lot of pictures with smaller children which further bolstered his confidence about hiring her. All in all, she seemed like a sweet young woman. But he reminded himself that social media only showed the best—often times artificial—sides of people.

No one was sweet all the time. Like everyone else, she probably had a side that wasn't so nice, and maybe she even had a side that hid a little spice.

His brain raced somewhere he had no business trespassing and he shut his laptop. Best not to think of her that way. She was the last hope as far as local childcare went, and he really needed this to work out—for Addison's sake.

Jasper Falls had a daycare issue that needed to be addressed. He'd tried to get the funding to open a pre-K, but a public pre-school wasn't in the budget. Until that changed, he was stuck looking for private help like everyone else with children under age five.

Shoving aside his forgotten sandwich, he flipped open

his portfolio. Erin typically left a print out of his schedule for the next day and any notes he might need to prepare for meetings. His gaze snagged on a handwritten message.

Adel's landlord called again. She still hasn't paid November's rent and December's is now overdue.

He sighed. It never ended.

Returning to his laptop, he directed an email back to Erin—subject line: PRIORITY.

Get a rundown of what Adel owes and see if you can get her on the phone. I need to find out what's going on. I also don't want to pay anything unless everything is working properly at the apartment. Make sure the heater's been inspected and that all the porch lights have working bulbs. And put together another grocery order for her. Make it a generous one. The holidays are coming. Use my personal card.

He sent the message then cursed, opening up a second email to his assistant—subject line: ALSO...

The new nanny starts today. I'd like you to pop in on her whenever you can, just to see that everything is running smoothly and answer any questions she might have.

With the election coming, I can't afford to lose this one. I want her to feel at home and as comfortable as possible in her new position.

He glanced at the refrigerator, not needing to open the door to recall it basically housed a jar of mustard, cold cuts, and some leftovers.

Unlike Jan, his secretary, Erin wasn't on the town's payroll. Erin worked specifically for him as his right hand, so he had no issue imposing on her. She picked up his dry cleaning, did his shopping, and even helped him find popular toys for Addison during the holiday season.

Erin had a way of anticipating his every need and inserting herself at exactly the right moment. He'd be lost without her.

One of the bedrooms will have to be prepared. She can choose any of the unused ones. Have her make a list of any additional items she might need to help her settle in.

There isn't much food in the fridge. Please take the morning to replenish the pantry and fully stock the kitchen with anything Ms. Marcelli might require. I trust you know what to get. I want her to feel at home, since she will be staying. If there's anything else you think of, you have my credit card.

He closed the email with an inside joke about her ever-growing Christmas bonus. He had no doubt Erin would see to everything he asked.

This time, Rhett would make sure the new governess had every amenity she could want and no chance of getting burnt out like the last four nannies. He trusted Erin to see to her comfort.

4

STEPPING outside of the café with her peppermint coffee in hand, Skylar breathed in the crisp winter air and grinned. The wind held the bite of snow, and the sky was swathed in wispy clouds.

Across the street, Christmas trees crowded the parking lot of O'Malley's Pub, and salt sprinkled the roads in anticipation of that first dusting of white.

Gazing at the mayor's mansion at the other end of Main Street, just beyond the Town Hall, a swirl of excitement gathered in Skylar's belly. She'd been so keyed up about her new job—and new salary—she barely slept a wink last night.

Bouncing out of bed around five, she showered and dressed in a carefully selected first day of work outfit. Her salary raised the expectations and she didn't want to disappoint, so she tried for a professional look that wasn't too schoolmarm-ish. She wanted to impress her boss, but she also wanted to dress in a way a four-year-old would view as approachable.

Rocking a gray wool skirt she snagged from the thrift shop last winter, she paired it with black tights and a white turtleneck sweater. The whole outfit put off great governess vibes, and she was pleased with the end result.

...Pleased with herself.

She was a governess...

It started to flurry once she returned with her coffee to her car. She had so many fun ideas for activities to do with Addison, and if it snowed, she could dig into her winter collection of crafts and games.

Skylar wasn't quite sure what to expect of her new boss. He seemed busy and important, but also human in a refreshingly humble sort of way.

Maybe she should feel more intimidated around him, but yesterday he seemed so frazzled and in need of help, she could only see him as a dad in need of a female's touch. *For his daughter, of course!* There would be no touching him. He was her boss.

She backed out of her parking spot and carefully navigated the traffic.

Should she call him Mayor Buchanan? Or Mr. Buchanan? Or was it okay to call him Rhett?

She never thought much about the mayor. Before, he had just been the guy who beat her grandfather in the election. She'd done some campaigning on Pop's behalf and helped stuff envelopes, but Rhett Buchanan had the magnetic sort of charisma women especially seemed to love.

He could speak about bridges and park benches and stir the most inspired response among the town's people. A lot of the men bristled at his natural charm, but Skylar believed that was just poorly disguised envy, because all the women in Jasper Falls—married and single—remarked about how handsome he was.

He was indisputably striking in a timeless way, but she gave him more credit than simply having good genes and a nice voice. He was a visionary and a doer. Since becoming mayor, their little town had improved in ways she never imagined.

She'd never admit it out loud, but she thought Rhett Buchanan proved the better man for the job. She adored her grandfather, but Mr. Buchanan had accomplished so much in such a short time, she believed he possessed a true gift for civil service.

Since he'd taken office, the residents seemed happier. And now she was happier, because she would finally be earning enough money to finance her bachelor's degree and eventually finish her education.

It didn't matter that she would be going to college virtually. She still got to experience living out from under her parents' roof. That was a start in the right direction of finding her independence. And the amount of money she'd be saving on room and board alone made her job worthwhile. But then he had offered her a fabulous starting salary on top of that. If she budgeted and saved her money, she might actually graduate with no student debt, which was practically unheard of.

She hadn't even started yet and she loved her new job. She loved her little town and loved the fact that it was snowing. Nothing but sugar-sifted skies and green lights guided her way up Main Street.

However, those cozy small-town sensations died the moment she arrived at his property. Sure, this house boasted stunning architecture and the landscaping was clean, even for winter, but there was something cold and unlived-in about the place, something she had never noticed from the town's view.

It was almost eerie. The shutters were painted a gleaming black that contrasted beautifully against the white brick, but something was off. She couldn't put her finger on it.

As she parked the car beside an old oak tree, she stared

up at the looming home and a shiver chased down her spine. The hollow vibe was so unexpected it threw her confidence.

Maybe it was just the house and had nothing to do with the family inside. After all, the home had housed a hundred mayors, each one replacing the last with a portion of the town's tax dollars going toward the historic property's upkeep. It didn't technically belong to the Buchanans. It belonged to Jasper Falls, so any creepy vibes she sensed shouldn't be held against them.

Leaving the boxes of supplies in her car, she climbed the brick steps and knocked. A grand glass chandelier hung overhead, reminding her of the one in the Rose Garden at the White House.

The door swung open and her gaze climbed the front of her new boss. The wall of his chest seemed broader than the day before, and an expanse of tanned skin peeked out where his collar was undone.

His hair was damp and the air smelled of soap and mint. His brow creased and his eyes focused on something over her shoulder.

Had she parked in a bad place?

"Good morning. Am I too early?" Peeking around his body, she did a quick scan of the home. The inside was worse. Empty and vacant of life. Cold.

It wasn't the size of the home. Her family had lots of big houses and none of them felt as expressionless as this.

"Morning." His distracted gaze scanned the yard. "Is that snow?"

"Yup!"

"Great." His dry tone contradicted her cheer. "Come in."

She stomped her feet on the mat before stepping into the cavernous foyer. It might be a house, but it didn't feel like much of a home.

As far as personal touches went, there weren't any that

she could see. Polished floors and a mammoth staircase dotted with ancient furniture upholstered in cold satins and stiff batting. She couldn't process why it felt so chilly when the outside was twice as cold.

Removing her coat and hat, she shook the flurries out of her hair. "Not a winter person?"

"Snow creates chaos."

She supposed it did. "But it's so pretty."

He paused and gave her a strange look, then pivoted and walked deeper into the house, each step of his fancy shoes echoing off the polished floor. "You can hang your coat on the hook in the foyer. Addison is still sleeping."

She did as he instructed and quickly caught up to him. He glanced down at her as she kept pace by his side. Did he not expect her to follow?

She paused and considered the time. "I expected Addison to be awake. Does she usually sleep this late?"

"She usually rises somewhere between nine and eleven, unless I wake her. Are you a morning person?"

Skylar liked to think of herself as an *everything* person, a sort of *go with the current* kind of gal. "That's a wide range." She considered how important structure and routine was for children Addison's age. "What time does she usually go to bed?"

"Whenever I head up. Last night I was looking over grant proposals until after midnight."

Her eyes widened. Didn't he know that children Addison's age needed sleep for proper development? "You let her stay up until after midnight?"

"She usually crashes on the sofa, but doesn't like to go to bed until I do."

Skylar followed him into what appeared to be the family room. The couch was actually something designed after the eighteenth century and she found great comfort in the sight of a messy toybox in the corner.

"She can be a little cranky in the mornings," he warned. "She usually has her cereal in here and watches a few hours of television to wake up."

"A few *hours*?"

"I know." He at least had the self-awareness to look semi-guilty. "I read all the articles about limiting children's screen time, but it's just easier. As a single dad, I'm sort of stretched thin. You're welcome to adapt her schedule however you see fit. God knows it won't hurt."

"I appreciate that. Does Addison have any allergies I need to know about?"

Skylar would typically take this time to inform him that she was CPR certified and offer other credentials to put him at ease, but she was getting the impression that he truly had been desperate for any capable body to help care for his kid.

"No, but she's never been stung by a bee, so I guess there's that." He looked unsure for a moment, a total contradiction to his powerful posture and the sleek part of his hair. "Just call 9-1-1 if anything goes wrong. And I should give you my number as well."

"That would be good."

She'd followed him into a cavernous kitchen. It appeared recently renovated, as the appliances were all stainless and state of the art, but the cabinetry looked handcrafted and old world. He gave her a brief tour of the drawers and shelves, pointing out where the silverware was and inviting her to help herself to anything in the pantry.

"Erin will be by to set you up with groceries. I want you to make yourself at home. If there's anything you need, please add it to the shopping list. I know moving into a new home will be an adjustment, but I don't want you to feel restricted to your room. Which reminds me, Erin came by early this morning and made up one of the bedrooms for you."

"Erin?" She recalled the woman, but hadn't been

formally introduced yet. She wasn't sure what her relationship was to Rhett.

"My PA. You should have her number, too. I'll send it to you. She can answer any questions you might have—probably better than me. She controls my schedule, handles all my daily tasks, and basically keeps me from losing my mind."

"Wow."

He paused. They had circled through the cavernous house and returned to the foot of the winding staircase. "Wow?"

She shrugged. "It must be nice to have someone that attentive all the time." He must be pretty important to have so much going on that he *needed* an Erin in his life. Skylar mostly navigated day-to-day living on her own.

He grinned. "Erin's a real asset." He didn't say more, but she suspected there might be something more than a business relationship there.

Following him around was like the scene in *Annie* when she arrives at Daddy Warbucks's house. It was an overwhelming orientation and she was certain she'd need things repeated, but he seemed in such a rush to give her a tour, she simply tried to absorb as much as possible.

The second floor had six large bedrooms. "The door on the far end is the master. The middle one is Addison's. Let me text Erin and see which room she made up for you."

The bedrooms were all enormous with grand windows and antique furniture. She'd never slept in a large space and worried it might feel like resting in a tomb more than the cozy, cramped bedroom she'd grown up in.

His phone pinged and he frowned. "Huh—I guess she was thinking of privacy. She set you up on the third floor."

At the end of the hall, opposite the master bedroom, was a narrow door leading to an even narrower staircase that curved at the bottom. She followed him up the slim wooden steps and instantly thought of *Flowers in the Attic.*

Bare wood floors and a large window gave the room a sense of vacancy. The furniture was simple and dark wood. The bed was a twin with only a quilt folded on top. There was an antique wardrobe cabinet on the far wall and a private bathroom with a claw-foot tub behind the other.

The fireplace in the corner had been painted over with white and no longer appeared functional, but the room seemed warm enough, aside from the draft she felt by the front window. The glass was old and marbled, beautiful but drafty. Nothing some curtains wouldn't fix.

"I'm sure you'll have plenty of belongings to bring."

Not really. "It's lovely. Thank you."

"Feel free to personalize the space to suit your taste." He paused and studied her. "I should be the one thanking you. I was fresh out of options and had been running help wanted ads for two weeks trying to find someone to help with Addison. It's not good for her to be cooped up in an office all day. Kids should be busy running around and playing. I'm grateful you found us."

She agreed, children needed freedom and supervision to safely explore. "I'm sure we'll have a great time getting to know each other."

His head tipped as his stare turned curious. "Did you always want to work with kids?"

"Ever since I learned that a unicorn doctor isn't a thing, and a bride is just a one day job."

A smile climbed to his eyes. "A bride?"

She shrugged. "Moms are a big deal in my family. When I was little, I just assumed you needed to be a bride to be a mom."

"So, you want kids."

"I think so—someday."

"How old are you?"

She flushed, hoping he wasn't asking because she sounded immature or overly whimsical, which she sometimes was. "I'm twenty-one."

He blinked as if this surprised him. "I assumed you were a little older." He took a subtle step back, but she felt the intentional distance, unsure how to translate such body language.

"Is my age a problem?"

"Not at all. Just a surprise."

An awkward moment passed where neither of them seemed to know how to gracefully move on. "I have all my paperwork in the car," she blurted, painfully aware of the strange shift in energy.

"Ah. Good. Erin will need that."

Right. Erin.

Maybe dealing with Erin would be less awkward than dealing with him. Maybe it was this house. The charismatic mayor she glimpsed on the streets of Jasper Falls didn't seem the same as the man standing in front of her now.

He held himself so stiff, he appeared almost brittle. And the gaping voids of conversation filled with long silent seconds passed like a handful of sand down a windpipe. She desperately wished Addison would wake up. Children were easier to read than adults.

Following him downstairs, she studied the layout of the house and asked questions pertinent to the job. He went over a few of Addison's preferences as far as food choices and cartoons.

Skylar got the impression that they ate a lot of takeout and TV dinners. Aside from the occasional meal at her grandfather's restaurant, which was technically homemade, her family never ordered out or ate anything out of a box. Her grandmother and great-aunts wouldn't allow it.

A collection of freshly laundered dry cleaning hung on a hook in the foyer, beside her coat. He flipped through the many suits and located a collection of ties, selecting a winter green one that matched his eyes.

She hadn't meant to stare, but coming from a family that mostly wore flannel or cotton, she found his wardrobe fascinating. Sometimes her Uncle Braydon wore suits when he worked in the city, but those didn't seem to have the same effect Mr. Buchanan's suits were having on her now.

He knotted his tie with practiced ease. "You can call me or Erin with any questions throughout the day."

The air of the house still carried a chill, but her skin felt overheated. "I should be fine."

He slipped his arms into a pressed jacket and hitched it up his broad shoulders. "I try to wrap up at five every day, but I usually don't get home until sometime between six and eight. Is that okay?"

"Sure." Her throat dried and tightened. She assumed the job would be demanding, which was why she was eager to move her personal belongings into the house. "I haven't had time to pack, but I thought I could fully move my stuff in this weekend."

"Of course. The sooner the better." A collection of personal effects sat on a table by the door. A watch. A wallet. A few business cards.

She watched as he sorted and tucked each item into its place. His brisk movements seemed so methodical and practiced, thoughtless, but also extremely thought out. She couldn't help drawing comparisons between him and the men in her family, men who burped and kicked off their dusty boots and scratched themselves and grew beards out of sheer laziness and primitive habits.

There was nothing primitive about Rhett Buchanan. *Primal* seemed a much more fitting label. He was all man, but the most practiced, polished man she'd ever seen up close. She found him extremely intimidating and longed for the return of the humble, frazzled father she met yesterday.

Once he closed the clasp of his watch he turned to her, and his attention felt so hot and acute—almost accusing—her face burned and her gaze dropped to the floor. He totally caught her staring at him.

He cleared his throat. "You have everything you need?"

The pit of her belly hollowed with a sense of emptiness longing to be filled. She had all the information she needed to properly care for his child, but as far as having what she needed? She definitely felt like she did not. Her stomach muscles coiled around her core like hunger grabs hold of emptiness and squeezes. But she wasn't hungry, not in any way she'd suffered hunger before.

"Skylar?"

Her name traced his lips with gentle inquisitiveness but tightened her body like a reprimand. What the hell was wrong with her? "Um..." What had he asked? Her needs... "Yes. I'm good."

His stare latched onto hers, and his gaze softened and intensified at the same time as if he could see through her and read all the chaos racing through her mind. "Good."

Such a simple word, and she'd never enjoyed it more than when he said it to her.

Just then, Addison came downstairs, delivering a world of relief. Her presence was like a window opening, shooting a breath of fresh air into Skylar's constricting lungs. There was definitely something weird about this house.

Wearing the same mismatched outfit, she had on yesterday, Addison rocked a case of bedhead so bad there might have been a small animal living in her hair.

"Morning, sweetheart."

"Morning, Daddy." She climbed up his body like a monkey climbs a tree, and he hoisted her onto his hip.

The transformation in him fascinated Skylar as his unapproachable power suit conformed into nothing but thread. Seeing him through his daughter's eyes, he was just a daddy—safe, dependable, a rock of a pillow and a shoulder to lean on.

Skylar smiled.

"Addy, you remember Skylar, right?"

"Hi," she said, resting her head on his shoulder and pressing her little palm to his neatly shaved jaw.

Skylar wondered what it might be like to press her nose there and breathe deep. Did he smell like other men? She had a feeling he'd smell different. Better.

"I'm super excited to hang out with you today!" She needed to get control of her thoughts.

Addison nestled closer to her father, wreathing her arms around his neck. "I don't want you to go."

Skylar held her breath, waiting to see if he would brush her off or indulge her with some extra time. He did neither, and somehow delivered the best possible response.

He set her down and kissed her head. "Have to. I have an important meeting with the big guy at the North Pole today. It takes a lot of convincing to get him to come to our town's holiday party when he has the rest of the world begging for his presence."

Her mouth opened in awe. "Is he coming to the office?"

"No, he's too busy. We're having a phone meeting, but I don't want to be late."

"Will you tell him I've been extra good?"

"Of course, I will. And don't forget that he's watching, so be a good girl for Skylar, too."

"I will."

Skylar appreciated the help and took Addison's hand as they walked him to the door. Another shift happened as he gathered his coat. First, was the dramatic reminder that it had started to snow. By the sound of his wincing groan when he opened the door and saw the world dusted in white, he really didn't care for winter weather. But then, as he turned back and smiled at his daughter, and hesitated, Skylar saw the moment he wished he didn't have to go.

She wondered if he ever took the time to actually play in the snow with his little girl. Maybe he forgot how much fun a winter storm could be.

She wasn't sure if he was the type to take an afternoon off for a snow day or if he just didn't care, but she suspected he loved his daughter very much and, like most parents, found it difficult to leave her each day.

He suddenly seemed more nervous than Skylar about the arrangement. She took pity on him. "You have my number if you want to check in and see how we're making out."

"Right. And you have mine—and Erin's."

"Yes." She'd added the contacts into her phone during their tour.

Hesitating, he held the door cracked and let a few flurries drift in. Addison gasped at the sight of the snow. "I feel like I'm forgetting something."

"Daddy, go! Santa's waiting!" Addison practically pushed him out the door, and once that invisible line of connection was broken, he was off and on his way.

"So," Skylar said, shutting the door and leaving the drafty weather outside. "What do you want for breakfast?"

"Cotton candy!"

"Try again."

"I guess cereal."

"Good choice."

5

THE PANTRY WAS PRETTY PICKED over and there wasn't any produce in the house. Ketchup was the closest thing Skylar found to a vegetable. "Have you ever been to the farmer's market in town?"

"Do they sell pigs and horses?"

Skylar laughed. "No, but they have all kinds of home-grown veggies from my aunt's farm. We can go shopping and maybe make a fruit salad later."

"Okay!"

Addison put up a little fuss when Skylar told her she had to eat breakfast at the table. But she stood her ground and kept control of the situation.

When she brushed the knots out of her hair, however, their relationship took a turn for the worse. Skylar feared she might need scissors to cut out the center of the knot, and she really didn't want to go there on her first day.

"Doesn't Daddy ever do your hair?" she asked as she carefully separated the baby-fine strands from the rat's nest they formed.

"No." Her eyes still glistened where big, fat tears had fallen. "He doesn't know how."

She supposed that might be true. She didn't know if her brothers knew how to braid. "Well, don't you want to show him how pretty your hair can be?"

"No!"

She had hardly pulled, but some delicate hairs at her neck had been snagged and the fear of pain seemed more powerful than the actual act. She suspected Mr. Buchanan had done his fair share of untangling her hair and men weren't always the gentlest touch.

"I'll have to tell your dad to pick up some detangler."

"What's that?" Addison sniffled.

"You know what, we can probably make our own."

In the kitchen, Skylar found a jar. She brought it to the upstairs bathroom and poured a dollop of conditioner on the bottom and then diluted it with some water. It didn't work as well as a squirt bottle, but it did the trick.

Dipping a comb into the liquid, she gently worked through Addison's tangles. Soon, the strands tapered down her narrow back in loosely coiled order.

Skylar carefully worked the hair into a thin French braid and tied a ribbon on the tip then set it over her shoulder. "Take a look."

Addison peeked in the mirror and tilted her head. "I guess it's nice."

"You guess?"

Her smile grew the longer she admired her reflection. "Can we show Daddy?"

"Tonight, when he comes home. And, if you sleep with your hair in a braid, it won't be so knotty each morning."

Addison's closet was full of beautiful clothing, several items still pinned with retail tags. "You have so many new outfits."

"They don't fit." She pointed to the majority of dresses slung to the back of the closet. "These are too small."

"You mean big?"

"No, small."

Skylar frowned and checked a few tags. Sure enough, they were toddler sized. "How come you never wore these?"

"Daddy works too much. He's always busy. And my other nannies didn't want to ruin them." She pointed to the large dresser. "Play clothes are in there."

Skylar flipped through the hangers. "Oh, honey, life's too short. You have to wear the dress, eat the cake, and take the risk."

"Huh?"

Pulling a red corduroy dress from a plush hanger, she grabbed an adorable pair of fur boots off the floor. "You've just been upgraded to the most fashionable four-year-old in all of Jasper Falls."

Bonding over clothing proved a bonding ritual between females of all ages, and Addison was no exception. The child—a girl after Skylar's own heart—loved being a little *extra*. Once they were buttoned up in their peacoats, with all the wooly winter trimmings, they were ready to go.

Skylar opened the front door and let out a yelp at the woman standing on the other side. "Oh, you scared me."

"Hi, Erin!"

"Hey, peanut." The woman looked Skylar square in the eye. "We briefly met the other day. I'm Erin, Rhett's right hand."

So, this was *the* Erin. "Nice to meet you. I'm Skylar."

She stepped into the house and Skylar backtracked, shutting the front door to keep the cold out. She'd been dying to get out of the house and they were bundled to go, but Erin had information and supplies she needed.

"We can go in a few minutes, Addison. Keep your coat on, but you can go play with your toys."

Erin studied them with a tight-lipped smile that didn't quite reach her eyes. "You two are going out? The roads are getting snowy."

"Oh, well, we were just running to the farmer's market to get some produce. Technically, we could walk."

"Actually, Rhett suggested grocery shopping. The pantry's usually picked over by midweek and he wanted it fully stocked. He's *very* particular and gets moody if he has to scavenge. You know how men can be. He also wanted dinner ready when he gets home. After all, that's what he's paying you for."

Technically, he was paying her to take care of his daughter, but he'd mentioned light cooking and cleaning. Skylar just assumed he meant she'd be performing those acts for Addison.

Erin spoke of Skylar's salary as if it somehow offended her. Did she know how much he was paying her? Did she think it was too much?

Being that it was a substantial pay increase from what she was used to, Skylar felt immediately uncomfortable and over-valued. Pressure to prove she was worth every penny he'd offered made her eager to meet every expectation.

"Can you recommend some meals he likes?"

"Skylar, I wanna go..." Addison tugged at her coat.

Erin glanced down at her. "Honey, why don't you go grab a Coke from the fridge."

"Oh—" Before Skylar could object, Addison bolted into the kitchen. "Please tell me that's for you."

"Let me give you a little advice, from one friend to another."

"Okay."

"Mr. Buchanan is under a lot of stress and he really can't be bothered with distractions right now. He's generously compensating you for your services to avoid any unforeseeable complications. We have two events this month, and the holidays are always a little more hectic than other months. He wants to get through Christmas and start the New Year off on the right foot. I suggest staying out of his way, keeping

Addison happy and occupied. Don't ask too many questions."

Her stare once again intensified as she looked directly at her. Skylar had the urge to drop her gaze, but forced herself to hold the other woman's stare. She didn't want her to assume she couldn't handle the job.

"Rhett might seem like a patient man, but that's all part of the job," Erin continued. "It's my business to adjust his life where needed, whenever needed, so he doesn't have to. That's the way he likes it. He tells me what needs to be done and I do it, so he can maintain diplomacy at all times. That includes the supervision, hiring, and firing of his staff. Understand?"

Skylar blinked like a cartoon, not used to this sort of abrasive intensity from others. She wasn't sure what Erin thought of her, but it seemed clear she didn't care for her. Skylar wasn't even sure she viewed her as a person, but it seemed clear she didn't see her as an equal.

At the moment, she felt a little like a trespassing spider Erin had decided to let live—for now.

"I understand." How else could she respond? Her attitude was completely unexpected and unfamiliar. Seriously, who spoke to people like that?

"Good." The word had a completely different impact than when Rhett had used it as a form of praise earlier.

Skylar swallowed, a little afraid to blink.

Erin reached into her purse and removed a manilla folder. "Here's your paperwork. Paychecks get electronically deposited every Thursday." She removed a one-hundred-dollar bill from her wallet. "And this is for this week's groceries."

Skylar never shopped for a family before, but quick math told her a hundred dollars wouldn't be enough for three people requiring three meals a day for a solid seven days, especially if she wanted to feed them more than junk.

Maybe when he said meals, he expected her to pay for her own. She should have thought of that. And he probably skipped breakfast and grabbed lunch in town.

"Is there a list?"

"Rule number one, Skylar, no one has time to hold your hand and walk you through every step. You'll only survive in this position if you know how to be assertive and get things done." She cocked her head and made the most patronizing pout. "Is that something you think you can handle?"

She wanted to snatch the money out of her hand and tell her to fuck off, but she simply smiled, some deep seated voice of maternal wisdom telling her that the strongest women didn't need salty language to face off with a bully. But the hillbilly in her really wanted to hogtie the bitch and shove a frog in her mouth. "I think I can handle it."

"Good."

Just then, Addison came running back into the foyer. She had a brown mustache and a spill down the front of her fuzzy, white coat.

Erin tsked. "Oh, honey, what have you done?"

Addison put her chin to her chest and frowned. "Whoopsie. I spilled."

"Your Daddy's going to be very upset if he sees that. That's your good coat." The child pouted and Erin turned to Skylar. "You'll have to get that cleaned. Mr. Buchanan wouldn't want his daughter walking around town in dirty clothes."

Really? Because yesterday she was running around in thirty degree weather without a jacket, in a mismatched outfit, with unbrushed hair. "I'll take care of it."

By the time Erin left, Skylar felt like she needed a nap. What had started as a fun outing, now felt like a heavily weighted assignment that could make or break her.

She blew out a breath and Addison did the same, mimicking her post-tornado posture. "Is she always like that?"

Addison shook her head at the door, imitating Skylar's tone. "Is she always like that?"

Skylar chuckled, needing the slight comic relief. Addison had a decent sense of humor for her age and they were going to have a nice day together, stains or not.

"Come on, kid. Let's change your coat and get going. We have a lot of stops to make."

❄

Being that she was only given a hundred dollar allowance to feed a family for a week, Skylar had to get creative. Luckily, she came from a long line of women who could feed an army on a dime and make pretty much anything from scratch.

She stocked the pantry with the basics, splurged on produce from the farmer's market, and went to the butcher for some cheap cuts of meat she could disguise with fancy side dishes.

A whirlwind of efficiency, she managed to do all the shopping, drop Addison's white coat off at the cleaners, swing by her Aunt Colleen's to grab a jar of Italian Mary's sauce, and get everything back to the house and unloaded before the snow truly started to stick.

Addison was getting cranky and Skylar figured she could probably use a nap, but naps weren't something the child was accustomed to.

"But it's daytime," she whined.

Skylar pulled the curtains closed in her bedroom, blocking out the sunlight. "I understand. But if you want to stay up and see Daddy tonight, you need to rest."

"I'm not tired!"

It hadn't taken long to realize Addison was used to getting everything she wanted and, often, spoiled as a supplement to actual structure. Skylar couldn't work like that.

"Today we're starting a new routine. This is quiet time. You can come down in one hour, and I'll have everything ready in the kitchen so we can make dessert for tonight."

Purple moons showed under her big brown eyes. Despite her objections, Addison slouched on her pillow. Her bedroom was decorated like something out of a magazine, giant plush animals spilling out of tiny chairs, a perfect tea set arranged for her dollies. Princess costumes hung from silk hangers, and her library was large enough to supply a school.

Skylar selected an old favorite from the shelf. "I love this story. How about we read it?" The book creaked as if it had never been opened and she wondered if the stories were as unused as the clothing in Addison's closet.

Lowering to the mattress, she sat on the edge of the bed and drew the covers over Addison's shoulders. "*In the great green room there was a telephone and a red balloon...*"

By the time she reached the middle of *Goodnight Moon*, Addison's eyelids were heavy. She slowly blinked, listening to the story and fell asleep before the last few page when Skylar whispered, *"Goodnight stars... Goodnight moon..."*

She quietly shut the book and left it for Addison to look at later, then backed out of the dim room.

Skylar was grateful for the break. It gave her time to freshen up, explore the house, and get more oriented with her new home.

Creeping through the second floor, she peeked through doorways and mentally catalogued each room. She wondered why she wasn't given one of the more luxurious guest rooms, but she supposed she was the help, and they wanted to keep their personal space private for the weekends and other family time.

At the end of the hall, where the master bedroom was

located, she stood outside the tall double doors. She wanted to see what was on the other side, but knew this was Mr. Buchanan's private space.

Her hand reached for the ornate handle and she paused. What if he had cameras?

She glanced at the ceilings and walls, not seeing any sort of surveillance. The house was old, so she didn't suspect it was wired for top secret spying. And this was Jasper Falls, after all.

Turning the knob, the latch clicked open. Cool air swept over her face as she crossed the threshold and stepped into the shadows.

A masculine scent, mixed with traces of soap, clung to the air. The furniture was carved, heavy wood, and the linens were midnight blue. The walls, papered in a gold and navy demask, suited the room for a king.

In the corner, a cherry wood secretary desk stood open. Tiny compartments and drawers held stationary, but there wasn't much paperwork scattered about. Just a notepad with an address scribbled on it, and a ledger of some sort. She scanned the numbers and frowned.

$1150 Rent
$425 Back Rent
$677 Medical
$82 Rx
$2,456 Collections
$96 Septa Pass
$82 Rx
$4,892 Brightview Treatment Center...

The list of expenses went on and on, but she didn't understand who was charging such things. There were countless prescription charges and medical bills, and very expensive treatment centers. Was someone sick? Perhaps Mr. Buchanan's parents?

She shouldn't have come in here. Backing out of the room—

She paused, her gaze snagging on something familiar.

Drifting across the carpet, she stared at her scarf, neatly folded and resting on the corner of his night stand. The pillows still wore the indentation from his head. Why was her scarf in here?

It belonged to her. Should she take it?

She couldn't, not without alerting him that she'd trespassed into his room. What was she doing?
Without touching anything, she quietly shut the door and turned—*"Mr. Buchanan."*

Her heart plummeted to her feet and she gasped.

"Skylar?" His gaze trailed down her front, dropping to her hand.

She followed his gaze and regret squeezed her insides as she stared at her hand still holding the knob of his door.

6

Skylar's bones seemed to shrink within her skin. It was as if her body was literally trying to implode through a black-hole and disappear. "I, uh, was looking for the towels."

It was clear he knew she was lying. She saw the awareness in his eyes. He knew it. She knew it. There was no covering the truth. Caught snooping, red handed. Ugh, he should just fire her now and get it over with.

Crossing the hall, he opened the door to the laundry room and removed a stack of white fluffy towels from a basket. "Where's Addy?"

"Addy?" She couldn't move. She was still standing with her back against his bedroom doors, the lingering scent of his morning shower still stuffed up her traitorous, snooping, nosey nose.

"My daughter, Addison."

"Oh, Addison. She's napping."

His stern, censoring stare was replaced with surprise. "Is she?" Surprise morphed into concern. "Was she feeling all right?"

She nodded. "Four-year-olds need naps."

"And she went down for you okay?"

She nodded again. Any second now, he'd remember she was outside of his door and fire her. "I read her a story and we had a busy morning."

"So, things are going well?"

They were. She swallowed. Should she just admit she'd been doing something bad and face the consequence?

Would he reprimand her? Punish her? Spank her? Dear God, where the holy hell had that image come from? She dropped her head back against the door and looked up, pleading for some sort of divine intervention to deliver her out of this mess.

He held out the stack of towels.

She took them and pulled the soft material to her chest. What the hell had he asked? Oh, if things were going well. "Yes."

"Yes?"

She panicked. "Yes...*sir*?"

His jade eyes darkened emerald as his pupils swelled. Oh shit. Maybe she pissed him off. "You asked if things were going well."

His head jerked and he breathed out a laugh. "Right. Sorry."

Now he was apologizing? She was the one who owed him an apology. "Mr. Buchanan—"

"Rhett."

Her throat had narrowed to a pipe cleaner. "Rhett..."

The longer he stared at her the harder it became to speak. "Skylar."

"Yes?"

"I need to get something out of my bedroom."

It finally happened. She was as certifiable as the rest of her family. Ducking out of reach, she moved to the adjacent wall. "Sorry."

The side of his full lips quirked into a half grin and disappeared inside the master bedroom. A moment later, he returned to the hall, holding a blue checkbook she recognized from the desk.

"I shouldn't be too late tonight. You can expect me a little after seven."

He wasn't going to fire her? "We'll see you then."

"Perfect. Enjoy the rest of your day."

He took the winding staircase with a youthful pace that didn't quite match the impression Erin gave of him earlier.

When the front door closed, Skylar exhaled all the breath she'd been holding and deflated, sliding down the wall until her butt hit the floor. She rolled to her side and smooshed her face in the pile of towels then groaned. "I'm such an idiot."

❄

She definitely underestimated her mom, aunts, and grandmothers.

"It smells like fire!" Addison scrunched her nose and fanned away the smoke bellowing out of the oven.

"Shit, shit, shit, shit..."

"Ooooh, you said shit!"

Skylar removed the charred casserole from the rack and tossed it onto the stove. "Well, don't repeat me!"

Addison angled her head and stretched her neck to better see the ruined dish. "You killed it."

Skylar sighed. Cooking was not supposed to be this difficult.

She glanced at the time. It was almost seven—not enough time to make something new, and no possibility of fixing the burned casserole. "Shit."

"You said shit again."

"Stop repeating me!"

"Then stop saying potty words!"

"Sorry." Skylar rubbed a hand through her sweaty hair.

Lifting Addison off the counter, she said, "Go get your shoes. We're running out."

It was dark and the roads were wet with slush and snow. Luckily, Jasper Falls was only four miles long, so they didn't have far to go.

"Are we eating here?" Addison asked as they parked outside of Vincenzo's.

"No, we're just picking something up." She'd called ahead and told her Aunt Angela it was an emergency.

The front windows of the restaurant fogged with oregano and garlic scented steam. The heat drew them inside, and the sound of Dean Martin crooning from the speakers made her feel right at home—something she hadn't felt all day.

Skylar momentarily wondered if it was a mistake, leaving the familiarity of family and venturing into this new job. There was a good chance that Mr. Buchanan might still fire her. Maybe he just didn't want to do it in the middle of the day and be left stranded without child care. Maybe he was waiting for Erin to do it, since she seemed to claim hiring and firing as her forte.

Aunt Nicky's head poked through the kitchen window. "Hey, your order's not finished yet." Without waiting for a reply, she turned and yelled, "Sky's here. Where are my chicken cutlets?"

"Well, well, well, look who's returned." Her grandfather, dressed in black, flour-dusted pants, a white tank top, and a sauce-stained kitchen apron, appeared. The gray hair on his chest was so thick and wild, it also carpeted his shoulders. Gold chains glinted under the florescent lighting as he stepped into the front dining room.

"Who's this little *bellezza*?"

"Hi Pop. This is Addison. Addy, this is my grandfather, Vincenzo."

"*The* Vincenzo?"

Her grandfather nodded. "This is my place. Here. You taste this." He snatched a pizza fritta knot from under the glass display and sprinkled it with sugar.

Addison accepted the offering and sniffed it before tasting. Her face lit up when she chewed.

"Good?" Pop asked and she nodded. He narrowed his eyes at Skylar. "So, you've come back?"

"I had a kitchen emergency."

"Everyone comes back. They say they want to leave, but in the end, they always return. You know why? Because you can always count on family."

Her grandmother, Camilla, appeared carrying a large box of food. "Leave her alone, Vincenzo." She slid the box onto the counter. "I put a piece of cardboard between the salads so they don't get hot, but don't leave them in there for too long."

"Thanks, Nonna."

"She's paying for that. We don't feed outsiders for free," Pop said.

He made no secret of his disapproval. Not only did he prefer his daughters and granddaughters working in the family business, he openly despised Rhett Buchanan, the man who single-handedly beat him in the last election.

"Get back in the kitchen," Nonna snapped as she punched something into the register. As soon as Pop grumbled his way through the swinging door, the register opened and she slammed it shut. "I'll still give you a little discount —just between us."

Aunt Angela appeared and Aunt Nicky followed. "So, how is it?"

"What's he like?"

Skylar shrugged. "I'm still getting settled. And to be honest, he's a little intimidating at times. I don't know how to read him."

Nicky tipped her chin toward Addison, who was

drawing pictures in the steam on the front window. "That the rug rat?"

"That's Addison."

"She's cute. Is she good?"

"So far I haven't had any major problems."

"Make sure they pay, Camilla. That man doesn't deserve my food," her grandfather's voice yelled from the kitchen window.

"Get out of here!" Nonna snapped, then punched a few keys in the register again. "Forty-two-ninety-one."

Skylar inwardly winced. It was more than fifty percent off, but still a lot for one meal. She really needed to improve her cooking skills.

Reaching into her purse, she removed her debit card and handed it to her grandmother. The three women glanced at it and scowled.

"Why are you paying for their dinner?" Nicky asked.

Skylar flushed and lied, "I get reimbursed."

The truth was, she already spent the grocery budget and burned tonight's dinner, so she had to make things right. She didn't plan on telling Mr. Buchanan about it.

"I should hope so!"

"And really, Skylar," Nonna said, ringing her out. "You should be preparing meals yourself. You know how to cook."

"I know. It's just the first day." She couldn't afford take-out, anyway, not on the grocery allowance Mr. Buchanan was providing.

She gathered the box and her aunt held the door, walking them out to the car. "Watch the snow. It's slippery."

Once she had Addison buckled and the food secured on the back seat, she faced Nicky. "What?"

Her aunt, who was only in her late twenties, smiled. "What's he like?"

"I haven't really interacted with him. He's always busy."

Her eyes rolled back. "He's so sexy. You should really mention that you have a single aunt."

Actually, Skylar had three, but that didn't matter. "I think he's sleeping with his personal assistant."

Her dreamy expression twisted into revulsion. "Who? Erin Montgomery?"

"Yeah."

"No way. Ugh, that just knocked him down a rung."

"Do you know her?"

"She used to date your Uncle Finn."

Skylar's eyes bulged. "Erin did?"

"Yeah, before Aunt Mallory came around. She was horrible to him. And I'm pretty sure she slept around behind his back."

"Do you think she knows I'm Finn's niece?"

"I'm sure. There isn't much that gets past her. God, I can't imagine him hooking up with that witch. He can do so much better."

Skylar wanted more details about the woman tied to her boss's life, but she was running out of time and had to get back. "You'll have to fill me in on her later."

"Definitely." Aunt Nicky kissed her cheek and instructed her to drive safe.

On the way back to the mayor's house, she couldn't stop thinking about how revolted her aunt looked at the mention of Erin. It actually helped, because after their interaction that morning, Skylar felt a little off-kilter. She sensed something passive-aggressive hiding under her surface, but couldn't figure out why Erin disliked her when they only just met.

Now, it made more sense. It wasn't Skylar. It was her family. Strangely, she could accept that. Her family could be *a lot* at times.

They made it back to the house, and she had everything transferred to serving dishes and on the table when Mr.

Buchanan arrived. He entered the dining room and stilled, seeming surprised to find the table set.

"Wow."

"Daddy!" Addison charged out of the kitchen and catapulted into her father's arms.

"Look at you!" He kissed her cheek and hoisted her onto his hip, inspecting her hair and outfit. "You're all dressed up."

"Skylar did my hair."

"I can tell. It's beautiful." He smiled and the expression climbed all the way to his eyes. "I'm impressed."

She didn't know why his praise flustered her, so she ducked her head and mumbled that it was nothing as she put the chicken cutlets on the table.

He placed Addison in a chair and grinned. "This looks amazing. And it smells terrific."

She fidgeted like a klutz and dropped a serving fork with a loud clatter, catching it awkwardly before it landed on the floor. She should confess she didn't make the food. "Well, enjoy."

"Wait a minute. You have to eat, too."

She paused at the door, hesitating. This was his time with Addison and she had a sink full of scorched dishes to handle. "That's okay—"

"Nonsense. Take a seat."

"Yeah, Skylar, sit down," Addison commanded with a bright smile. The nap had served her well today.

Before she could make another excuse, Mr. Buchanan gripped her shoulders and steered her toward the table. The weight and heat of his large hands frayed the last of her wits and she dropped into a seat without objection. It was the chair meant for him.

"I only set two places," she murmured.

"I'll grab another plate." Already on his way to the door, he glanced over his shoulder and pointed at her. "Stay put. I want to hear all about the day you two had." He disappeared into the kitchen, and she regretted the mess he found on the other side of the door.

As soon as he returned, she confessed, "I had a little trouble with the oven. I'm not used to cooking with gas."

He glanced at the feast laid out before them. "If this is what trouble looks like, I think we're fine."

"I can't take responsibility for this. It's from my family's restaurant."

"Vincenzo made it!" Addison announced.

Mr. Buchanan paused from serving. "Vincenzo Marcelli?"

Skylar bit her lip. "I hope that's okay."

He hesitated then laughed. "Well, this finally gives me a chance to taste his cooking. Everyone's always raving about it." He didn't need to state that he wasn't welcome in the restaurant. Her grandfather made that clear enough. "So, tell me what you two did today."

His genuine interest was unexpected, as was his enthusiasm for the meal. It made it worth all the trouble of cooking.

Addison reviewed every detail of their day while they ate. Not only did Mr. Buchanan enjoy the meal, he had seconds followed by thirds. It was safe to say he loved it.

"Well, it sounds like you two are off to a great start."

"Tomorrow, we're making a snowman! And Skylar promised to teach me how to bake a pie!"

"A pie?" His attention returned to Skylar, and his eyes smoldered as his voice dropped low. "I love pie."

Addison bounced with excitement. "It's gonna be an apple pie! We bought the apples today at the farmer's market and I made friends with Hunter, the farmer's son. The farmer's a girl, daddy!"

Captivated by his daughter's enthusiasm, he glanced at Skylar and smirked. "Who is this Hunter?"

She laughed. "He's my cousin. He helps out at the market."

"Ah, I think I know who he is."

Hunter was older, but had a very young heart and a unique mind. He loved their town and every person in it. She wasn't surprised that he was thrilled to meet Addison today. Now that he associated the young girl with Skylar, he'd likely ask about her every time they crossed paths.

After dinner, Skylar cleared the table while Addison retold the story they read before her nap. "Will you read it to me, again, Daddy?"

"I'd love to."

Skylar pressed a hand to her heart as she slipped into the kitchen, giving the father and daughter some privacy. Mr. Buchanan was a good father for the simple fact that he showed so much interest in the things that interested Addison.

Rinsing off the plates, Skylar set the dishes on the rack to dry and scooped out three servings of fruit salad, topping each one with a dollop of whipped cream they made from scratch.

The door opened and Mr. Buchanan appeared, startling her. "Addison's using the bathroom."

"Oh." Awkwardly balancing the three bowls in her arms, she waited for him to hold the door or step aside. He did neither. "I was just going to bring out dessert."

He stared at her, stared at the fruit salad, and the mess behind her in the kitchen. Then he frowned.

"I'm sorry about the mess. I'll clean it—"

"Forget the mess."

Her breath hitched. Was this it, the moment he'd call her out for trespassing in his private room and being a no good snoop?

"I want to thank you."

"Huh?"

"This is... I can't remember the last time we shared a meal like this, at a table, with actual conversation."

Was there another way to eat? In her family, meals were the only way they communicated. "It's no big deal."

He caught her arm. "It is a big deal, Skylar. It's a big deal for Addy and I should have realized that. She doesn't always know what she's missing because she's young, but I should know better. I appreciate you reminding me of the ways I can do better by her."

If he only knew how disinterested some fathers were in their daughter's lives. Skylar had been lucky. She always had a dad close by, showing her how to hook bait on a line but also up for combing her dolly's hair if that's what was on the agenda. But some girls were simply ignored. "I think you're already doing a great job."

"I can always do better."

"Don't be so hard on yourself. The most important thing is that you love her, and it's clear you do."

"Thank you. For everything."

Her cheeks heated. "Well...you're welcome."

He didn't move and she tried her best to patiently wait and ignore the strawberry juice slipping down her thumb.

"I think you're the best choice I've made for my daughter in a long time."

His words struck a chord deep within her heart and her gaze lowered. "Thank you."

The silence expanded, tightening the energy around them like a rubber band she feared might snap. Her stomach swooped and she held her breath as his feet moved closer. When his hand slowly lifted, her heart beat wildly and her knees shook. "Mr. Buchanan—"

"Let me help you with this." He relieved her of the fruit salad cups and pushed open the door, holding it with his body so she could slip by.

Okay, totally misread the situation.

Her face flamed as she slipped by him, her back slightly brushing his front—one hundred percent by accident—but she swore she heard his breath catch in a masculine sort of grunt.

What was a grunt? She wasn't versed in grunting. Had she misread him? She was picking up all sorts of mixed signals.

Job. This was her job. She was harboring completely inappropriate thoughts. *Head out of the gutter, Marcelli!*

Addison skipped back to the table and bounced into her chair. "All clean!" she announced holding out her freshly washed hands.

Mr. Buchanan set the fruit cups on the table and Addison gasped.

"Daddy, we made the whipped cream with scratch!"

"*From* scratch," Skylar corrected.

"It looks amazing!" He set out three spoons and glanced over his shoulder. "You coming?"

Skylar bustled to the table and sat down rougher than intended, jostling the glasses. "Sorry."

He grinned. "This looks delicious. What did you put in here, Addy?"

"We put cantaloupe, blueberries, strawberries..." As she listed all the fruit, Skylar studied him. It was a perfect moment until his cell phone rang.

"Sorry, sweetheart, I have to take this." He lifted the phone to his ear. "Erin?" The mumbled voice on the other end spoke and he chuckled. "And that's why I need you. Thanks for reminding me."

Skylar slipped into the kitchen and started on the rest of the dishes. Addison helped, claiming that her dad was still on the phone about work.

Once they had the kitchen returned to its usual order, she drew a bath for Addison, adding a little lavender to settle her. After the bath, Skylar combed out her hair and braided it.

They returned to the den once Addison was buffed to a shine and in her ruffled nightgown ready for bed. Mr. Buchanan blinked in surprise as if he hardly recognized his own daughter. "Look at you!"

Addison raced over to him and flung her body against his in a gush of giggles and hugs. Skylar smiled and left them alone for a bit, so they could have some time together.

At bedtime, she lured Addison upstairs with the promise of another story. Tucked in and listening attentively, her heavy, brown eyes watched the pages turn as Skylar read.

A floorboard creaked and Skylar sensed they had an audience, which distracted her. Sure enough, Mr. Buchanan observed them from the door but didn't enter or interrupt.

At the end of the story, Skylar brushed a hand over Addison's hair and wished her sweet dreams. Only then, did Mr. Buchanan enter the room to kiss his daughter goodnight.

Skylar waited in the hall as he quietly backed out of the room and shut the door.

"You really have a gift with children."

"Thank you."

He hesitated. "Was she good for you, today? I know she can be challenging at times."

She could, but so could every four-year-old. "She was an angel."

He chuckled. "I know my daughter, Skylar. It's okay to tell me the truth."

"Mr. Buchanan, she was perfect. I'd tell you if there were any issues."

"Rhett."

She bit her lip. It was the second time he reminded her to use his first name, but Erin had adamantly referred to him as Mr. Buchanan when addressing Skylar. Still, he was her boss, not Erin. "Rhett." She couldn't survive another awkward silence. "If it's okay with you, I'm going to head home. I still have to pack and—"

"Of course." He took a wide step back and averted his stare to the other end of the hall. "I hope we didn't detain you."

"Oh no, dinner was nice, and I intended to help get her to bed. That's my job, after all." It was, wasn't it? She really wasn't clear about when she should step in and when she should back off when Rhett was around.

"Well, thank you for a great first day. We'll expect you at the same time tomorrow?"

"I'll be here."

He watched as she bundled up, and she wondered what sort of thoughts he hid in the wide-open silence. It would be less awkward once she moved in and could just slip away to her room to avoid these strange moments that sort of made her feel like an exhibit at the zoo. Did he always stare so much?

It had been a long day and she'd hardly slept the night before. Typically, when she finished a shift, she liked to zone out and forget about work, but she thought about the Buchanans the entire drive home—especially her boss.

The strange thing about Rhett Buchanan was his ability to put others at ease. He'd redeveloped their forgotten town into a storybook village, complete with all the bells and whistles. Yet, in his own home, he seemed completely at odds. Personal accents and assets remained tightly packaged and tagged, as if he never truly settled in.

The mansion was cold because it was simply a house. It boggled her mind that a man who could transform their entire town couldn't turn his own house into a home.

They didn't have any Christmas decorations or personal photographs sitting around, and some of the rooms, like hers, looked completely untouched. She questioned if tonight was the first time they actually sat down for a meal in the dining room.

As she navigated the snowy roads home, she considered all of these things. And while she'd taken the job to take care of a little girl, she decided it wouldn't do any harm to go a little further, and take care of Addison's father as well.

7

RHETT GLANCED at his watch as Erin continued to review her notes from today's meeting with the school board. She'd been droning on and on about the gymnasium renovation at the middle school for nearly an hour.

"I think we have everything," he interrupted, earning a confused stare from his assistant.

"You still have to vote on the—"

"Just say yes."

"Rhett, this is a big deal—"

"It's for the kids, Erin. The town can afford it." He didn't mean to rush the decision, but he wanted to get home. Lately, he'd been anxious to return to his house and discover what awaited him.

Last night, the girls baked a blueberry cobbler from scratch. It was still hot from the oven when Skylar topped it with a scoop of vanilla bean ice cream.

His mouth watered even now as he recalled the way her auburn hair fell over her shoulder. When she tucked it behind her ear, she got a smudge of caramel filling on her cheek. That little smear distracted him for twenty solid minutes, until he finally had to tell her so she'd wipe it off.

She blushed and used her fingers to smudge it away. Then she sucked the tip of her finger into her mouth and laughed. Such a simple, natural motion, yet it unraveled him.

He was a total cliché, lusting for the nanny, but he couldn't help it. At first, because of her age, he expected a certain level of maturity. But that wasn't the case. If anything, Skylar was more mature than women his own age.

Then, because she was a teacher and into things like popsicle stick crafts and tissue paper collages, he hoped she'd be a little too corny, in a sort of well-intentioned, dorky way, but maybe he was the dork because he found every project she and Addy created absolutely fascinating.

Skylar was so damn clever and creative. She made a butterfly out of a coffee filter, some Smarties, and a clothespin. This couldn't be the stuff they taught in college. She had a use for everything.

Her age wasn't repellant, because no matter how he did the math she was a legal, adult woman. And her personality wasn't stopping his mind from playing a non-stop game of strip the nanny in his head. And her cooking, well hell, every time he tasted her food he wanted to taste all of her.

Last night he had a full blown fantasy about taking a swipe of that caramel filling on his own fingers and feeding them slowly into her hot little mouth. He wanted to leave her nipples sticky and wet and kiss his way right down to the hot apple pie between Skylar's legs.

He was so fucked.

It hadn't even been a week. How the hell would he put up with her proximity long term. And he couldn't mess this up, because she was seriously the best governess Addy ever had.

Besides, who was to say she'd be interested in him? She was too pretty, too smart, and too damn sweet. He kept waiting for her to do something immoral, something a little shitty that proved she wasn't perfect, and she almost did.

While goofing around with Addison, trying to make a game out of cleaning up her toys, Skylar impersonated an ogre by hiking up her pants, messing up her hair, snorting like an animal, and wobbling all over the den.

She hadn't realized he'd come home and was completely unaware she had an audience. Her play acting was so unguarded, he should have felt embarrassed for her. Instead, he found it endearing. He supposed he had a thing for sexy ogres.

He'd sat up most of the night doing math problems in his head. But numbers didn't lie. If Skylar was twenty-one and he was thirty-six, he was fifteen years her senior, and therefore a very creepy old man who should not be thinking of her that way.

"Hello? Earth to Rhett."

He blinked at Erin, clueless of whatever she'd just said. "Sorry, I got distracted."

"I'll say. What's up with you today?"

"It's the holidays." True, but not why he'd been distracted. Now that he thought about it, he had nothing ready for Christmas. Skylar had distracted him in that department, too.

"I'm still working on a list for Addy. Any progress with the chinchilla thing?" Addison wanted some computerized chinchilla pet that needed artificial food and care to survive. It was the item of the season, and they were having a tough time finding one.

"Not good." Erin flicked her pen against the notes she held. "I found a few on eBay, but they're going for hundreds and there's no guarantee they're unused. She'll want a brand new one, so it's programmed specifically to understand her."

That wasn't the news he wanted. "Well, keep working on that." He stood and went to the coat rack.

"What about the rest of this stuff?" She gestured to the stack of files waiting on his desk. "We really need to go over everything. I could order out."

He didn't want to keep the girls waiting. It wasn't abnormal for him to stay late and share takeout with Erin, but things had been so *normal* this week, he wanted to see how long he could keep that up, especially for his daughter's sake.

"I promised Addy I'd be home by seven." He gathered up the files in his bin and transferred them to his briefcase. "I can look these over at home."

"Do you want me to follow you there?"

"No, you go ahead and clock out. I'm sure you have plenty to do."

She appeared a little stunned that he was wrapping up early, but he was hungry for another home-cooked meal.

❄

When Rhett got home, the house smelled divine. A savory, honey glazed ham waited on the dining room table and Christmas carols played from the kitchen. Addison greeted him with her usual excitement. Today, her hair was pulled up in pigtails with curly red and green ribbons.

"Daddy! We made Christmas cookies!"

"You did?" He scanned the kitchen for Skylar and smiled when she appeared from the pantry.

"Hi." A dusting of flour clung to her jaw and she wore a red ruffled apron.

Her dark auburn hair was pulled up into some sort of wild knot at the crown of her head but a few strands had escaped. Most distracting of all, was the strap of her bra showing where the collar of her shirt had shifted askew. It was hot pink.

"Hi." The word escaped like gravel, and he felt raw with the desire to throw her back into the pantry and fuck her right against the pasta and rice.

She smiled, setting a heavy mixer on the counter. "We're still cleaning up."

He frowned, not recognizing the appliance. "What's that?"

"Oh, I borrowed it from my mom. You don't have a mixer."

"I don't?"

She shook her head and untied her apron. "Usually, I'd just do it by hand, but these were sugar cookies and they take a lot of mixing to get the dough right."

"I see." She put the heavy mixing machine into a box and he frowned when her purse appeared. "Are you leaving?"

"If it's okay with you. My mom called, and she needs the mixer back. Something about a cookie swap and having to make fifteen dozen of Russian Tea cakes by morning. Plus, I still have some packing to do for tomorrow."

That's right, this weekend she would move in and live there full-time. Something eager pulled in his stomach. "You aren't staying for dinner then?"

"I wish I could, but my mom will shoot me if I don't get the mixer back to her."

He followed her to the foyer where she slung on her coat and wrapped her scarf. She hugged Addison, and he grinned at the bond they'd formed in such a short time. He couldn't recall his daughter taking to any of her previous sitters so quickly.

"Let me get that for you." He lifted the box with the mixer, surprised by how heavy it was, and followed her out to her car.

The temperature was in the twenties and her windshield

had a layer of ice and snow on the glass. "I should have warmed up my car."

"You need an automatic starter."

She laughed. "I think my car's too old for that sort of technology." The ice covering the door cracked when she opened it. She ducked inside and started the engine. It sputtered like an asthmatic kitten.

"Take my car."

She frowned, holding a pathetic little ice scraper. "What?"

He took the scraper out of her hands and reached for his keys. "I have four-wheel drive and my car's still warm."

"I can't take your car."

"Why not? You'll bring it back in the morning. You're only on the other end of town." Her family lived on the mountain, and he didn't want her sliding around on the back roads. "How are your tires?" If she was driving Addison around, he should probably make sure her vehicle was safe."

"My tires?"

He reached into her car and shut off the engine, pocketing the keys. Lifting the box with the mixer, he walked it over to his SUV and put it inside. With the press of a button, the Escalade started.

"I'll feel better if you take this. The roads are icy." He held open the driver's side door and she hesitated. "Please."

She looked completely unsure, but he wanted her to take the car. He would feel safer. Somehow, she had become someone essential to his daughter's life and his happiness, and he needed to keep her out of danger.

"Take the car, Skylar."

She bit her lower lip and his cock twitched. "You're sure?"

He was sure he wanted her body in his vehicle, her

hands on his gears, and her scent trapped there for days. God, he was pathetic. He nodded and she climbed in.

He stood inside the door and watched as she buckled the seatbelt and adjusted the seat and mirrors, wishing he could do the simple task for her so he'd have an excuse to touch her. Something about seeing her held securely in place made him want to lean in and kiss her. Would she slap him if he tried?

Probably. He cleared his throat and forced himself to take a step back.

She gripped the wheel and gave an awkward smile. "This is weird."

Distracted by the flour still dusting her jaw, he reached for her. "You have flour..."

She glanced in the mirror. "Oh." Licking her thumb, she scrubbed the powder off. "I'm a graceless chef."

More like *graceful*. He'd go as far as calling her angelic. More than usual, she smelled like cookies.

"Well, goodnight," she whispered softly.

"Drive safe."

"I will." She glanced back at the house. "Your dinner's getting cold."

And Addy was waiting. He stepped back and shut the door, standing in the bitter wind until the taillights disappeared. Surprisingly, he wasn't cold.

8

"DON'T TAKE things from this house without asking, Skylar. I spent an hour looking for that mixer. Like I don't have enough on my mind."

"Sorry. You weren't here and I didn't want to bother you at work."

Her mother plugged in the mixer and dumped a bunch of dry ingredients into the bowl, not measuring a single one. "Doesn't he have his own appliances?"

"Not really. The house is pretty empty."

"That big house? That can't be true. He's not the first mayor to live there."

"I'm telling you, it's not lived in. They have furniture and books and curtains, but it feels more like a museum than a home."

Her mother cracked several eggs and plopped a stick of softened butter into the bowl, then set it to low. "Well, it's not your job to provide these things. You're going to have to be more assertive and ask him for the supplies you need. I'm going to be up until midnight making these cookies for Vinny's class, now."

This wasn't about cookies. This was about one more

thing filling her mother's plate when she was already overworked, under rested, and stressed to the max. "I'll help you."

"I thought you had to pack."

"I do, but I have all weekend."

Her mom sighed. "Thank you."

For the next two hours they worked diligently mixing, baking, and powdering several hundred Russian Tea cake cookies. Hannah interrupted once, needing help with an algebra assignment. Vinny and Ciera disturbed their process several times, asking for snacks and drinks until their mom threatened to call Santa if they didn't go play. And James just camped out at their feet, playing with trucks, spatulas, and pots and pans.

The kids were all sleeping by the time the last batch was boxed up, and Skylar's feet were killing her. Just after eleven, when they moved the boxes onto the table in the hall, her father came home, looking just as exhausted as her mom.

"Hey, Sky, what's all this?" He hung his coat on the cluttered rack and toed off his shoes by the door.

"Cookies for Vinny's cookie swap."

"Any left?"

Her mom appeared with the last stack of boxes. "Dinner's in the microwave."

Her dad pressed a kiss to her mom's head and Skylar smiled. No matter how busy or stressed life got for the two of them, they never forgot to show affection.

"Who's Escalade's in the driveway?"

Skylar blushed. "It's the mayor's. My car was iced over and he insisted I take his SUV instead. I'm driving it back first thing in the morning."

"Huh." Her dad nodded with approval. "That was nice of him. Sounds like a decent guy."

She thought so. "Did you get anywhere today?" Skylar asked, changing the subject and hoping her father made the breakthrough he'd been trying to accomplish for the last eight months.

As an epidemiologist, he spent hours researching. He'd been working on a proposal for a new treatment, but their funding was running out and the grant money hadn't come through yet. He finally had to tap into the family savings, which put everyone on edge.

With Frankie away at Penn State and Hannah looking at colleges, Skylar once again figured it would be a relief when she moved out. Though her family would never admit it was a struggle to feed, clothe, and shelter so many kids, she knew her absence could lighten their burden.

"Nothing yet," he said, heating up his plate and carrying it to the table. "How's the new job?"

She smiled. "I like it. Addison is adorable and my boss is nice."

He took a bite and raised a brow. "Don't say that around your grandfather."

She rolled her eyes.

He patted her hand and gave it a squeeze. "I'm proud of you, Sky. This is a big step, and it'll be good for you to make some real money."

She grinned, hoping it helped take some of the pressure off his back. Not only was he spending countless hours at the lab, he sometimes picked up extra shifts at the lumber-yard. No wonder he was exhausted.

"I won't have rent, so maybe I can help out once I start getting paid—"

"Hey, stop that. We're fine. You put that money away for your future, you hear?"

She nodded.

"Besides, once my grant gets approved and I get this lab up and fully running, we'll make our money back tenfold."

Her eyes widened. "Really?"

"What do I always say about big pharma?"

"It's bigger than our human brains can calculate."

"Exactly."

Her room was dark and Hannah snored from a lump of blankets on the bed shoved against the wall. Skylar's side was the tidy one.

Boxes were stacked by the door and only a few items remained in her closet, but it was too late to pack now. She told Rhett she'd be moved in by Saturday, which was only two days away.

She could swing it. More than anything, she needed sleep.

Climbing into bed, she turned out the light and stared at the shadows cast on the wall from the window. Specks of snow flurries danced in the moonlight as she went through a mental list of everything she needed to accomplish.

As she fell asleep, her last thought was of her boss, and how he insisted she take his car home. She smiled, a warm sensation she didn't recognize filling her chest. She secretly admitted she couldn't wait to return to work, tomorrow.

9

ADDISON GASPED as the log cabin came into view. "Is this the North Pole?"

"Not quite." Skylar parked beside her grandmother's ancient, wood-paneled Jeep Cherokee and helped Addison out of the back seat.

Gran had called that morning to inform Skylar that the kids were working on a gingerbread house. Being that her grandmother watched all the little ones who had not yet reached school age, Skylar figured this would be a good chance for Addison to make some new friends.

As they climbed the steps of the big house, Addison asked a hundred questions. "Does Santa live here? Where is this place? How many chimneys do they have? Were those reindeer or regular deer we saw on the way in? What if I have to go potty? Do they have a toilet? How did you find this place? What's in that barn over there? Do they have horses?"

Gran greeted them at the door, wearing her usual warm smile, threadbare apron, plain house dress, and, of course, a battered pair of work boots.

"Well, you must be Addison. Aren't you just as cute as a

bug's ear? Come up here and let me have a good look at you, love."

Suddenly shy, Addison clung to Skylar's leg. She nudged her forward. "Addy, this is my grandmother. You can call her Miss Maureen."

Gran crouched in the doorway. "I was just making the kids some hot cocoa. Would you like some?" When Addison didn't answer she said, "I need a special helper to drop the marshmallows in. Do you think you could do that?"

The screen door on the other end of the porch swung and snapped. Little footsteps raced closer and Ciera jumped into view from around the corner of the wrap around porch. "I'm Rudolph!"

Skylar laughed at her little sister's red nose and Gran stood. "I let them use my lipstick."

"Cute." Skylar glanced down at Addison. "This is my sister, Ciera."

Addison studied her for a moment, then she seemed to come to the conclusion that Ciera was safe. She walked over, belly first, and gave her a closer inspection. "Do you like cats?"

Ciera shrugged. "I guess."

"Do you have a cat?"

Her sister shook her head. "My mom says we have too many kids to have a pet."

"I don't have a cat either."

"Do you have a dog?"

"No."

"Do you like pizza?"

"Yes."

Ciera smiled. "My Grandpa Marcelli makes the best pizza. He can make you some." And just like that they were friends.

Ciera led Addison into the house through the kitchen

door to meet the others. Skylar looked back at Gran and smiled.

"Busy?"

"Like a one-legged man in a butt kicking contest." She smiled. "Christmas is upon us."

Looping her arm through Skylar's, she walked her in through the front door. The scent of fresh baked gingerbread mingled with fresh cut evergreens. The railing of the main staircase was wound with thick garland, strung cranberries, and pinecones.

Carols played from the den where wood crackled in the fireplace. She loved that Gran still hung stockings for all seven of her kids. The tree was lit with lights, but the ornaments wouldn't be hung until the whole family came together on Christmas Eve.

Little voices chattered from the kitchen and Skylar knew exactly what she'd find once she entered. Children crammed around an old farm table loaded with candies and piping bags full of homemade frosting. Gran had been following the same traditions since Skylar, Hannah, and Frankie were babies, and she probably started them with her kids.

Aiden, Bethany, Michael, James, Alexia, and Lennon crowded the long table, dipping sticky fingers into bowls of gumdrops and chocolates. Ciera and Addison sat together, both girls perched with their knees planted on the long bench and their upper bodies hoisted over their elbows as they crowded the table, pushing right into the gingerbread action.

Four years ago, their family had a bit of a baby boom, and Gran had been fully booked as the childcare provider ever since. She ran a tight ship, but there was no escaping the noise, mess, and occasional outburst of tears when someone wasn't playing fair.

Of all the grandchildren Gran had helped raise, Skylar

liked to believe she and Gran shared the strongest bond. She idolized her mother's mother, and spent more time with her than any of her cousins. They shared similar interests and, like her own mother, had a deep maternal manner. Skylar often stopped by to lend a hand with the kids, because like Gran, she loved watching the little ones learn and grow.

Once the walls of the house were glued with icing, absolute chaos ensued.

"Ciera, give James a chance to stick a piece of candy on the house," Skylar said, as her little brother tried once again to poke his body between their sister and Addison.

"He can't do it."

"So, help him. Be a big sister."

"Fine."

Addison watched Ciera assist James, but Ciera wasn't the most patient with their little brother. A rush of pride filled her when Addison stepped in.

"Like this." Using her little hand, she closed it over the piping bag and showed James how to squeeze out the frosting. The sugary paste snaked out of the tip and only a small glob connected to the gingerbread, but it was enough. "Now stick the candy there."

James focused hard on gluing the gumdrop into place and he was so pleased when it stayed put. Addison smiled with him, until James leaned forward and bit his hard work right off the gingerbread wall.

"Why'd you do that?"

"I was hungry."

Addison smacked her palm to her head and rolled her eyes. Then she gave him another gumdrop, which he eventually ate as well.

Skylar and Gran helped the kids attach candies with globs of frosting, trying hard to keep the mess to a minimum and deal with several meltdowns when an ornamental piece fell in the occasional frosting landslide. After so many years of child-rearing, Gran's patience always amazed her.

When the gingerbread house was finished it looked like Frosty threw up on it.

"Beautiful!" Gran praised. "Now, go wash your hands, then see if you can find Pop-Pop."

Addison went with the others, and Skylar and Gran lingered in the kitchen, cleaning up the mess left on the table.

"She seems like a nice little lass."

"She is."

"Shy."

"Not usually. She warms up." She wiped down the table. "What happens with this, now?"

Gran sighed. "Your grandfather will pick at it and then I'll throw it out back for the animals. I tell the kids it's for Santa's reindeer. You remember."

She did. Gran always added so much magic to Christmas, which was why the big house was her favorite place to hang each December.

As Gran dumped the remaining candy and washed the dishes, Skylar dried and put them away, as comfortable in this kitchen as she was in her mom's, and now in the Buchanan's.

"Colin told me you're taking a class at Shippensburg, is that right?"

"It's just an online course."

"Still counts, dear."

Skylar grinned. Despite having dozens of grandchildren to keep track of, her grandmother never missed a beat.

"This new job will help with tuition. By the time Addison starts school, I should have enough saved to finish my bachelor's degree—debt free."

"Do you need that to open a preschool?"

Technically, she only needed an associate's to run a day

care, which she had, but she also needed a substantial amount of seed money. And currently she was broke.

"It's the money. Mr. Buchanan is paying me well, and I want to work for a while so that I have enough saved to design a school house exactly how I've dreamed." She shrugged. "If I keep working for him until Addison goes to Kindergarten, I can save a lot of money and manage a few more virtual courses." As a teacher, her education would continue until she retired, so going to school while working in a classroom wasn't abnormal.

"It'll all work out." Gran passed her the last bowl to dry.

Once the kitchen was clean, they bundled the kids up and let them play in the snow for a while, which gave her grandmother a chance to get off her feet. While Gran enjoyed a mug of hot tea and honey on one of the rocking chairs, Skylar tried to build a snowman with the kids.

When their rosy cheeks were chapped and their mittens soaked with melted ice, Gran set them up by the fire with popcorn and a Christmas movie.

Addison was wiped out by the time they left, and asleep by the time they made it home. Skylar carried her into the living room and covered her with a blanket on the couch. That night she slept right through dinner.

The house was quiet when her boss arrived and Skylar wasn't sure if her presence was needed any longer. Hovering by the door, she began to make her exit.

"Stay," Rhett said, as he realized he'd be eating alone.

Skylar hesitated. Dining alone with her boss... It seemed too intimate.

"If you go, I'll end up making a plate and taking it to the study where I'll get lost in work and let it go cold."

"Well, don't do that." She laughed, knowing he was trying to guilt her into staying.

"I can't make any promises. I'm a creature of habit."

Was he? He definitely followed a routine, but he was

fairly easy to derail. Skylar had yet to meet the hardheaded, particular boss Erin implied he would be.

"Stay," he repeated, voice dropping low. "We can call it a business meeting and you can update me on how you're settling in to your new position."

There was that charismatic mayor charm people couldn't resist. "Fine."

They settled at the kitchen table rather than using the dining room. At first the conversation was hollow, punctuated mostly by Rhett's animated response to her cooking. The man could get excited about a can of corn.

"What were you eating before I started working for you?"

"Nothing good. Way too much greasy fast food and a lot of dry sandwiches. One week and you've spoiled me. You're an excellent cook."

"Hardly."

He paused and raised a brow.

"I'm adequate," she admitted modestly, thinking of her mother's, aunts' and Gran's incredible skills.

"Does praise make you uncomfortable?"

His question did. She shrugged.

When she didn't verbalize an answer, he waited her out and the silence became stifling.

Finally, she admitted, "I think it has to do with being one little part of a very big family. It humbles you or it ruins you. I'm not the bitter sort, so I go with the flow."

"Interesting." He cleared his plate and filled it with seconds of everything. "So, you don't like being the center of attention."

"I'm just not used to it."

He studied her, staring into her eyes until her gaze dropped to her plate. She'd only eaten a little bit. He made her nervous—not necessarily in a bad way, but in a way that made her lose interest in food.

She didn't want to miss anything he said and his interest kept her on her toes.

"Do you have a boyfriend?"

Startled by his question, her skin heated, a blush burning to her chest. "Um, no. I'm single."

"How come?"

She frowned at his unexpected curiosity and turned the question back on him. "How come *you're* single?" As soon as the words left her mouth, she regretted them. "I mean… I just assumed…Never mind."

He chuckled. "It's fine. I am single." He set his fork on the plate and leaned back, crossing his arms over his chest in a contemplative pose. "Relationships are complicated. My focus is Addy. She's my number one priority."

She nodded, respecting and understanding his excuse.

"Now you."

Her chest tightened. "I, um…" What was her excuse? She considered the boys she knew from high school and the lack of chemistry. College wasn't much better, because she was always rushing to class then off to work. "No one asked."

He scoffed. "I find that hard to believe."

"Why?"

"You're a beautiful woman."

Her cheeks caught fire.

"Sorry. I didn't mean to make you uncomfortable. It was just an observation."

Every muscle in her body tightened, but she somehow felt loose and flimsy and hot. A smile pulled at her lips, but she was afraid to give in to the emotions piping through her veins, afraid to come off over excited from one silly compliment. "Thank you."

His stare remained focused on her face. "Smile."

The urge to do so disappeared. Blinking at him in confusion, she wondered what this was. Was she putting herself in an inappropriate position? Was he being inappropriate?

Was she reading too much into things? They were both adults.

She stared at him in question, unsure if he was like this with everyone or if there was something happening here. Her lungs felt shallow and tight. "I don't know how to read you."

"You'll learn."

That felt...promising. She swallowed, and slowly forced her guard down. A shy smile curved her mouth and he mirrored the expression.

"Beautiful. You shouldn't hide your smile. It lights up the whole room."

Her cheeks stretched and she laughed. "You're embarrassing me."

"Why?"

"I don't know."

"It's the attention." He chuckled, as if amused by her shyness.

She used the sense of closeness to her advantage and asked, "Does Addison ever see her mom?"

The energy of the room drastically shifted and chilled. He stood, catching her off guard.

Collecting his plate and hers, he cleared the table. "The boys in this town must be nuts to have paid such little attention to you. Shame on them."

A divot formed in her brow as he obviously dodged her question and turned the focus back on her. She got the unmistakable impression that her boss didn't like to share personal details of his past. She'd try to remember that.

He turned on the faucet and proceeded to wash the dishes, leaving her there to process the abrupt change in him. He'd gone from acutely curious to completely disinterested and she regretted prying into his personal life.

Yet, he took no issue with speaking about hers. She desperately wanted to know if he was simply making observations about her or if he was implying something more—saying something without saying anything at all.

Maybe there was something wrong with her, because deep down she wanted it to be the latter.

Was it wrong that part of her was eager to answer anything he might ask? She should be more guarded with her secrets but she wasn't. She wanted to trade all of hers—not that she had many—for a measly few of his.

His behavior made it clear that he had secrets and those secrets were off limits. Of course, that caused her to covet them even more.

10

Skylar spent the weekend hauling boxes up to the third floor and settling into her room. She used an old card table Gran had loaned her to set up a work station in the corner of her bedroom and a mason jar to hold her pens and highlighters.

She liked the sense of a fresh start and decorated the space with a minimalist's touch, opting for open areas of sunlight over clutter and accents in white and beige. At the farmer's market, Aunt Ashlynn gave her a small houseplant as a moving present, and Skylar set it on the built in seat by the big window in her bedroom.

By Sunday, her laundry was done and she was fully unpacked and settled in. Rhett had some work to do, so he was gone most of the day. Skylar used Addison's nap time to work on a paper for her winter course.

When Addison woke from her nap, they had a snack and practiced her letters. They had finally settled into somewhat of a routine, and Addison was showing great affection for learning.

In the mornings they did a craft, usually one with a holiday theme. Then they practiced counting. They read a story in the afternoon, practiced her reading throughout the day, and usually went on an outing in town to get Addison out of the house. In the evenings they cooked together.

There was always something exciting happening, but Addison's favorite part of the day was the moment her father came home. Skylar also looked forward to that part of the day and sometimes caught herself watching the clock or catching her breath when the sound of a car pulled into the driveway.

She didn't overthink it and tried not to feed into her feelings too much.

Rhett was a handsome man. Of course, she noticed him. And he was kind and charming in a way she'd never experienced before. He was unique.

Did she have a crush on him? Yes, maybe a little. Did that mean she was going to act on her attraction? No.

Her job was to care for and educate Addison, so when her feelings for her boss became especially distracting, she pushed herself deeper into her work.

Skylar started labeling items around the house, using a red marker for the first letter of each word. Addison was learning that S was for sink and T was for television. Rhett was impressed with how quickly his daughter could acquire knowledge.

Sunday evening, Skylar made pasta with Italian Mary's special meat sauce. Rhett came home at six-twenty. Each day it seemed a little earlier.

She enjoyed cooking for him because he ate with such curiosity and enthusiasm. Addison loved telling him about her day during dinner. In a way, Skylar felt like an intruder, but Rhett insisted she eat with them every night—unless she had other plans.

She didn't know what it meant that she'd purposely cooked dinner on a Sunday, when every Sunday of her twenty-one years had been spent eating dinner with her family at the big house. Deep down, she assumed it spoke volumes about her being exactly where she wanted to be. But there would be hell to pay for missing a Sunday dinner at Gran's. Not to mention that she also missed church to avoid any preemptive lecture about skipping dinner.

"I saw Santa's reindeer!" Addison announced before slurping a large bit of spaghetti through her lips. As the noodles disappeared with a slither of red sauce leaving her mouth a mess, she scooted higher in her seat. Italian Mary's gravy was obviously a hit.

"Where was this?" Rhett asked, maneuvering his pasta with a much more refined twirl against his spoon.

"Up on a gigantic mountain, Daddy! 'Member? I told you! There was a barn, and we saw three reindeer. We made a gingerbread house that was as tall as me, and Miss Maureen said I can come back any time. I made lots of friends."

He glanced at Skylar and grinned. "Your relatives?"

"The McCullough side." It was sort of a joke around Jasper Falls that there were more McCulloughs than all the other townsfolk combined.

"Ah, well, it sounds like you two had a fantastic week."

"Why don't we have a Christmas tree?" Addison asked, abruptly shifting gears.

Rhett made an expression Skylar couldn't read, which wasn't anything new. But something protective came over her, and she wanted to save him from whatever put that look on his face.

"My Gran showed Addison our family's ornaments. She was a bit enchanted by them."

His brow kinked. "We have the one out front."

"That's not the same, Daddy. We need one inside, so Santa can put the presents under it."

"Santa puts the gifts by the hearth."

Addison's stern expression made Skylar chuckle. It

became perfectly clear this was no longer acceptable in her book.

"Well, I guess we need a tree." He glanced at Skylar. "I'm holding you responsible for this."

"Me?" She laughed. "She got here on her own."

"Oh, please." He eyed the red and green paper-chain garland they made earlier that week and the paper snowflakes hanging from the chandelier over the table. "Every day this place looks more like Santa's workshop. I'm convinced I'm not your only boss, and you're working personally for the big guy."

Addison's eyes widened. "Do you work for Santa, too?"

"No." She shook her head at Rhett. "Your daddy's starting rumors."

"What's a rumor?"

"A fib, sort of like when people call your daddy a grinch."

She gasped. "My daddy's not the grinch!"

"Ouch," Rhett laughed. "Okay, maybe I have some work to do."

After dinner, they bundled up and drove down to the tree lot in the O'Malley's pub parking lot. Classic rock filled the SUV and Skylar frowned.

"You're doing this all wrong." With a twist of the dial, she set the station to Christmas carols. Addison bounced and sang in her seat. So did Skylar. She wondered how it was possible for a man Rhett's age not to know the words. Maybe he just didn't like to sing.

Tree hunting was one of Skylar's favorite pastimes. The scent of pine needles and the strung lights overhead… It was all so very Charlie Brown.

Rhett had no idea how to go about getting a tree. His questions confused her.

"How do they stay upright?"

"You get a stand. Haven't you ever had a Christmas tree before?"

"No."

She stared at him completely perplexed. They celebrated Christmas, so she didn't think it was a religious thing. Before she could ask why he never had a tree, Addison ran over to a bulky Douglas fir and declared it their tree.

"Ooh, I like this one!" She returned to Rhett's side and dragged him closer to the tree. "Sniff it, Daddy!"

"Why?"

Addison frowned. "You gotta."

Skylar walked over to the fir. "Because it smells like Christmas, silly." She stuck her face close to the pine needles, shut her eyes, and breathed in the magical fragrance.

Ah, Christmas...

Rhett didn't appear convinced, but his daughter's insistence got him there. Skylar helped by giving the back of his head a little nudge.

"Really get your face in there. Grab a lungful."

He looked at her like she was crazy. "A lungful of what?"

"Just do it," Addison snapped.

He shut his eyes and breathed deep. Then he looked at them. "Now what?"

Skylar shook her head. "Grinch."

Addison also shook her head. "Yeah, Daddy. Can't you smell it?"

"What? It's a tree!" He held out his hands, but she and Addison left to go find an attendant to string up the branches and tie their Douglas fir to the roof of the SUV.

The tree was enormous, but they had the room for it in that big, empty house. Once they got it inside and centered on the new tree stand, Rhett inspected it like one might scrutinize a monolith. Addison had gone upstairs to change into her pajamas.

"This is a good one, Skylar?"

"Sure. It's definitely a big one."

"Big's good, right?"

Such a masculine assumption. He was adorable. "In my family, you either go big or go home."

He nodded with agreement, appearing pleased. "Big is good."

"Do you have ornaments?" When he gave her a panicked stare, she asked, "Lights?"

"Crap."

He really never had a Christmas tree before. "McGinty's is still open."

Addison returned to the den in her pajamas. "Get your coat. We're going back out."

"But I'm in my jammies."

"Just put your snow boots on. No one will notice."

Bundled back up, they drove to McGinty's. Rhett went a little overboard, buying every possible Christmas decoration he found. He even bought a mixer, since they didn't have one at the house. The SUV was packed to the gills, and Skylar was a little sick over what he must have paid at the register.

"You're a little extreme," she said, as they carried in the bags and formed a mountain of packages in the foyer.

Rhett shrugged. "It's for Addy. I want her to have all the perfect memories kids should have."

She studied him as he examined the instructions for an inflatable lawn snowman. "I don't know if *perfect* is how I'd describe holiday memories."

"No?"

She shook her head. "*Chaotic* seems more fitting."

His smile was slow as he turned to look at her. "Maybe chaotic is the perfect way it should be. Maybe that's normal."

He used the word normal as if he didn't fit the category.

Her family was absolutely abnormal, but in a way that made them extremely regular in a very dysfunctional yet normal way.

"How would you describe your Christmases?"

"Empty." He opened a box of lights.

Something pinched in her chest and she took a step closer to him. The strangest urge to hug him took hold of her, but she forced her arms to stay planted at her sides.

She looked directly into his eyes. "Did your family—"

"What do you say we string these in the front hedges?" Once again, he'd purposefully dodged any questions about his past.

"Yay!" Addison bounced off the floor and followed him out front, leaving Skylar standing in the foyer, unsure of the secrets her boss so obviously wanted to hide.

His holidays were *empty?* The word *empty* seemed bursting with hidden meaning.

Where had he lived before coming to Jasper Falls? And how did someone who called his memories *empty*, bring so much charm to their little town?

They left the ornaments in the foyer and spent the night decking the yard with blue spotlights, colorful twinkle lights, and tacky, inflatable decorations. Skylar didn't dare broach the subject of his past again.

By ten o'clock, Addison was cranky and ready for bed.

"I'll take her up," she offered, and as she held her, Rhett kissed his daughter goodnight. The scent of his hair and skin filled her lungs, and she might have enjoyed breathing him in as much as she loved sniffing Christmas trees.

Addison didn't make it through two pages of a story. When Skylar returned downstairs, Rhett had organized the ornaments by type and color.

"I guess we'll do this part tomorrow night." He glanced at her. "You'll help, right?"

"Sure." She hovered by the arm of the couch, content to

simply watch him. Painfully curious about who he was and what made him tick.

As if he could feel her observing him, he stopped arranging the boxes and self-consciously gripped the back of his neck. "Thanks for coming with us tonight."

"No problem." She gathered up the trash and walked it to the kitchen to throw away. Rhett followed.

"You're really wonderful with this stuff."

She put on a kettle of water and unpacked a box of chamomile tea. "Thanks. I love Christmas."

"It shows."

She studied him for a moment, setting the water to boil. Feeling courageous, she returned to their earlier conversation. "Earlier, when you said your Christmas memories were empty, what did you mean by that?"

He took the box of tea and read the label. "Nothing."

It was clear he didn't want to answer, so she took pity on him and let it go. "Do you want some tea?"

He put down the box. "Sure."

She took two mugs down from the cabinet and waited for the kettle to whistle. It was taking forever.

Rhett opened the cupboard and set honey next to the mugs. "You take it with honey, right?"

He'd noticed how she took her tea at night? For some reason this information made her stupidly giddy. She hid a smile. "Right." Her heart raced as she once again remembered him telling her not to hide her smiles because they could light up a room.

"Did I say something wrong?"

"No, you're just very observant."

He retrieved the milk, anticipating her every move. "You have a routine."

She flushed. "I like structure."

Returning to the stove where the kettle heated, his gaze held hers. "I noticed."

They were only standing a few inches apart, and if she moved, he would notice and possibly take it as rude. But maybe she should step back anyway.

Her breasts felt heavy and every shallow breath seemed to lift them. It was as if her body was instinctively reaching for him. She needed something to drink.

Mirroring her stance, they stood between the island and the stove, each with a hand resting on the counter. His palm glided over the granite and his fingers brushed against hers.

Intentional. Very intentional.

Her breath caught and her gaze turned questioning.

A thousand logical responses pranced through her head. They had a professional relationship. This was inappropriate. They were playing with fire. Addison could get hurt if they went there...

They all made sense but she didn't want to acknowledge a single one. She wanted him, plain and simple.

"Tell me no."

She couldn't. Her body felt heavy and hungry. She'd never had such a response to a man. She hardly knew him. Her heart wanted her to be reckless anyway.

"Skylar..."

No, she wouldn't tell him no. She said nothing, refused to blink, making it perfectly clear the answer was yes.

"Tell me a secret," she challenged. "Something people don't know about you."

Shock registered in his eyes and she expected him to shut down whatever this was, but instead, he shifted closer and whispered, "The prettiest place I've ever slept was under the North Carolina sky. The stars are so big and bright there, they make the shadows glow."

"Is that where you grew up."

His eyes turned guarded. "I lived there for a time. I lived in a lot of different places. Until finding Jasper Falls, North Carolina was my favorite."

"Why Jasper Falls?"

"You said a secret. I gave you one."

But he didn't necessarily share anything personal and now he watched her as if silently asking what she would give him in return. Her heart fluttered into a canter as she tried to translate his body language.

His socked feet shifted closer and his fingers once again brushed hers. "Why are you so fascinating to me?"

"I'm boring."

"I can think of a hundred ways to describe you, but boring isn't one of them."

"What would you choose?" She wanted to know what he thought of her, how he saw her.

"Stunning. Patient. Sweet. Warm."

Her lips pulled into a smile and her face heated. "Thank you."

"How do you see me?"

Her brow creased. "You're...my boss." She couldn't confess all the things he made her feel, especially when she didn't know how he managed to stir such emotions in such a short time.

He blinked, and something close to disappointment flashed in his eyes. "Is that all?"

He was testing her. Pushing her. It might have been the most adult conversation she'd ever had, but her body was quaking with uncertainty and her heart was terrified she might say the wrong thing out loud and be mortified the next morning.

She dropped her gaze, erring on the side of caution. "You're a good father to Addison."

Hooking a long finger under her chin, he raised her face, forcing her to hold his stare. He grinned with genuine pride. "Thank you."

His touch lingered, and he stepped another inch closer.

"Rhett..."

"I just have to see something..."

Her lungs filled with a deep breath as he closed the distance and brushed his lips against hers. Such simple contact, but her body caught fire. Chills raced down her spine and her nipples pulled tight.

Maybe it was because they were doing something wrong. Maybe it was their age difference that made the press of his lips to her feel a little taboo, a little too tempting. But the truth was, they weren't breaking any laws, and she had every right to stand there in his kitchen and let him kiss her if she wanted him to.

And oh...she wanted...

A wave of dizziness swept over her, knocking her slightly off balance in a true to God swoon. The next breath she took hitched past her lips in a delicate gasp.

He eyed her closely, catching every blink and breath and pulsing ache she couldn't seem to hide. His hand slipped beneath the curtain of her hair, softly cupping the back of her neck, and everything inside of her clenched with anticipation.

She expected a kiss, but nothing could have prepared her for the one he delivered. He didn't just press his mouth to hers. He pressed his entire body to her body. Hard, hungry muscle against soft, needy curves.

His height and breadth crowded her as he took complete control, turning her back to the island and angling his body over hers as his tongue broke the seal of their lips and stole into her mouth. She let him lead, wanting to see how far he would take things.

Deep, masculine groans met her delicate mews, and he challenged her to meet his passion. Her pulse fluttered wildly as his hands sifted through her hair and over her curves. Soft lips ran delicately over her jaw, teasing and coaxing, licking and nipping. The heat of his body surrounded her.

Her breasts smashed against the hard wall of his chest, and she reveled in the sturdy feel of him, wanting—no, *needing*—more. His desires dominated her senses. His height dwarfed her small form. He filled her with a riotous sense of wildness, yet made her increasingly aware of her fragility.

He was big, she was small. He was strong, she was delicate. He was fire and desire, she was cherished and revered. He was experienced, she was not. But, oh, she wanted to learn from him.

His thigh wedged between her legs, pressing exactly where she needed pressure. His mouth returned to hers and he deepened the kiss, her body burned from the inside out, heating her skin in a fiery flush.

No matter how aggressively he kissed her, his touch remained sensual and inviting. He didn't kiss like the other guys she'd made out with. He touched her like a man, with skill and familiarity and dark intentions. He didn't just kiss and caress her, he consumed her.

His skill should have scared her or intimidated her but, instead, it made her feel delicate yet safe. Arching her body closer to the island, she wanted to wrap her legs around his hips and pull him down to the floor. At the very least, she wanted him to lift her to the counter and spread her body out beneath him and have his way with her.

She wanted more. Needed him to hold nothing back. Wanted all of his strength and power and—

The sharp whistle of the tea kettle was like a bucket of ice water spilling over the moment, and they broke apart. Rhett blinked and frowned at her as if he'd forgotten who he had been mauling a second ago.

Not the look she wanted from her employer.

Shit. He was her boss.

Logic sank in hard and fast, like a bolder breaking through a placid bond. She moved to the stove and removed the screaming kettle from the heat, clicking off the burner and waiting for the ripple effect to come and mess everything up.

"I shouldn't have done that."

She winced, glad she hadn't turned to face him. Anger bubbled inside of her. "Then why did you?"

"I don't know."

Well, it happened and now they had to live with it.

Why hadn't she listened to her more rational instincts? Now what? Would they pretend nothing happened? Act like everything was normal?

"Are you mad?"

She was irritated that he seemed to be ashamed of his actions and didn't like the way his regret made her feel like a dirty *thing* he shouldn't touch. "I thought it was...nice."

"It was inappropriate."

Ouch. She pivoted and found him scowling so she scowled, too. "It was your idea!"

He jerked back at the unhidden censure in her voice. "I'm aware. I wasn't thinking."

She scoffed and narrowed her eyes as he tried to shrug off any accountability. "You *were* thinking."

Both of them had been thinking about this for some time, thinking of all the reasons why they shouldn't act on desire, thinking how good it would feel to be reckless, consequences be damned.

"It was a spontaneous impulse."

Unbelievable. "How about a little self-awareness and accountability, next time."

Affronted that she'd call him out on his bullshit, his jaw hardened. "There won't be a next time."

"Good!" she snapped, slinking past him and marching out of the kitchen.

"What about your tea?" he yelled after her.

"You drink it! Or was that also a spontaneous impulse you had no intention of seeing through?"

He said nothing else and she didn't stop scowling until she reached the third floor. Once safely inside the privacy of her room, she dropped her face into her hand and groaned. The mortification she'd predicted arrived with a gut swilling nausea that made it hard to breathe.

11

RHETT WAS FURIOUS WITH HIMSELF. Of all the foolish things he could have done, this one took the cake. Skylar was perfect for Addison, and they were finally finding their groove, finally accomplishing all those normal homelife activities he had missed growing up. Then screwed everything up by kissing her.

Not just kissed her. That was no ordinary kiss. He took her. Held her. Consumed and savored her. If not for that damn tea kettle, he would have fucked her right on the kitchen floor.

His body hardened at the mere thought. Would she have let him?

No! No more thinking of the nanny that way!

He should have never gone so long without female company. As the mayor, he avoided the women of Jasper Falls, preferring to see to his needs in the next town over. But it had been some time since he'd taken a night to himself.

After Addison was born, any thoughts of long term relationships fizzled. His daughter was too special and he didn't want to complicate their situation by bringing random women around. Nor did he want to get involved with the wrong woman.

Skylar was his daughter's nanny, therefore she was the wrong woman. But he couldn't stop seeing her as perfect.

And when he kissed her...

His cock hardened and he groaned, locking his jaw and shoving the vision away. She was for his daughter, not for him!

He avoided his home for most of the week and worked late, even on nights he had no excuse to stay after six. Every night, he walked through the door to find a wrapped plate of food on the counter beside a picture Addison had drawn. She was getting better at writing her letters and printing her name.

Skylar was nowhere to be found in the evenings after Addison went to bed, but he sensed her presence everywhere. It was in the carefully positioned pillows on the couch that now smelled like her. The flowers on the kitchen island he assumed were her doing. Her wool hat and coat hanging in the foyer beside Addison's made their entryway look homier than it had ever been. She was everywhere.

She was in the air, in his house, in his mind, and now she seemed to be burning in his blood. The light from the third floor seeped under the narrow door. What was she doing up there?

If the lights were on, she wouldn't be sleeping. He didn't think she had a television up there. Was she reading? On her phone? Morbidly curious about her search history, he wanted to know every secret she kept.

She hadn't been guarded until he put up some guards of his own. He wanted to know more about her, but feared she might discover too much in return.

No one honestly knew him in Jasper Falls and he preferred it that way. His past was ugly, like a patch of broken sidewalk that people shouldn't step on. It didn't fit with the picturesque image of Jasper Falls. Being the mayor of such a town, meant grooming his reputation to fit with the brand he was trying to sell.

No, he wasn't ready to let others in. His privacy was just that—private.

Yet, no matter how much he knew better, he still wanted to get to know her. Why was she so alluring? He had to find out, had to—

Once again his train of thought had gone off track in the wrong direction.

Not going to happen. He shouldn't even be looking in her direction. She was an employee, a member of his staff. His curiosity and interest blatantly disrespected her personal space. He needed to back off.

Why was he so obsessed with her anyway? Sure, she was beautiful and sweet and there was a playfulness about her he hadn't found in many grown women. But there was something else.

She impressed him. She did things differently, always adding extra care and a personal touch to any task. She was old-fashioned, despite being young.

And when he kissed her... The heat of her touch stunned him. Sweet little Skylar had a fire in her. The moment he laid his hands on her, pressed his body against hers, arched her back over the counter, and groped those tight curves he was lost like a moth to a flame, and he'd been burning for her ever since.

Avoidance seemed the only answer. For days, he kept himself occupied with work, but his thoughts always returned to her. Skylar was not an easy woman to forget.

Addison had been eager to decorate the tree they bought, but he'd been making excuses all week. Kissing Skylar had been a mistake—and one he'd love to repeat. But for the sake of his daughter, he had to cool things off with the nanny.

Addison needed her. *He* needed her—and *not* in the way he truly wanted her. He needed her for his daughter. He couldn't afford to mess that up.

After a few days of avoiding the house, he hoped they could leave the kiss in the past and move on. She seemed to be avoiding him as well, so the decision to overlook his misstep seemed to be a mutual one. But once the weekend started, he'd have to face the music.

When he came home Thursday night, he found the house quiet, per their new normal. He heated up his plate and ate alone at the counter.

The kitchen door pushed open and Skylar stilled. "Oh, I didn't hear you come in."

She had her hair pulled up in another one of those messy buns. A loose sweatshirt hung off her frame and her legs were covered in red and white candy cane striped leggings. Her feet wore the bulkiest socks, the casual vision sending him over the edge.

His throat dried. "I just got home."

She looked away and pulled a mug from the cabinet, but rather than make her usual bedtime tea, she set the coffee pot to brew. Seeing her stand where they kissed did things to his body, things he had a hard time hiding.

He positioned himself behind the granite island. "No tea?"

"Not tonight." She fidgeted with the mug, adding a scoop of sugar and a dash of cream. "I have to study."

He frowned. "For?"

"I have an exam tomorrow."

Had he missed something? "You're still in class?" He'd assumed the semester had ended. "I thought..."

"That I finished? That was at the community college where I got my associate's. I'm starting on my bachelor's, now, but it will take years to finish—especially since I can't afford to go full time." When she looked up at him, her eyes appeared huge. "I'm only taking one class online through Shippensburg at the moment."

"What class?"

"Behavioral Management."

Another layer peeled back, revealing more intimate details about who she was and what she might be doing up in that room after eight each evening. The thought of her studying triggered a slew of librarian fantasies, reminding him that she was an intellectual as well as playful.

Smart, beautiful, silly, and an incredible kisser... He was doomed.

He needed to know more. "Is the class difficult?"

She shrugged and her shoulder peeked a little further out of the collar of her sweatshirt. "It's not easy, but I'll pass. I just have to study if I want to keep my GPA up."

She wasn't wearing a bra. That bare shoulder tormented him, and if he dropped his gaze, he bet he'd see her pert little nipples pressing against the fabric, loose and hungry to be held.

Do not drop your gaze!

He looked.

It was like a punch in the gut. He wanted to slide his hand under the sweatshirt, up her warm skin and cup those sweet curves. She'd let him, too, because she was a good girl who liked being kissed. She liked being naughty.

His cock hardened and his mouth watered as he imagined pulling her sweet, pink nipples into his mouth and sucking them until they were wet and cherry red. He'd lick them over and over, pulling the tips and making her beg—

"You didn't like it?"

His fantasy screeched to a stop and he followed her gaze to his plate. "I haven't tasted it yet." He'd been too distracted and hungry for something else.

Her brow pinched and her lips formed a soft pout. "You don't have to lie."

He wasn't lying. "I'm not."

"It's fine. I'm not great with roasts and I think I overcooked it anyway. I can make you something else." She grabbed the plate as if she intended to dump it in the trash, and he caught her wrist.

"Skylar, leave it." Touching her was a mistake.

The air snapped with hot energy, and his skin prickled at her nearness. He could so easily bend his head and kiss that exposed shoulder. Her collar bone called to his mouth, begging to be licked.

She looked at his fingers wrapped around her wrist and didn't tell him to let go. On the contrary, she relaxed her arm, subtly giving in to his hold. He tugged her wrist to his chest and she gasped, staggering into him.

Her eyes looked up, questioning and unsure.

He remembered studying. It was on the tip of his tongue to offer to help her, just so he could work an invitation into her room. He wanted to ask her questions on little flashcards and see her handwriting and watch her think. He wanted her on her knees looking up at him with those big blue eyes.

The coffee pot beeped and the softness in her gaze disappeared. He was keeping her from her books. And he was backtracking.

Days of avoidance down the drain because he couldn't control himself. What was this hold she had on him?

He released her wrist and she turned away. She poured a cup of coffee with a shaky hand, and he couldn't bear the idea of causing her any discomfort.

When she put the coffee pot down, he brushed a finger down the back of her exposed shoulder, feather light and gone in less than a second. She tensed. "I'm sorry."

"You don't have to apologize."

"I do."

She wouldn't look at him and it was his fault he'd made her uncomfortable in a home that was now hers.

"The other night..."

"Please," she begged, her gaze glued to the counter, her voice shaken and desperate. "I let it happen."

"Why?"

Her shoulders moved with each steady breath. "Does it matter? You changed your mind in the end."

And he'd been torturing himself ever since—changing it back and forth so many times he was giving himself whiplash. She was right. It didn't matter how it started.

He stepped away, giving her an appropriate amount of space. "Forgive me. I'll let you get back to your schoolwork."

He pivoted and marched out of the kitchen, not stopping until he was locked away in his study, sick with regret and harder than steal. He was fucked.

❄

Skylar released a trembling breath as soon as he left the kitchen. She'd be lucky if she still had a job come Monday. This entire week had been a nightmare.

Since their kiss last weekend, they had both been avoiding each other. But this was *his* home. She wasn't sure who was the pariah.

They had both participated in the kiss. Maybe he had started it, but she had been fully invested in finishing it. Even now, simply being in the same room as him made her body ignite.

When he looked at her with those hungry eyes, her self-control disappeared. She'd never been one to self-sabotage, so she didn't understand why she would risk the best job she'd ever had by flirting with her boss.

They were too close, too intimate. That had to be what was confusing her. She needed to establish boundaries that made it impossible to overlook the fact that she was his employee.

She knew better than to touch him, but what about when he touched her? What about when he stood close and her brain lost focus as it repeated the mantra *touch me, touch me, touch me...*

Was it bad if she let him touch her?

Yes! Ugh. The fact that he *shouldn't* touch her only made her want his hands on her more. This was a disaster.

Taking her coffee up to the third floor, she shut the door and tried to focus on her studying. But thoughts of Rhett kept intruding.

What was he doing? When he said sorry, what exactly was he sorry for? Was he seeing someone? What kind of women did he date? And why the hell did she think his plans were any of her business?

She was the nanny. Her job was keeping his kid safe and teaching her things she would need to know before kindergarten. Her job was not kissing the sexy mayor.

She was no better than the rest of the women in this town. That's all this was, a simple crush. Rhett Buchanan was an attractive man in an authoritative position. He was charming, because the job required it of him. Women probably threw themselves at him all the time.

How many times would she have to bear the humiliation of his rejection and withstand that awful look of regret in his eyes before it sunk in. He didn't want her that way, and that was for the best, because—*hello*—she worked for him!

The following day, she'd let Addison watch an extra hour of television so that she could finish her test before noon. It was open book but mostly essays, so she really needed to focus.

When she finished, Skylar shut her laptop and checked on Addison. "Okay, how about we—Oh, no, what happened?"

"I decorated the tree!"

Fragile ornaments were strewn all over the floor and garland was knotted in the branches. The tree leaned cock-eyed against the wall, and she rushed over to straighten it before it completely fell over.

"You have to wait for your father to do the tree."

"But he's always working."

"I understand, but he'll be home this weekend." A glass ball fell and shattered near Addison's bare feet. "Don't move. I have to get the broom."

When she returned, Addison wasn't happy. That made two of them.

Skylar spent the next hour putting ornaments back into boxes and trying to reason with a disgruntled four-year-old. She wished she could explain why men were so complicated, but that was something even Skylar didn't fully understand.

Once everything was put away, she made Addison a PB and J sandwich and promised they could play in the snow after lunch. But before they made it out the door, Erin showed up.

Skylar was used to her sporadic visits at this point but would prefer if she knew ahead of time when the woman was coming. It would make planning errands a lot easier if she knew which day of the week she'd have money for groceries.

"Mr. Buchanan needs you to work on something for him," Erin said, after giving her another hundred dollars for next week's groceries.

Skylar glanced at the money and did a double take. "This is two hundred."

"Right. Like I said, Mr. Buchanan has a job for you."

A job on top of her usual job? "What is it?" The inexplicable urge to please him frustrated her on some level, but she wanted to make him proud. She wanted to make him smile and look at her and hear him say, *"Good job, Skylar."* She suppressed a smile. Maybe he wouldn't say good job. Maybe he'd say, *"Good girl... Show me what a good girl you are... show me what else you'll do to make me..."*

No, no, no, no, no! God, what was wrong with her?

Erin glanced at Addison who was struggling to put her snow boots on the wrong feet. "Peanut, why don't you go get yourself a Coke."

"No!" Skylar barked then softened her voice. "You can have a juice box from the fridge. No soda."

Addison pouted but still went to fetch a juice.

"I'd prefer it if she didn't drink soda."

Erin raised a brow but didn't comment. "Anyway, Mr. Buchanan wants you to find a Charming Chinchilla. It's on Addison's Christmas list, and he doesn't have time to search for one. Do you know what they are?"

Being that all of her aunts and uncles were up at the butt crack of dawn on Black Friday trying to find one, yes, she was familiar with the toy. How was she supposed to get one?

She frowned at Erin, unsure if she understood the sort of challenge this would be. "They're really rare, especially this time of year." She might have to order one from an auction site. "A hundred dollars might not be enough, especially if it's coming from the black market."

"Really, Skylar, it's a toy. I think you can manage. Do you have a laptop? I'll show you the one she wants."

She really disliked the patronizing way she spoke to her but didn't want to drag out the woman's stay by confronting her. "It's in the den."

Erin followed her to the den. Skylar opened her laptop and put in the passcode. Addison returned, needing help punching her straw into her juice box. As Skylar helped her, she heard an email notification ping. "Just minimize my inbox and open a new search." She handed Addison the juice box. "Drink this in the kitchen. I have to help Miss Erin with something for a few minutes. We'll go outside as soon as I'm finished, okay?"

"Okay."

Erin had the site pulled up and pointed. "It's this yellow one."

"Does it have to be that exact one?"

Erin looked up at her as if she was an idiot. "Do you think Santa would make a mistake?"

"No, but I also think he'd have his elves fill the order months ago, not his nanny three weeks before Christmas."

Erin shut the laptop. "It's the yellow one. When you get it, let me know. I do all the wrapping at the office."

Every time the PA left, the house felt a little cooler. Skylar quickly reopened her laptop to check her mail, but her inbox was empty. Weird, she thought she heard something. Tucking it away, she went to find Addison.

12

IT TOOK all weekend to find the chinchilla Addison wanted for Christmas, and when Skylar finally found it, the delivery would be hit-or-miss, since it was coming from overseas. Not to mention, with the expense of shipping and handling, the toy would cost close to one hundred and forty dollars. The things some parents did for their kids...

Skylar ordered it using her personal credit card and texted Erin a screenshot of the total, so she'd know she was owed forty dollars. After that, she spent the day working on a project for her class that required her to come up with an entire unit to teach "Respect in the Classroom" with corresponding lesson plans and sample materials.

Since the class was virtual, she had to not only provide the lesson plans but put together three videos of her teaching sample lessons with materials. This gave Rhett and Addison plenty of time alone to decorate the tree.

She was practically brain-dead when she emerged from her room late Sunday night. She'd taken most of the weekend to do schoolwork, and Rhett had used her absence as a chance to order takeout from every restaurant in Jasper Falls—except for Vincenzo's, of course.

He sat on the couch, reading over paperwork as Addison cuddled into his side. Skylar tried not to intrude, but there was no getting to the kitchen without passing the den.

"Skylar," Addison yelled when she spotted her. It was late and Skylar hadn't expected her to be awake. Addison slid off the couch and ran over to give her a hug. "Where were you?"

"I was doing schoolwork."

"Wanna watch *Elf* with us?"

"Oh, I can't honey. I just came down to get something to eat and then I have to get back to work."

She pouted, her hair unbrushed and her clothing mismatched. "But we haven't seen you in days."

Her gaze met Rhett's and she regretted looking in his direction immediately. It was the first time she caught him in casual clothes. Barefoot and wearing *only* loose fitting gray sweatpants, he looked...delicious, like the love child of Magic Mike and a modern day Baron von Trapp.

Her ovaries did a little jig as she pictured him dancing like Channing Tatum to a naughty rendition of *Edelweiss.* No wonder there were so many classics about men making love to their governesses. The combination of his authority and good looks was a potent cocktail, and she'd gotten drunk by the mere sight of him enough times to now recognize that she had a problem. She was addicted to staring at and fantasizing about her boss.

Reading glasses perched low on his straight nose, he looked perfectly disheveled and poetically masculine all at the same time. How was this man still single?

She glanced at the tree and smiled. It was hideous. The decorations were expensive and lovely, but the garland had been thrown on with amateur effort, and the lights were blinking and racing fast enough to cause a seizure.

"What do you think?" he asked, closing the file that

rested on his lap and tossing it onto the pile of paperwork to his left.

"I think it's perfect, exactly how a family decorated tree should be."

"We waited for you to do the angel," Addison announced. "Daddy said we should take a picture."

"Oh, okay." Skylar pulled out her phone and opened the camera.

Rhett stood and her mouth went dry. His trim waist was carved with muscle and tight from his hips to his broad chest. "Ready?" He hoisted Addison into the air, lifting her higher than his shoulders.

Strong arms roped with thick sinew twisted into smooth, bulging shoulders. The softest tuft of hair flashed under his arm.

Addison lifted the angel and Skylar focused the camera. Rhett leaned close to the tree and Addison reached for the top, sinking the angel's coned skirt over the tallest branch.

Skylar snapped several pictures—anything to hide how overheated she suddenly felt. "I'll send these to you."

"Thanks." After he put Addison back on the ground, he adjusted the angel and asked, "Is that straight?"

"Hmm?" She'd been sorting through the pictures and zooming in on certain pectoral points of interests, not paying attention to what was actually happening. "Huh? What? Yes, looks straight to me."

She needed to get out of there.

As soon as she made herself a snack, she went back to her room to finish up what she could. The project would take another week to complete, but she was making great headway. She also thought she did well on her exam, so all in all, this was adding up to be a pretty decent class, one she hoped to get an A in.

The next day, Erin stopped by unannounced again as they were eating lunch. Skylar assumed it was to drop off the forty dollars she was owed but that would make too much sense. Every time Erin came by the house, she disrupted the happy, peaceful vibe.

"Tonight's the town Jingle Ball," Erin said, as if Skylar should know what that meant.

She was aware that for the last three years Jasper Falls had hosted a Jingle Ball, but it wasn't something she ever attended. "And?"

Erin scoffed. "Addison needs a new dress. Santa will be there, and all the kids will have their pictures taken with Santa and the mayor."

"Santa's coming?" Addison perked up from where she'd been coloring at the table. "I want to go!"

"O-okay. What time should she be ready?"

"You'll have to bring her there by five. And Mr. Buchanan expects you to work late. He'll be busy meeting families and taking photographs and you'll have to keep Addison occupied at the event. Here are your tickets to get in the door. Don't lose them."

"He wants me to *attend* the Jingle Ball?"

"Are you listening to me? Yes, he wants you there to keep an eye on Addison."

"But I don't have clothing for a ball."

"Really, Skylar, no one's going to be looking at you. You're just there to keep an eye on Addison. Wear whatever you want."

Her mom and dad went to the ball the year James was born, and they both got really gussied up. Her dad even rented a tux.

The first hour of the evening was really the only part geared toward the children. The rest of the night was like a wedding reception with music and dancing while white-gloved butlers served hors d'oeuvres. As an employee of the mayor, who was technically the host, it would be inappropriate to wear anything other than a dress or a suit.

Erin left without paying her the forty dollars for the chinchilla or offering money to buy Addison a dress. Skylar sighed. "Looks like we're going shopping."

They drove to McGinty's and found Addison a white dress with a red ruffled petticoat underneath. She also needed shoes and tights, which were easy enough to find, but the store had nothing in terms of women's formal wear.

In a panic, she called her sister. "Hannah, I need to borrow a gown. Something black and simple."

"Sky, I don't have anything like that. The closest I have to a black gown is the dark blue cocktail dress I wore to the winter formal last year, but your boobs are bigger than mine. It might not fit."

She didn't have time to be picky. "Is it clean?"

"I think so. It's in my closet."

"Perfect. I'm swinging by to borrow it for tonight."

"Where are you going?"

"The Jingle Ball."

"For real?"

"Don't ask. Thanks for the dress. I owe you one."

Bundling up Addison, she hurried out. Once at her childhood home, she ransacked her sister's closet for shoes and also stole some jewelry. She would make an excellent burglar, being that she was in and out in five minutes flat. They were back to the mansion by four, and she needed to get Addison bathed, buffed, brushed, and shined for the ball.

Once Skylar had her little charge ready, she set her on the couch and turned on cartoons. "Stay here and don't touch anything that can get you dirty. I have to get changed."

She raced up the stairs and basically freshened up with what her grandmother called a whore's bath in the sink, then squeezed into Hannah's dress. It was gorgeous, but her sister wasn't kidding when she said the top might be tight. Skylar's boobs were bursting out of the plunging neckline and there wasn't much she could do to smoosh them down.

She flipped her head over, slicked back her hair, and teased the rest into a bun. Nude silk stockings and midnight blue satin heels finished the look, but she needed something more. Digging through her makeup case, she found a black brow pencil and quickly smoked out her eyes. Her sister's fake diamond earrings added that final sparkle and she was ready to go.

Addison gasped when she came down the stairs. "Wow, you look like a princess."

"Thanks. So do you. Ready?"

"I didn't get dirty."

"Good." Skylar buttoned Addison in her white dress coat. She wished she owned a nicer coat to go with her outfit, but her usual wool peacoat would have to do.

Walking through snow in heels was always fun. Luckily, she made it to the rec center behind Town Hall without breaking her neck.

The Jingle Ball was super fancy for their town. They even had valet drivers to park the cars.

Town Hall was illuminated with classic white twinkle lights, and candles lit each window. The rec center was dressed in hundreds of red poinsettias, and everything was draped in evergreen branches that glittered with gold satin bows.

Children raced around in beautiful clothing, the little boys with their clip-on ties and the girls in their shiny patent leather shoes. The choir had been arranged on the staircase leading to the second floor and people gathered around the landing as they sang "Silent Night".

Families lined up to have their pictures taken with Santa. The air smelled of winter festivities. And guests sipped champagne while the sky outside started to snow.

"Let's try to find your father." They checked their coats

and searched for Rhett, but Skylar didn't see him anywhere. She did, however, spot Erin in a red dress by the bar.

A drink sounded great. Skylar led Addison through the crowd and into the banquet hall. Chef tables glowed from every corner as caterers readied carving stations and candy bars and even an omelet kiosk. A string quartet started to play while a DJ set up behind them.

"Wow," Addison said, echoing Skylar's thoughts.

No wonder this event was so pricey. The town pulled out all the stops. "This way."

When they reached the bar, Erin spotted them and frowned. "What are you wearing?" Her gaze dropped to Skylar's neckline.

Skylar glanced at her exaggerated bustline and flushed. "It was all I had last minute."

"It's a little low cut."

It was, but it also wasn't indecent. She smiled tightly. "Do you know where Rhett is?"

"*Mr. Buchanan* is speaking with constituents over by the ice sculpture. He won't want to be disturbed while he's networking."

She was getting tired of this woman always trying to micromanage her every move. "His daughter wants to say hello."

"I'd wait—"

"Come on, Addy. I see him." She didn't really care what Erin had to say at that point. The witch had already insulted her attire. And she still owed her forty bucks, which Skylar never expected to see.

As they pushed through the crowd, Rhett came into view. Dressed in his tuxedo, he looked like everything Bruce Wayne wished he could be. The man was absolutely perfect, the truest definition of debonair.

When he spotted them, his attention snagged and whatever he'd been saying seemed to fall right out of his head. A group of townies followed the mayor's stare as he smiled to greet her and Addison.

"You look incredible," he said, the moment Skylar approached. His eyes dropped to his daughter. "And look at you! Two princesses." He scooped up Addison and kissed her cheek.

"Mayor Buchanan, can we get a picture?"

He turned and a man with a wide lens camera snapped his photo. Nearby, women gushed over what a handsome, doting father he was.

Skylar backed into the shadows, letting him have this moment, figuring it was good for his image and good for his daughter to share in his spotlight a little. It was also a good reminder of how out of her league and impressive he was when he wasn't fumbling over Christmas ornaments and eating his fill of her apple pie. This was the real Rhett Buchanan, and it would serve her well to remember that.

In true wallflower fashion, she sampled every appetizer that passed and gathered quite a collection of cocktail napkins and toothpicks. A butler delivered a flute of champagne and she gratefully accepted it, using the empty flute to stuff her trash in when she sucked the bubbly fizz dry.

"Skylar?"

She turned at the sound of her name, startled to see a familiar face in the mix. "Uncle Colin!" She spotted her aunt. "Wow, Aunt Sammy, I love your dress!"

"And look at you," her aunt said, taking her hand and pulling her into a half twirl. "I hardly recognized you."

Skylar flushed. "It's Hannah's dress. Sort of a last-minute thing."

"Well, you're stunning." She kissed Skylar's cheek. "I guess you're here for your new job?"

She nodded and pointed to her charge who still clung to her father's side. "That's Addison."

"She's a cutie." Sammy raised her brows and leaned close to whisper, "Just like her father."

She needed no reminder that the mayor was considered the town's most eligible bachelor. Women of all ages found him charming and classically handsome. Apparently, even the happily married ones weren't immune.

Rhett turned and smiled at them, then broke away from the conversation to walk over and say hello. "Colin, Samantha, it's nice to see you again."

"You too, Rhett," Colin greeted, shaking the mayor's hand. "How's your newest employee doing?"

Sammy rolled her eyes and gave Skylar an apologetic glance. But Rhett played it off and simply said, "She's wonderful. Fitting right in."

"Hi, Addison, I'm Sammy. You met my son Michael the other day." Her aunt crouched down so that she was at the little girl's eye level. "Do you want me to show you where he is?"

Addison frowned and Skylar reminded, "You remember Michael, don't you? He helped you make the gingerbread house at Miss Maureen's."

"Oh, yeah!"

They broke off from the men and found Michael playing in the banquet hall with some other children. Addison jumped right into the fun.

"Champagne?" A server appeared and she and Aunt Sammy eagerly accepted two glasses.

"Thank you."

Aunt Sammy watched her and chuckled. "I'm not used to seeing you drink."

"I'm twenty-one now, so..."

"I know, but when I met you, you were just a little girl. I still see you that way sometimes."

She remembered when her Aunt Sammy first came to visit. She'd actually come to the mountain with her Uncle

Braydon, but there was a whole twisted story there, and she ended up with her Uncle Colin, who, at the time, was supposed to become a priest.

She smirked into her champagne flute. Every family had their secrets.

"So, how's the new job?"

"Pretty good. I love Addison."

"How's her father?"

"He's fine. His assistant leaves something to be desired."

She stared across the room where Erin appeared to be lecturing some of the catering staff. It was the first time she got to take in the other woman's dress. She had a lot of nerve making a comment about Skylar's dress when she was basically wearing a skintight, red candy wrapper.

"Erin Montgomery?" Sammy asked, her expression similar to the one Aunt Nicky had made.

"Do you know her?"

"Unfortunately." Sammy hid her mouth behind another glass of champagne. "I'm not a fan."

That seemed to be the verdict for most.

Just then, Erin noticed them and crossed the dance floor. "Skylar, Addison's wearing white. She's going to get dirty before pictures. I specifically told you to watch her."

"She's playing with the other kids."

"Well, the other kids aren't the mayor's children."

"Hello, Erin," Sammy interrupted. She'd never witnessed or believed her aunt had a cold side, but the chilly look she sent Erin proved every woman was capable of an icy stare.

"Samantha. How are you?"

"Wonderful. You?"

"Great."

Skylar wasn't sure how some women managed to use pleasantries as passive aggressive daggers, but her aunt was proving a master. The more she smiled and chose nice words, the more evident it was that she despised Erin. Aunt Sammy was a passive powerhouse, and Skylar was beyond impressed.

Erin's brittle smile turned back to Skylar. "Get Addison off the floor." With that she stalked away.

Skylar rolled her eyes. "Was she always a bitch?"

"She's always been…something special. Let's get more champagne."

Skylar needed to get food in Addison's stomach.

They hit the buffet and made plates for the kids. After that, they moved to the line for Santa.

Michael and Addison were adorable together. They danced and twirled and took great interest in each other, which kept Addison occupied and happy most of the night. It also gave Skylar a chance to catch up with her aunt. The evening turned out to be a lot of fun.

Once they made it to Santa Claus, she called Rhett over and he got an adorable family photo with his daughter and the big guy, but then it was back to playing mayor. When Sammy and Colin left, Skylar was on her own and back to the usual business of keeping Addison occupied.

Now on a schedule, her little charge yawned at exactly nine o'clock. Skylar found an upholstered chair in the hall and sat down with her. It wasn't long before Addison passed out in her arms.

Skylar was getting tired as well, so she didn't mind sitting in the shadows and watching the people go by. It was the first time she truly rested in two weeks. No dinner to make, no lesson to plan, and no books to study. She was officially off the hook and able to relax, which she did, for the next two hours.

As the party cleared out and the DJ played the last song, the hallway clogged with guests waiting at the coat check for their items. Valets fetched cars and vendors packed up.

Erin didn't see her sitting off to the side, but Skylar definitely saw her as she slipped her number to a man. The man leaned close, whispered something in her ear, and for the first time ever, Skylar saw the woman smile.

She no longer believed the woman had something going on with Rhett. Mainly because Rhett said he was unattached, but also because she didn't believe he was the sort to kiss other women while in a relationship—casual or otherwise.

But she still believed Erin wished there was something there. Not only was she overly protective and territorial around him, the PA shamelessly flirted with him at every opportunity. She also worked hard to leave the impression that no one knew Rhett as well as she did. But the truth was, everything Erin told her about Rhett didn't add up to the man Skylar knew.

Either the woman was misinformed or the man was pretending to be someone he wasn't. Skylar didn't care about proving Erin wrong, but she did care about revealing the real Rhett Buchanan.

When the crowd thinned and most of the guests were gone, only the staff and those on the mayor's payroll remained. Erin shifted into her coat, finally noticing Skylar and Addison sitting in the corner.

"You're still here?"

Where would she have gone? "We've been enjoying the music."

She frowned. "It's past Addison's bedtime."

The woman truly treated her like the worst nanny in the world. "She's fine. She's been sleeping for the last hour and a half."

Erin rolled her eyes. "Here comes Rhett, now." She crossed the hall—likely to tell on her—and said something to their boss.

His gaze lifted, connected with Skylar's, and his eyes widened. Then he scowled.

Doubt knifed through Skylar. Maybe Erin *did* know him better. He looked shocked to see they were still there. With a swish of her hips, the PA pivoted and walked out of the hall, smirking with her nose held high as she passed.

Skylar couldn't believe it. The woman actually tattled on her. What a little snitch. And now her boss was stalking toward her, face drawn with a frown.

"How long have you been sitting here?"

"A little over an hour. It's fine. Addison fell asleep and I didn't want to disturb her."

His lips pressed into a thin line and he bent down to collect his daughter in his arms.

The absence of Addison's weight left Skylar feeling a little numb and off balance. She stood and brushed the wrinkles out of her dress.

Rhett watched her and his frown deepened. "I thought you two left a while ago."

"You were busy."

He glanced at the empty coat check closet. The attendant had left and only a few garments remained. "Do you mind fetching the coats?"

"Of course." She lifted the trap door and retrieved their items.

Once she had her coat on, she draped Addison's over her little, sleeping body and hesitated, unsure what to do with Rhett's. "Um..." Should she put it over his shoulders?

"Can you carry it for me?"

"Sure." The material was heavy wool and the lining smelled like his cologne. She might have taken a few extra breaths when he wasn't looking.

She followed him out of the hall. Her little car and a black limo idled by the curb, all the other vehicles were gone. The limo driver opened the door and he set Addison inside. "You next."

"Oh, my car's right—"

"The roads are a sheet of ice. We can get it in the morning. In you go."

She hesitated a moment, but he pressed a firm hand on her bare shoulder and she immediately obeyed. When he touched her, no matter how casually, her body turned into absolute mush.

The valet returned her car to the lot as soon as Rhett waved him off.

Slipping into the warm limousine, she pulled Addison onto her lap like a shield. Rhett used the other door, and once the chauffeur put the car in gear, they rode in silence.

If he was upset with her, she wished he would just come out and say it. She didn't come from a family that stewed silently. Both sides of her family liked to air their grievances and move on.

Silent treatment was a slow sort of torture she wasn't used to. He was killing her, and the drive home was taking forever due to the icy condition of the roads.

The closer they came to the mansion the more she sensed his stare on her, burning through the shadows, through the material of her dress, and into her skin. Okay, maybe not through her dress, but a girl could dream.

He obviously wasn't happy with her. A person could choke on the tension in the air.

Her finger nudged the window button and the cool breeze hit her skin like a gulp of water eases thirst.

"Hot?"

Every breath filled her belly and she seemed to breathe faster than usual. "A little."

A low grunt was his only reply.

She wanted to kick Erin for getting her in trouble. But why was she in trouble? She'd done exactly what was asked of her, every time, for precisely two weeks. If he was really all that particular when it came to his out of the house mayor functions, he should give her more notice and clarify his expectations in advance.

She hated taking orders from Erin. As a matter of fact, she hated the way Erin constantly tried to overthrow her authority where Addison was involved. Who was the governess here? Addison was her job, and Skylar had done nothing short of care for her properly since the moment she accepted the job.

Attending balls was above her pay grade. She hadn't complained. She'd found a last-minute dress and made it all work. She even worked late, so that the mayor wouldn't be *disrupted,* which was really the only instructions she'd been given. It wasn't her fault no one told her when to leave.

"If you didn't want me there, why did you insist I come?" she suddenly snapped.

But as soon as the words left her mouth, as soon as she found herself finally looking at him, the hard lines of his beautiful face cast in moonlit shadows and the hungry glow of his eyes, she realized she'd drastically misjudged the situation.

13

DID she think she could hide behind Addison all night? Even with his daughter sleeping in her lap she was barely covered.

Skylar's breasts were practically spilling out of that dress, and the moonlight accented every dip and curve. She looked too young, too innocent, and too damn tempting for him to deal. And what was this about him not wanting her there?

The limo pulled into the driveway. There wouldn't be enough time to discuss her little outburst now, and the roads were too shitty to simply joyride and talk out the misunderstanding. But he couldn't let it go.

Who knew how much time they would have once they made it inside the house? According to their recent behavior, she'd likely put Addison to bed then disappear to the third floor. He couldn't let that happen.

"Let's get one thing straight, Skylar. If I don't want something, I don't do it. You were there, because I *wanted* you there." The limo parked. "We're home."

The driver opened her door before she could muster a

response, and the next several minutes were focused on navigating the icy walkway, unlocking the house, and getting Addison undressed and into bed.

His daughter didn't stir once through the process as he hovered, watching Skylar the entire time, not giving her a single shot of escaping the upcoming confrontation. The longer he observed her moving about in that sexier than sin dress, caring for his child, blushing under his inspection because she knew damn well he stared, the more he wanted her.

He was through denying his attraction.

Tonight, when she first arrived and smiled at him, he caught something in her stare. Her presence made his pulse fluttered with awareness whenever they were within a few feet of each other, and he was coming to guess that her temperamental moods were less to do with the fact that he'd kissed and touched her, and more to do with the fact that he'd stopped before finishing what they started.

Fuck propriety. He wanted her every which way and then some.

He wanted her under him, on her knees in front of him, riding him, stroking him, screaming for him. Hell, he even wanted her sweet for him. He wanted the freedom to kiss her at will when she danced around in cute little aprons. He wanted to trap her under mistletoe and lick her cheek when she made a mess of herself while baking. He wanted to feel her up when she was soft, in her pajamas, sneaking down for a cup of bedtime tea, and steal into her room when she tried to hide from him.

He wanted her sexiness, but also her softness. Perhaps that was where it all began. She was such a nurturer at heart, he wanted her to take care of him.

She had become an obsession he'd quickly grown tired of trying to ignore. His fixation with her had multiplied every day, to the point that he was distracted at work and fighting the constant threat of an erection.

She didn't even have to try for sexy. The woman achieved it effortlessly. Hell, even her bulky winter socks did it for him.

Backing out of the nursery, he gave her space to emerge when she was ready. As Skylar turned, the look in her eyes made it clear she understood his intentions. They were addressing the tension between them *tonight*.

She shut the nursery door and paused. Her hair had tumbled loose and her shoes were in her hand. Stocking-covered feet pointed toward him, small and delicate. Christ, there wasn't one part of her that didn't captivate him.

She glanced at the floor, appearing unsure.

Run, little girl... a hungry voice in his head growled, mostly because the thought of chasing her turned him on even more.

"I don't understand what you want from me," she whispered, her gaze lifting and slaying him in one glance.

"Does it matter?"

She studied him for a quiet moment. "Yes. I want to know."

Her appeal to understand him gave him so much more than he had a right to ask for, more than she likely realized she was offering. He wasn't perfect. That didn't mean she had to accept him, but he felt her desire to do just that. He truly believed she wouldn't be satisfied until she understood every hidden part of him, and it was her curious interest in him that fed something starved inside.

"Why would you think I didn't want you there tonight?" She'd become a part of them. She made them function better as a family, and she was exceptionally patient with Addy. Of course, he wanted her there.

Her brows drew together in a fiercely adorable scowl. "You aren't clear about your expectations. You had no right to get pissed that I stayed. Addison was sleeping. We weren't in the way."

"I never said you were."

"Well, Erin..." Her words faded away and her lips pressed tight.

"Erin what?"

She shook her head. "It doesn't matter. I know you were frustrated on the way out of there tonight. What did I do to frustrate you?"

Would she be able to handle the truth? He needed to find out. "You existed."

"What?" Her head drew back.

"Skylar... I wasn't angry that you stayed late. I felt like a shmuck for being too preoccupied to see that you and Addy made it home safe and at a reasonable hour. I was pissed at myself."

She looked away in confusion. "But my existence frustrates you?" When her stare returned to his, she was pissed. "Are you firing me?"

Startled she'd jump to such a conclusion, he panicked. "No. The thought never crossed my mind. Do you want to quit?"

Her head shook, but her eyes hid secrets.

"Tell me what you're thinking." His voice stayed low and neutral, but he'd beg for her thoughts if he had to. He wanted to crowd her and touch her, but they needed to clarify a few things first.

Her lips pursed with a tight little scowl. "We never discussed what happened in the kitchen."

"So, let's discuss it now."

A deep blush crested her sharp cheeks, drawing his attention to the beauty mark by her eye. She looked incredible tonight. Beautiful in a different way. Her eyes were done up with black coal and the blue irises popped in contrast.

She looked dangerous, and for the first time, he admitted that this woman could actually hurt him.

She was the whole package and she deserved the same. As much as he wanted to get to know her, he now understood that women like Skylar Marcelli deserved a man's full attention. They were an investment, because women like her could ruin men for all others. And once he had her, he was certain it would be a long time before he'd let her go.

"I kissed you because I wanted to. I stopped because I didn't want you to feel pressured. You're my employee."

"You didn't pressure me." Her voice softened and he held his breath to hear every raspy word as she confessed, "I wanted it."

His body tightened to a point of pain. "And now?"

Her gaze lifted, stark blue eyes driving home a challenge. "I don't want to get hurt."

"I won't hurt you." It was more likely that she'd be the one to hurt him in the end.

He stepped closer, dropping his voice and grazing his fingers along the delicate heart shape of her jaw. When she didn't back away, he whispered, "But I'm not sure I can be gentle."

"I don't want gentle."

God, help him. "What do you want?"

You... The silent word screamed from her eyes but he needed to hear her say it.

"Tell me."

Her shyness, or perhaps it was inexperience, stole her voice.

"Your job is safe, Skylar. Whatever this is, it's separate."

She gave a subtle nod, which he translated as relief, consent, and a dark desire to continue.

"If you let me have this, I promise I'll make it good for you."

Her full lips trembled as she looked up at him giving

another subtle nod. "Tell me what *you* want," she rasped, her voice a throaty temptation that drove him wild.

It had been a long time since he wanted someone the way he desired her. Tonight, in the limo, he finally admitted, resistance was futile.

"I want everything you're willing to offer."

Her breasts pressed against the blue silk as her breath noticeably quickened. She glanced at the double doors to his bedroom and his gut clenched with need. He wanted to devour her, and he was running out of patience. He'd die if she turned him down now.

"Make a choice, Skylar. Left, you go to your room, shut the door, and go to sleep. Right… You're awake all night and nothing's the same in the morning."

Her brow puckered. "What about Addison?"

"I told you, your job's safe either way. I'm not a shmuck. My daughter loves you. You're good for her. You're good for us."

She stepped around him and his heart ripped into a hard beat, pounding behind his ribs until she turned left. His mood plummeted and his body raged at her rejection as she slowly walked toward her bedroom door.

How had he so massively misread the situation? He shouldn't be surprised. He wasn't new to rejection and—

She paused at the end of the hall, but she didn't open the door. Setting her shoes beside the carpet, she turned, her footsteps silently treading over the runner as she walked back to him.

His throat went dry and desire spiraled through him. That look. Did she even realize how much she tempted him?

His body vibrated with needy hunger as she took a step. His breath caught as she slowly walked toward him, returning to him. Rivers of midnight blue taffeta rippled from her narrow hips as she took her time, drawing out his torture.

She stopped two feet in front of him and met his stare. "Addison can't know. I don't want her getting hurt."

"Agreed."

A nervous smile teased her lips but didn't hold. "Okay then."

"Okay?" He had to be sure.

She nodded. "I'm ready."

He closed the distance, trapping her face in his hands and stealing her mouth with a darkly promising kiss. She lifted to her toes, pressing into him with a soft moan. He pulled her close, delving his tongue deeper and forcing her to open for him. She complied with a sort of elegant grace that was his undoing.

She was incredibly easy going, but she left him hard by simply breathing. Their chemistry seemed absolutely effortless. It was the simplest connection he'd ever experienced with a woman, and that terrified him.

"How far are we taking this, Skylar?"

If there was any chance they'd have to slow down, he needed to know now. He already knew, once they started, it would be excruciating to stop.

She lifted a delicate shoulder and blushed. "How far do you want to go?"

She was too agreeable for her own good. "With you? I can't imagine ever hitting a limit."

This time she let her full smile show, radiant and flawless, and his knees nearly buckled with need.

"Show me," she challenged, her smile playful and curious.

He caught her tempting body in an unbreakable hold and slammed her to the wall, his mouth crashing over hers and delivering a sinful kiss that promised she'd be a wiser woman come morning.

Biting her full lip, he tipped up her face and vowed, "You're mine."

Grinding his body against hers, he showed her what she did to him. His mouth dropped to her throat, nipping and tasting, tongue sliding over her racing pulse until he groaned with desperation, needing to be inside of her.

Her kisses were addicting. Soft, leading, teasing. He pulled away and growled, resenting their clothing and the trek they still had to make to his bed.

"Your mouth makes me crazy," he confessed, dragging the pad of his thumb over the pillow of her lower lip.

She pressed her cheek to his touch and parted her lips, letting the digit slip inside. His eyes rolled back, and he groaned.

"Don't tease me."

"I'm not."

When she looked up at him with those smokey blue eyes, he nearly came in his tux. Tugging her away from the wall, he lifted her off the ground, anchoring her body to his so that her legs twisted around his hips.

His face buried in her throat, sinking kisses over every exposed inch of tempting flesh as he crossed the threshold and kicked the door shut. He didn't stop kissing her until he tumbled her to the bed, sinking his weight over her, pinning her in a purely possessive way.

She laughed, the sound sweet and nervous, and he valued that she didn't scare easily. He caught her jaw in an unbreakable hold, then loosened his grip to stroke the long, tempting line of her throat.

She sobered under his intense stare and moaned softly when he flexed his hips, giving her a slow kiss that left her pliant and warm. God, she tasted like Eden, and her skin smelled like heaven on fire.

Dragging his mouth lower, he teased his tongue along

the seam of her bodice. Her body was a symphony of springtime that lured him like a spell.

Straddling her hips, he stared down at her tousled beauty. Her pure skin was rosy from his five o'clock shadow, and he took great satisfaction in seeing markings from his touch on her flesh.

"No going back now." He peeled away the plunging neckline of her dress and her nipples sprung free. "Jesus."

Pert, tight little buds, begging to be touched. Her curves were lush and inviting. His palm cradled the soft flesh as his thumb teased the hardened tips. Lips parting, back slightly arching in a plea for more, her eyes grew heavy with need.

His mouth closed over the turgid tip, his teeth nipping with a teasing pull as he sucked hard and greedily. She gasped and a startled moan escaped in breathy relief. He looked up at her, only to find her watching him with innocent curiosity.

He recalled being a boy in his early twenties. The fumbling, the lack of endurance, and the selfish need. It had been a while since he took a woman to bed, but he was certain he could open her eyes to the joys of sleeping with an experienced man.

"I warn you now, I'm greedy, but also generous."

His tongue licked over the tip of her nipple, now a deeper cherry red from his rough pulls. He pinched the other, and she inhaled sharply. Then he released the tip and captured it in his mouth, bathing the abused flesh with warm, wet kisses.

He worked a hand under the endless layers of her skirt as he feasted on her breasts. Teasing and tormenting, training her responses and showing her how easily her body answered to his touch.

Her thighs were lush and supple, stirring an endless hunger in him. He teased his fingers close to the seam of her panties but never made contact, drawing out the excruciating hunger they shared.

"Rhett, please..."

Her plea poisoned his patience and his hips reflexively rocked with urgent need. He'd tormented them long enough. He rolled to his side, but still angled his body over hers, still played at teasing her into a soft but hungry frenzy.

Silken legs scissored against the duvet, as he traced his nails to the top of her pantyhose and slowly rolled the covering away. This stunning woman, drowning in waves of gossamer, was easily the sexiest female he'd ever touched. If he didn't get her naked soon, he was going to embarrass himself.

He chuckled. "I think your dress is growing the more I try to get you out of it."

She laughed and he couldn't resist that mouth. Dropping his lips to hers, he kissed her slowly, devouring her with every swipe of his tongue. Soft, kitten-like mews left her throat as his hands explored her bare thighs, hips, and stomach.

She was burning hot, and every inch of her skin called to him. His life revolved around being the perfect, politically correct civilian, but the things he wanted to do to her in that moment were a far cry from civilized.

Her thighs opened, silently begging him to stop teasing her. The swatch of silk covering her sex was damp with arousal. He pressed the material against her skin, showing her that he found the evidence of her desire.

Another stunning blush.

He rubbed the silk of her damp panties, finding the tight bud of her clit through the material and adding enough pressure to drive her mad.

"Rhett!"

"Do you want me?"

She nodded.

He stripped her of the panties, leaving the dress twisted around her waist, and grinned. "Show me. Open your legs for me."

His fingers traced a line from her ankle up her shin, and her knees drifted apart. Sharp breaths panted past her lips, and her eyes were wild as his touch dragged higher.

Her body unfurled like a flower, hinting at the sweetest honey. He dipped a finger between her folds, keeping his touch shallow and teasing. Her body arched, pressing into his hand, and he chuckled again, pleased by her eagerness.

"More?"

"*Please*." She panted.

"So polite."

He plunged a finger into her heat, stopping only when his palm cupped her sex. Warm cream coated his knuckles and together they groaned. He held still for a moment, allowing the anticipation to build.

The touch of his thumb slipped over the bud of her sex, and then he was sliding into her delicate folds, adding another finger, and drawing the softest cries from her throat.

She was tight. Petite. He took his time, stretching her and stoking that fiery need. Returning to her tempting breasts, he kissed and teased, never letting his fingers slide fully out of the hot grip of her sex.

His mouth shifted to her lips and she kissed him back with such desperation, he knew it was time.

He moved between her legs and pushed her thighs wide, dragging his tongue through her slit and closing his lips over her sensitive flesh. He continued to tease and pleasure her, loved when her fingers boldly raked through his hair, pulling hard at the strands and anchoring his mouth to her sex. His other hand toyed with her breasts and her body fluttered and responded to every touch.

"You're almost there." He stroked and kissed faster and her breath hitched.

He teased her into a frenzy until her cries crested into a breathtaking crescendo and her body came alive, arching against the mattress, back bowed and quivering, calling his name as heat gushed over his fingers.

Her hands knotted in the coverlet. Her body wore a feminine dew of sweat and arousal. The scent of her desire was a drug to him. And he was an instant addict, needing more.

He kept going, kissing her swollen flesh and pumping his fingers. He drank every drop of her sweet release and pushed her to give him more.

He was a glutton for her pleasure, needy to impress her and prove himself the best she'd ever had. He lost count of how many times she cried out in pleasure and her body grew weak. Her limbs draped over the covers and her moans were near delirious.

Taking pity on her, he softened his licks to gentle kisses and removed his probing fingers, simply petting her delicate, but swollen folds.

"You're so pretty here. Pretty everywhere. But here... seeing your soft, pink skin, swollen from my mouth, wet from my touch... I'm aching to be inside of you."

She sighed and gave a smile sculpted of the sweetest secrets. "Then why aren't you?"

When she showed that direct side of her, assertively content in her sexual need and undaunted by the fact that she was a hot, red-blooded woman, he craved her a hundred times more.

Fascinated, he laughed and whispered, "Where did you come from?"

She smiled. "Jasper Falls."

Yet, no one in the town could claim half her beauty, match her wit, or entice him so completely. Maybe there was some sort of magic hiding in the water up on that mountain where her family lived, something sacred.

"I've never met anyone like you."

She smiled and the flush on her cheeks darkened. "I hope you know I'm not usually this, um...forward with men."

He leaned in and gently kissed her. "Don't move. I'll be right back."

In the bathroom, he stripped off his tux and opened a condom. She waited in a rumpled heap of blue on the bed, her tapered limbs and tempting curves on full display, her still tight nipples glistening in the moonlight.

She opened her eyes as he pulled her to sit up. "I should have taken this off before we started." He searched for the zipper as satin and taffeta pooled around her waist.

Her body was pliant, her smile soft and satisfied. He slid the material to the floor, revealing her flawless shape. She was utter perfection in that she appeared so beautifully human with rounded curves and a healthy softness around her hips and thighs.

He joined her on the bed and kissed her tenderly. Their bodies aligned and she looped her arms around his neck, staring deep into his eyes. He settled his weight on his knees, careful not to crush her.

He wanted her without barriers. The hot slide of her sex against the tip of his erection made him resent having to use protection, something he never resented since becoming a father.

He reached between their bodies and guided himself close, sliding along the seam of her sex without fully penetrating.

Her brow creased and he worried he might have been too rough during their foreplay.

"Did I hurt you?"

She shook her head. "No. Keep going."

He nudged deeper, stretching her, careful to take it slow. Her brow tightened again and he paused. He pressed a kiss to her temple and whispered, "Do you want me to stop?"

"No. It's just..." Her breath teased his ear. "You're really big."

He chuckled. "That sort of flattery will only make me bigger."

She laughed then sobered. "Just... hold me tight. I want to keep going."

He gathered her in his arms and kissed her. Her body momentarily tensed as he nudged forward, and then he was in. "I've got you."

The sinking feeling that this might be her first time haunted him, but he chased the thought away, as it made her seem too young and innocent, when so far she'd matched his desires every beat of the way.

He drew back and slid forward slowly, holding her just as she asked and staring into her eyes. It was incredibly intimate and he felt strangely bonded to her in a way he'd never experienced with past lovers.

Once she matched his rhythm and grew accustomed to his size, her body came alive. She gave him everything. When he kissed her, she met his kisses with equal fervor, and when he touched her, she melted into his caresses. He couldn't recall ever being with such a responsive woman. It was like she was made for him.

Her nails dug into his shoulders as he shifted his hips and angled his body deeper. She clung to him, moved with him, actively tried to give him as much as she possibly could.

When he stared into her eyes, finding a storm of emotion swirling in shades of midnight blue, he feared losing himself there and battled with the instinct to hold part of himself back.

Yet, he wanted to give her everything, the good, the

decent, the dark, and the depraved. He wanted to see if she was truly as accepting as she seemed.

Her lashes lowered and the link they shared broke, leaving him emotionally flailing for the connection he'd just felt.

"Look at me," he commanded, and her eyes opened. "Keep looking at me, just like you were." He thrust deep and she cried out. He was a selfish prick, but he needed whatever she stirred in him to stay alive. He'd never felt something so soothing before.

Holding himself still, buried inside of her to the hilt, he struggled to tamp down the surge of emotion rising in his chest. The pad of his thumb traced over her delicate throat, landing softly on her rapid pulse.

"I want you to feel me inside of you tomorrow and remember this moment."

"Oh, I don't think that'll be a problem," she teased, her body clenching tightly around him.

He nearly finished and the constricted grasp of her body and pushed his hips deeper, until it was impossible to sink any further into her. She was so petite in his hold, so delicate and tempting, yet so sensual and hungry for more. He sensed her desire building as her body shifted and adjusted to his intrusive presence.

They hadn't even started and he was greedy for more. He feared he'd never have enough of her. "Will you let me have you again?"

"Yes."

He drew back and pumped his hips hard, drawing a gasp from her lips. "And again."

"Yes."

"Every time I want to feel your body wrapped around me, will you let me have you?"

"Yes!"

He lifted his weight and thrust in and out, driving fast

strokes of his hard body into her tight sex. "All of you? You'll hold nothing back?"

"Nothing."

"That's how I want you. Do you hear me? I want you just like this. Open. Needy. Raw. *Mine.*"

He pushed himself to the edge, foregoing the pressure to be gracious and ever-diplomatic. That's not the man he wanted her to know in his bed. He wanted her to see the real him, because he actually believed she might accept him. She might like the man he showed the town, but he suspected she wanted to meet the parts of himself he hid, the parts that were private that no one else knew.

Then a possessive thought occurred. "This is us, Skylar. No one else touches you this way while we're doing this. Understand?"

She nodded. "Just us."

"Good girl. And if there's something you need, you tell me and I'll do it. I'll take care of you so long as you take care of me."

Maybe that was it. Maybe some sick and twisted, unloved part of him envied how completely she cared for others. She was so good at anticipating people's needs.

He gripped her thigh possessively, digging his fingertips into her flesh and stroking her tempting curves. "Will you take care of me?"

"Yes." Her legs wrapped around his hips. "Tell me what you need."

His nostrils flared. Was it really that easy?

He caught her wrists and pinned them over her head. "I need this." He drove into her and she gasped.

Her breasts swayed with every hard thrust. The more vulnerable she appeared, the more he wanted her surrender. The more accommodating she became, the more he wanted her care and affection, her acceptance.

He'd never dared to act so freely with another. He was

greedy. Needy. And he, without a doubt, would shamelessly take every act of care she willingly offered.

"I want all of it. Every inch of you. Every minute of the day. And I want it without asking." He released her arms and cupped her breasts, plumping the flesh hard enough to leave bruises. More than anything, he wanted the freedom to be himself with her and know she'd like him anyway.

"I don't want to have to be a gentleman with you, but I'll never disrespect you. I want all my desires to be perfectly okay with you." He hesitated, then confessed, "I've never been that open with anyone before."

Her arms gracefully fell to the bed, a show of utter surrender and beauty. "I want the real you, Rhett. If you cross a line, I'll let you know. But until then...hold nothing back."

He stilled and swallowed. This was a very dangerous game they were playing. Too dangerous.

His conscience beseeched him to reconsider his request, but her body felt too damn good, tightly wrapped around his, clenching and milking the last of his logic away.

He pulled out and jumped off the bed. She opened her mouth to protest, but before she could form a single word he caught her ankles and dragged her ass to the edge, wrenched her legs wide. "I'm sorry. You're gonna be sore tomorrow."

He plunged into her wet sex, angling his body deeper and thrusting hard. He lost himself in the following moments, drunk on lust and pushing with unquenchable need, greedy for every comfort she could offer, every comfort he could steal.

Her body trembled in his arms and he sensed her close to finishing. He pushed her, wringing out every ounce of her pleasure until the last moment when she shattered.

He held her through the storm, cradled her close, sheltered her in his strength, and once he knew she was done, he let himself go.

No experience came close to what they just shared. He was in uncharted territory, and when the final chills of his release vibrated every muscle in his body, dancing wildly along his spine, he found himself compelled to do something else he'd never done. He pulled her close and held her in his arms.

14

SKYLAR TREMBLED as he clutched her shaken body to his. He was strength and heat and fire, and she was tender uncertainty and inexperience, gifted with trusting consent. She hoped she'd done everything the way she was supposed to.

When his body pulled out of hers, it seemed to steal a layer of her soul with it. She expected it to end after he finished, but he held her for a long time, stroking her arms with the soft side of his fingers and pressing kisses into her temple and hair.

A vacant ache filled her core. Swollen folds were tender and over sensitized, sore but satisfied. The tender muscle aches she anticipated were already setting in, but as he continued to caress her, she found her aching limbs an easy inconvenience to ignore.

She shivered, her body cooling as she came down from the rush. He pulled the covers over them, cradling her to the hard plane of his chest.

His hands traveled her body as he laid claim to parts of her no man had touched before. She drew comfort from the steady beat of his heart.

The room was dark, and her limbs ached with a gentle

throb she feared would grow in the hours ahead. He warned her she'd be sore in the morning, but at the time she hadn't cared. Now she wondered how sore. She wondered what it said about her that, despite her discomfort, she still wanted him again.

His breathing kept a steady rhythm in the silence, and her mind sung with every rise and fall of his chest. Safe. Sheltered. Desired. She'd never existed as the center of someone's attention before. It was heaven.

"Are you thirsty?" he asked, voice a low, delicious timbre from more than an hour of masculine moans.

She was thirsty, but she'd rather die a painful death of dehydration and hunger than ever leave the sanctuary of his arms. "I just want to stay here, like this."

He chuckled, sounding as relaxed as she felt. "Me too."

The tension in his muscles gave way to ease, and his body softened beneath her. She had no basis for comparison, but she had a strange hunch they just had *really* good sex. Maybe she was just being cocky. She smirked at her corny pun.

"What's that smile for?"

She cleared her throat, too embarrassed by her juvenile train of thought to share it. "Did you like it?"

He groaned, the sound rich with male satisfaction. "You're incredible. I'm convinced there isn't a single thing you don't do well."

Her lips curved into a full grin. Though she'd been rather shy in the beginning, his praise bolstered her confidence and she pressed a kiss to his chest. "I loved it."

His easy expression faltered as his face blanked.

Silence.

Chilly, frigid silence.

She should have chosen her words more carefully. She knew better than to casually toss out the L word to a man early on in the relationship, even if she had only been applying the adjective to the act. She'd seen enough spoiled plotlines to know that word was poison to anything concerning casual sex.

Although, they hadn't fully defined how casual this was. He'd mentioned not seeing other people, but that wasn't exactly a testament of affection as much as it had been a hot and sweaty, grunting display of territorial male ego.

Her heart raced as she desperately waited for him to say something back, *anything* to confirm he knew she was only saying she enjoyed the sex and that he understood she wasn't confessing love or anything so drastic.

His body shifted, and he gently transferred her to the pillows. "I'll get that water."

When he left the bed, it felt personal. An ache formed in her chest and part of her soul trembled as if about to cave in.

Aware of how overly delicate she suddenly seemed, she blamed it on too many hormones and the shaken effects of sex.

Don't you dare cry...

Clarifying anything or mentioning what she'd just said would only make matters worse, so she swallowed back the lump of fear forming in her throat and suffered through the lonesome silence as she waited for him to return.

It was unbearable. She scrambled off the bed, her legs nearly buckling under her weight as the ache in her overused muscles screamed. She quickly scooped up her sister's dress and draped it over the chair in the corner, sneaking into the bathroom to freshen up.

The bathroom lights were startlingly bright, casting her in an unflattering, clinical glow, and she winced. Her skin was rosy and whisker burned. Her makeup was smeared, making her eyes appear twice their usual size. And her hair was destroyed. No wonder he left her there.

She quickly washed her face and combed her fingers

through her hair, pulling down the bun and making matters worse. Tangled hair framed her face in a wild cloud of auburn.

She tsked, unsure how to fix such a mess without fully showering. But that would be weird, wouldn't it?

She heard a sound from the bedroom and did a three-sixty, searching for a towel or anything to cover nakedness. Why had she left the dress in the other room?

"Everything all right?"

"Everything's fine!" She winced at the shrill sound of her voice. She needed to chill.

Staring at her reflection, she propped a fist on her hip and adjusted her posture. Women walked around naked in front of men they had sex with, right? She rolled her eyes, not satisfied with any posture she tried.

She could play a lot of roles, but sophisticated bed partner might not be one of them. Peeking out of the bathroom, she looked for any possible way of making it back into the bed unseen.

Rhett placed a glass of water on the nightstand and paused when he caught sight of her.

Her blush burned from her cheeks to her breasts to her other cheeks, too much of a novice to bear the walk of shame.

"You don't have to be shy with me."

"I know." It was literally like the distance from the bathroom to the bed was growing. She typically wasn't shy. But she was naked and, well, a bit frizzy and blotchy—not that she was complaining. "If you could just turn around for a second—

"Not a chance." He crossed the floor and pulled her from behind the bathroom door then tipped up her chin, brushing a sensual kiss across her lips that quickly turned into more.

Her body unraveled and she leaned into him, never realizing kisses could be so sheltering. His reassurance was incredibly appreciated, bolstering her confidence and casting some of her doubts aside.

When he broke the kiss, she looked up at him and smiled. She'd been pretty good about denying her feelings up until now, but who was she kidding? He touched her and she turned into pudding.

"I got you water."

She was no longer thirsty—or she was, but she didn't want to break their stare because then he might look down and recall that she was naked.

Her hips shifted, casually stroking her body against his and his eyes darkened. "I think I like when you're not a gentleman," she confessed, and his nostrils flared. "Wow, you give great smolder."

The hardness in his jaw and the intensity of his stare shifted with a burst of laughter. "Is that what I was giving?"

"Mm-hm."

Everything about him seemed carved out of hard masculinity. He was an unmoving boulder, lodged in place by time, and she was a fleeting snowflake, tumbling recklessly down a knoll, collecting speed and rolling into an unstoppable avalanche.

She didn't need experience to know he'd eventually hurt her. She didn't need him to say a single word to predict that she would be the one to eventually say too much.

But she didn't care. She wanted to be real with him. She wanted to be reckless. And, for once, she wanted to do something solely for herself without thinking of others.

No one knew what was going on between them. Rhett was her deepest, darkest secret. And she was feeling especially indulgent.

She followed all the rules, lived on the *Nice List,* and always did what was expected. Up until tonight, she never got into trouble or did anything worth keeping secret.

"After tonight, I think we're definitely on the *Naughty List.*"

"There's still a chance for you to redeem yourself." His hands continued to map out her curves and she couldn't get enough of his caresses.

She could bask a lifetime in his attention. The thought of disappointing him in any way gutted her. She should probably examine the reaction she had to him and this strange need to please him, but, at the moment, she was too consumed with the desire to do as he asked.

"I'm glad you kissed me."

He cupped her jaw and stepped closer. She kept her eyes focused on his expression, which told her so much about the things he wanted. The hunger in his eyes lured her to him, tore down her insecurities, and filled her with a dark desire to please.

"I want you again."

Her breath hitched and the ache in her muscles vanished in place of desire. "I'm yours."

"Are you?"

She nodded and he reached for a pillow on the bed, tossing it to the floor.

"Show me."

Understanding dawned and she lowered to her knees. Unsure but not ignorant, she waited and let him take the lead. It was much more intimate than she expected. He was incredibly gentle, gliding his rigid flesh over her lips and guiding his length into her mouth. He watched her closely, eyes smoldering with desire, as if the sight was better than the actual act.

Soft, whispered commands told her what he liked and how to make it better. She pleased him and he praised her, his endless flattery raining over her like a baptism of intimate attention nothing else could match.

The longer it went on, the more frenzied his breathing

became. When he was close, he lifted her body off the floor and carried her to the bed. His mouth covered hers, kissing her swollen lips with bruising force, as he rolled on a condom and found his way back inside of her.

This time, when he took her, he took more than before. He moved with slow intensity, brow pressed to hers, hand gripped tightly at the back of her neck as he rocked into her with long, intentional strokes.

He took her mouth. He took her cries. He took her most secret desires. He may even have taken a piece of her soul. He was insatiable. He took everything.

In the end, she had nothing left of herself that felt untouched by him. But that also meant she had no space for regrets.

15

RHETT CHECKED his phone again and grimaced. The day was lagging, and it was killing him to sit in his office pretending to work when his mind was so clearly elsewhere.

"We're ordering Chinese for lunch. What do you want?"

He glanced at Erin standing in the doorway, a notebook and pen poised in her hands. "Nothing for me. I have to run an errand. I'll grab something while I'm out."

"This is the third day you've missed lunch. Eat, Rhett. I don't feel like dealing with your *hangry* ass when four o'clock rolls around."

"I will eat, just not here."

Her eyes narrowed, but she gave up and walked away.

He busied himself for twenty more minutes then sent a text, warning Skylar he was leaving soon.

He'd been a greedy bastard, taking every bit of comfort she offered. Never in his life had he been so insatiable with a woman—so satisfied. So grateful.

After their first night, he insisted she let him take care of her. Using a soft washcloth, he bathed her folds in warm water, wincing at how swollen he'd left her. She was too sweet to complain, but he knew enough to tell she was sore.

The following morning, he insisted she take the morning to soak in the master tub while he took Addison to breakfast in town. He truly tried to give Skylar time to recover, but he only made it a few hours before finding himself inside of her again.

He took her slowly. Tenderly. But Skylar said he was holding back. She ordered him to be real with her, and goddamn, he wanted to do just that. She was unlike any of the other women he'd met.

When the scent of Chinese food filled the office that was his cue to leave.

Grabbing his coat and keys, he mumbled an excuse and rushed out the door. Five minutes later he pulled into his driveway.

His heart raced and his body heated as he unlocked the door. He came in quietly.

Skylar appeared at the top of the stairs, her hair down and her smile shy. She wore black leggings and a pink fuzzy sweater with deer antlers sewn on the front, around a red sequin Rudolph nose. She was everything he shouldn't want, yet he'd never been more attracted to a woman.

"Is she asleep?"

"She just went down." Her socked feet silently descended the staircase, and his body hardened. "How much time do you have?"

"About twenty minutes."

"I made you a sandwich."

He'd been skipping lunch. Of course, she would see that he ate. She was just that kind of woman.

Like a dog after a bone, he followed her into the kitchen. His eyes tracked her every move, and his hunger grew by the second, *ravenous*, but he wasn't after lunch.

She pushed a plate across the island. The diagonal cut peanut butter and jelly sandwich made him chuckle. She'd even set three carrot sticks on the side. It was the perfect lunch, the kind made with tender loving care that his classmates used to bring to school, while he ate whatever the teachers gave him out of pity.

"Do I get a glass of milk with this?"

She turned to fetch the milk out of the fridge, and he rounded the island. Catching her arm, he pulled her to his chest, his front pressing hard against her back. His hand slipped under her soft sweater and cupped her breast through her bra. She sank her weight into him.

"I want you," he growled, teasing her nipple into a hard point.

"You have to eat."

"I'm hungry for you."

"Rhett..."

"Don't make me suffer. I waited all morning."

"Fine."

Thinking of how greedy he'd been, he delicately slid a hand into the front of her pants and teased her folds. "I want to kiss you here."

She moaned, her head leaning into his chest as her body softened with consent.

Pushing down the tight, cotton pants, he crouched in front of her, and yanked her to his mouth. Her hands caught his shoulders, holding on for balance as he licked the seam of her slit.

"You always taste amazing." With her leggings bunched at her knees, she had limited range of motion. Her hips cocked forward and he swiped his tongue deep inside her folds, tasting warm honey.

Her soft moan filled the kitchen and he tenderly worked her into a delicate frenzy. Her body was so responsive, so inviting. As her warm cream coated his tongue and she came, he smiled against her flesh, pressing a kiss to her throbbing clit.

"Beautiful."

Her eyes were dark and her cheeks flushed when he stood. She was a vision.

He pushed the plate aside and turned her body, pressing her forward, and guiding her hands onto the granite countertop until she rested her cheek on the surface. The clink of his belt buckle mixed with the soft hum of Christmas carols that seemed a constant backdrop since she arrived in their life.

His hand slipped into the waistband of her pants again, and her wet flesh greeted his returning touch. She was always ready for him. He removed a condom from his pocket, and filled her with one determined stroke.

She gasped and rose to her tiptoes, keening with every thrust. His clothes were bulky as he'd not even taken the time to remove his coat, but he couldn't stop now.

Her body welcomed his. She was a warm place that felt like home—even if he'd never understood what a *home* should feel like. He believed the warmth in his chest he experienced whenever she looked at him was what people meant. *Home.*

Her pliant body met his every stroke. He worked his fingers over her sensitive flesh as he approached finishing. When his pleasure mounted, he brought her with him.

Short, sweet, and exactly what he needed. But he wanted more. It wasn't just the sex he craved. He wanted to talk and hear how her day was going. He wanted to munch on carrot sticks and eat the lovingly prepared sandwich she made him. He wanted to sit around and simply watch her move throughout the house, magically turning every room she entered into a home.

His body folded over hers as he caught her chin and turned her mouth to his, showing her how much he enjoyed their stolen moments together. She was a secret sanctuary for him, a place of warmth and welcome he never wanted to leave.

But he had to.

Slowly, and regretfully, he pulled out and righted her clothing. She should hate him for being so abrupt and demanding, but she never complained.

They righted their clothing, and only then did he greet her properly, kissing her with gentle appreciation and smiling into her eyes. "Hi."

She grinned up at him.

"Join me for lunch?"

She sat beside him while he ate and told him about her morning. He loved the way her eyes lit up every time she mentioned his daughter. It was only second to the way she would get excited about some crafty idea she planned for the afternoon.

Now that he understood how natural she was with children, he harbored a bit of shame for keeping her all to himself. She should be in a classroom with dozens of kids, sharing all her wonderful skills and care.

But he was selfish and didn't want to share her. He never lived in a house that played music or hung finger paintings on the fridge. Other than business lunches, he hardly ever ate at a table before she came along.

Skylar was maternal in a way his mother had not been. She was civilized with antiquated charm. She was everything *good,* and he wanted to bask in the light she'd brought into their world.

After lunch, they chatted for a little longer, and he resented having to go back to work. She and Addy were making Christmas cards today, and he wanted to stay and watch them work.

He'd always taken an interest in his daughter's life, but before Skylar, that interest had mostly revolved around her safety and security. He never wanted her to feel ashamed of who she was. As a parent, his priority had always been making sure she had nice clothing, a safe home, and food in her belly.

But, to Skylar, caring for a child was so much more. She covered the basics, such as food and shelter, but she brought something more to the table, something he didn't know how to deliver. Everything Skylar did, no matter if it was something as simple as making a sandwich, she did with love.

Skylar *loved*. She injected love into every task and every chore. She listened with love in her eyes and spoke lovingly when she addressed others. The girl emanated love, and he, once again, felt like a thief because he was stealing all that love she offered with no chance of offering anything quite as valuable in return.

He was empty, unsure where people found such affection. Sooner or later, she'd discover the hollow secrets he hid. She'd learn that, like Jasper Falls, the illusion of normalcy was just an impression. Beneath the surface, he was nothing more than a basic man—a greedy one at that.

"The other night..."

Her words stole his attention and he held his breath waiting for her to finish her thought. He grinned when her face flushed with a fiery blush.

She drew in a breath and glanced at her lap. "You said that we...wouldn't see other people. Did you mean that?"

Hot-blooded male ego thrummed through his veins. He'd never been a territorial man. Never had a right to anyone that he could be territorial with.

"I won't share you." It wasn't sensible and he had no right to be so demanding, but something dark and greedy inside of him knew he'd kill anyone who tried to take her away from him.

Rather than appear concerned by his possessiveness, she smirked. "Well, I don't want to share you, either."

"You won't have to." All she had to do was accept him for who he was. It wasn't a tall order, yet no one had ever accomplished such a feat. Paranoia crept in. "Just...be honest with me."

She nodded. "Maybe now is a good time to discuss our past. I know you've been with Addison's mom, but I don't know if there's been anyone else."

His mind thrust a wall up, as if he could somehow protect himself from her questions. He stood and put on his coat. "It's getting late. I have a meeting—"

"Then we can finish this conversation after work. I want to know you, Rhett."

An uncomfortable knot formed in his gut. He briefly pressed a kiss to her lips and carried his plate to the sink. He didn't want to have this conversation now and he didn't want to have it after work.

"There's nothing to know."

"Sure, there is. Who were you before you were the mayor of Jasper Falls? Where did you live? Who was Addison's mom? Were you married? Did you love her?"

Love... The word landed like a grenade, pin pulled and spoiling the peaceful moment with the impending threat of disaster. Time to go.

"I worked with hedge funds before moving here and I lived in a lot of different places, none of them half as nice as Jasper Falls. I've never been married and Addison's mom is a person who lives in my past where she belongs. She didn't love me and I didn't love her, but she'll always be Addy's mother and that means something. Now, I have to go. Thanks for lunch."

He could see his cold, blunt response hurt her feelings, but he'd given her as much as he could manage. He hated feeling vulnerable and her questions left him exposed.

Why couldn't she just accept him, no questions asked? Why did she have to probe into his past? If she dug too deep, she'd end up like all the rest and he wasn't ready to lose her.

He hesitated at the door, looking back and reading the

confusion in her eyes. "I'm sorry. I'm just not...good with sharing."

"Okay."

But it wasn't okay. He felt like a total jerk. He wished he could give her something but he wasn't sure he had anything of real value to give. She deserved better.

Walking back to her, he kissed her softly, letting his affection come across in the caress. She smiled, the expression genuine and full of forgiveness he didn't deserve.

"Have a good rest of the day," she whispered, letting him off the hook.

Like a true coward, he accepted the out. "I'll see you tonight."

It wasn't her age or innocence, but her kindness that shamed him. He was taking advantage of her, using her softness to fulfill a void that had been gaping inside of him for years. Maybe she was healing him, but no matter how much she might make him a better man, he'd never be the kind of man she deserved. He'd never be good enough for a woman with her gentle heart.

Soon, she'd realize that.

But, for now, he wanted her. And like many other things he possessed in his adult life, he couldn't stop until he had her.

Love... that was something he knew nothing about, something she wouldn't find no matter how deeply she dug under his surface. Until her, he had never known love could fill a house like furniture, tangible and comforting. And while it fascinated him to watch her act so lovingly with others, he didn't have a clue how she did it.

Boundaries were good. They kept him in check and reminded him that everything had a shelf life. But even the most intentional lines started to blur after emotions got involved.

When he wasn't around her, she was on his mind. And

when they were together with Addison, they made a perfect picture, the sort a stranger might stop and stare at through a window.

But when they were alone, they were one. He spent what felt like lifetimes getting lost in her body, as if he could risk his own life for just one glimpse of her soul.

For seven days, everything was picture perfect. He should have known it wouldn't stay that way forever. He should have guessed that eventually reality would intrude and spoil everything.

16

"No, this can't be right." Skylar scanned the grades. Each one was listed next to a student ID, and hers was the lowest on the email.

She rifled through her books and paperwork, making sure she had the correct ID. Sure enough, that was hers. "How is this possible?"

Her vision blurred with unshed tears of frustration. She needed to fix this before she fell apart. There was no way she could be flunking this class. She'd studied her butt off and done every assignment.

Shaking, she signed into the Home Access Center and investigated. Her unit project was a mid B. Her homework assignments all showed complete. Then she found the problem. Her first exam, the one she'd spent days preparing for, was destroying her average. How the hell had she scored a forty-eight? How had she not realized until now?

She let out a jagged breath and quickly emailed the professor, asking for more information. Her hands were trembling so severely, she had a difficult time typing. If she failed this class, she'd never get invited back.

Addison was still sleeping when she heard the front

door open. Shutting her laptop, she wiped her eyes and tied back her hair. Rhett must have forgotten something because he typically didn't sneak home until Addison's nap time, and Skylar hadn't even finished her first cup of coffee yet.

Usually, rendezvous with Rhett were the highlight of her days, but right now, she didn't feel like seeing anyone. When she heard him enter the den, she again blotted her eyes but didn't turn around, not wanting him to see her cry.

"I can't today. I have some school stuff I need to handle."

"Can't what?"

Her gaze jerked to the doorway. "Erin." It seemed too early for a visit from the Wicked Witch of the West. There must be low broom traffic today.

The PA hitched her designer bag higher on her shoulder. "Were you expecting someone else?"

She wiped her nose, shoving down any emotion and stood. "No, I was just... I thought you were..."

The woman eyed her from head to toe. Skylar hadn't bothered to put on a bra that morning. With the fire burning, the house was warm, and she only wore shorts and a white camisole, which Rhett loved because he could see her nipples through the thin material. She now regretted her wardrobe choice.

"Is this how you walk around in your employer's home?"

It was her home, too. Skylar picked up her laptop, since it was the only thing within reach and clutched it to her chest. "I wasn't expecting anyone."

"It's in your best interest to dress as if you're always expecting company."

Her molars ground tightly. "What do you need?"

"I assume Mr. Buchanan informed you about the art gala tonight."

"He mentioned something about a fundraiser."

"Right, well, the event's been relocated to the mansion."

"Here?"

"Do you see another mansion? We only have nine hours to get everything up to par. All personal items will have to be hidden away, and the kitchen will need to be accessible to the catering staff."

"Hold on. I'm confused. Why is the gala being moved here?"

"A complication with the hotel. It's irrelevant. This is where we are now, and this fundraiser is important." She walked to the powder room door where Addison's tissue paper collage of a Christmas tree hung. "Unsightly decorations will all have to come down." She glanced at the actual tree. "I'll send someone over here to deal with this."

Skylar frowned. "That's the Buchanan's family tree. They decorated it that way."

"I don't have time to explain why that doesn't matter. I'm just here to give you a heads-up."

Well, at least that was a nice change, considering she usually got no warning at all about the schedule. "How formal is the event?"

Her head cocked and she smirked. "Very. It's an elegant fundraiser for the fine arts. Black ties and gowns, but that doesn't concern you. Mr. Buchanan asked that you stay out of sight for this one."

She drew back. "He said that?"

"Do I look like I'm joking?"

"What about Addison?"

"It's not for children."

"Oh." She didn't know why she was disappointed to be excluded. The last time she had to find a dress for an event, she'd been extremely stressed. She should be grateful she didn't have to participate.

"Your job will be to keep the little one completely out of sight. Do you think you can do that?"

According to Erin, she was wildly incompetent. "I think I can manage."

"Good." She tugged the picture of the Christmas tree off the door. "I'd start taking this stuff down. And get dressed. An event coordinator will be stopping by any minute."

Erin set up a temporary work station in the kitchen, so Skylar took Addison upstairs to get changed, not wanting to be anywhere near the other woman.

She wanted to call Rhett and hear his voice. Was Erin telling the truth about tonight? Did he really want her out of sight?

Once Addison was dressed, she told her to play in her room for a few minutes. Skylar went to the third floor to change and called Rhett.

He answered on the third ring and sounded harried. "Skylar, what's up?"

Jarred by his direct greeting, she hesitated. "Um... There's going to be a gala at the house tonight—"

"It's a total cluster fuck. Erin should be there soon to take care of everything. You just worry about you and Addy."

"She's already here." It amazed her how he never seemed to get the tyrant side of his PA the rest of them had to deal with.

"Oh. Well, good. Did you need something?"

He was obviously busy. "No, I just wanted to hear your voice."

"That's sweet." His tone softened. "We can talk after the event."

So, perhaps he didn't expect her to attend after all. "Okay. I'll see you later."

"See ya." The phone clicked in her ear and she felt more off balance than she'd been before she called.

The next three hours passed in a whirlwind of foot traffic and strangers. Rhett never stopped home, but the house was a hive of activity.

The usual furniture was moved into positions that

weren't functional for daily living. Sofas were steam cleaned and carpets were shampooed. There seemed a constant hum of machines running, as snow blowers tidied the walkways outside and catering companies built tents that extended off the back of the kitchen.

She and Addison escaped to her grandmother's. For the chaos of the big house to bring more peace and quiet than the mayor's mansion, proved how crazy things were.

The kids played with Addison as Gran sat in her chair stringing cranberries for the front porch garland. Pop snored in the recliner by the TV.

"They play nicely together," Gran commented, smiling at the children.

"They should. They're all the same age."

"I suppose they'll all go through school together. Just think, Addison could end up married to one of them."

Skylar grinned. Her grandmother had a romantic soul.

A car pulled up in the driveway and she went to the window to check who it was. "It's Uncle Colin."

"Oh, he's delivering the desserts I ordered from the school fundraiser. Be a dear and help him unload them. They'll need to go in the big freezer in the shed."

Skylar pulled on her coat and met her uncle out front.

"Skylar, what are you doing here?"

"We're just visiting. The kids are playing. Gran wants me to help you put the food in the big freezer."

She gave him a hand carrying the boxes. The shed was fairly tidy, but the freezer was packed with meat. They would have to reorganize if they wanted everything to fit.

"So, how's it going up at the mayor's place?"

Despite the cold air, her cheeks burned. "It's amazing."

Colin glanced at her and paused. "That great?"

Of all her uncles, Colin was her favorite, and she trusted him. "Rhett and I have really connected."

He frowned and stood up from where he'd been hunched over the opening of the freezer chest. "*Rhett?*"

She nodded. "Mr. Buchanan."

"You two are on a first name basis?"

They were on more than that. She couldn't hide her grin. "He's very..." She didn't want to get ahead of herself. "I like him a lot."

He lifted a box that looked to hold a frozen pie and slid it into the freezer. "Skylar, keep in mind that Mr. Buchanan is a lot older than you."

"I'm not a kid anymore, Colin."

"It's Uncle Colin. And you're more than a decade younger than your boss."

Actually, he was fifteen years her senior, but that didn't matter. They were both adults. "I don't need a lecture. I know what I'm doing."

"Do you?"

She bristled. "I thought you would be happy that I'm figuring things out."

"It's supposed to be a job, Skylar. I want to see you succeed. I want to see you get the experience you need to someday have your own preschool like we've discussed. I don't want to see you make mistakes early in your career that do long-term damage to your reputation. You need to keep it professional. I would hope that the mayor understands that, even if you don't."

Stunned that he could cut her down so quickly, it took everything inside of her not to stagger back.

He sighed. "I'm only telling you this because I care about you, Sky, and I want to see you make good decisions."

Her jaw hardened. "Were you making good decisions when you stole your brother's girlfriend?"

His sharp blue stare turned to ice. "What did you just say to me?"

They all heard the stories. She had been young when

Uncle Braydon brought Aunt Sammy home from school. Skylar still remembered everyone talking about his new girlfriend, but Uncle Colin had changed that in a matter of weeks.

Adrenaline shook her body as she held his stare. "I told you something personal because I trusted I could talk to you without judgement. But you're being a hypocrite. I'm not doing anything wrong. He's not married or dating anyone else. And I haven't promised my life to someone or *something*. So at least I have that going for me." She turned on her heel and stalked out of the shed.

"Skylar!"

She shook her head, furious with herself for sharing with him. He made her feel naive and stupid, like she'd done something terribly wrong—like she was just a dumb kid.

She didn't take off her coat when she returned to the house. "Addison, come on. We have to get going."

"But I don't want to leave."

"We have to."

"I wanna stay—"

"Addison, I said we're leaving."

Her grandmother frowned. "Is everything all right, love?"

God, she couldn't keep it together, and she didn't have the courage to make eye contact. "Everything's fine. I forgot about something I need to do."

"Well, you come back whenever you want. The kids like when you two visit."

"We will."

She rushed Addison out of the house just as Colin was closing up the shed.

"Come on. Into your seat." She quickly buckled her inside the car and shut the door.

Her uncle hovered a few feet away. "Skylar, I'm only

trying to give you some good advice. You're my niece. It's my job to look out for you."

She sniffled and shook her head. "Look out for me..." she mumbled. "That's what this family does. They say they're looking out, but really, they're just passing judgement, meddling where they don't belong, and gossiping. You're no better than the rest of them." She briefly met his stare and saw her words struck a nerve. "I don't need you *looking out* for me. I needed a friend."

He caught her arm and startled her. "I am your friend. I'm here. I'm sorry. Don't ever think you can't talk to me if you feel like you're in trouble."

She jerked her arm away and broke his grip. "Why do men always assume if a girl shares something personal, she must need some sort of saving?"

She climbed into her car and backed out of the driveway, losing the battle against her tears before she made it off the mountain.

❄

Skylar's professor finally got back to her, but she was more confused than ever. He said she failed the exam because she left a page blank. A page that happened to have several valuable essay questions on it.

She was a mess when she emailed him back, only maintaining a shred of calm by telling herself there was a solution for every problem. If she explained it was a mistake, a decent professor would give her a chance to make up the work.

Unfortunately, he already had.

She blinked stupidly at his response, feeling like she was suffering some sort of amnesia. He said he emailed her shortly after she submitted the exam, informing her that several questions were blank. He even gave her until the following Monday to resubmit the remainder of the test, but she never responded and he had no choice but to grade it as is.

At this point, it was too late to make any changes. Grades were calculated.

She never saw any such email. She was certain of it. But when she went through her inbox, sorting her archives, deleted messages, and spam, she found it.

Her heart sank, much like her grade. He'd given her a second chance and she'd somehow missed it. There would be no coming back from this. She was screwed.

"Skylar, why are you crying?" The angelic voice penetrated her meltdown.

She shut her laptop and tried to smile, but it was no use. "Because life is hard."

Addison gave her a hug. Skylar held her little body close, breathing in her sweet, youthful scent and pressing her lips to her silken hair.

Thank God the gala was tonight, because she didn't feel like seeing anyone. "What do you say we order a pizza, make some popcorn, put on our PJs, and make a fort in my bedroom so we can watch Christmas movies all night?"

"Yeah!"

It was still early, so they were able to sneak into the kitchen just before things got really hectic. Strangers wandered through the house, and she hated feeling on display.

She and Addison filled a laundry basket with drinks, snacks, crayons, and everything they could possibly need to make it through the night, including a small television from one of the other guestrooms.

When the pizza came, they carried it up to Skylar's bedroom and taped a sign on the door.

GIRLS ONLY! SLEEPOVER IN PROGRESS. NO BOYS ALLOWED!

17

"Erin, where are Skylar and Addison?"

His assistant looked up from her clipboard and hesitated a moment before answering. "They're on the third floor and asked not to be disturbed."

He frowned. It was almost Addy's bedtime. "Skylar's not attending the gala?"

"Sorry. She asked if she could pass. She said she hates these things."

"It's art..." he muttered but supposed that might not hold any appeal for some.

Who was he kidding? It was a fundraiser. She was a young woman. Of course, she wouldn't think campaign parties were fun. Even he got bored with them.

Caterers bustled through the kitchen, and he took that as his cue to head upstairs to shower and dress. Erin seemed to have everything covered.

He spotted a sign taped to Skylar's door and grinned when he read it. Their party would probably be more fun than hanging out with a bunch of stuffy art connoisseurs.

Once dressed, he sent her a text telling her he'd see her

after the party. She didn't reply, which was strange because she usually got right back to him.

When he returned to the first floor, he took in the total transformation of the house from the lighting to the formal holiday decorations to the makeover of their family tree. He frowned, looking for traces of Addison's winter artwork and toys. Where were the telltale signs of Skylar nearby?

Artificial walls had been erected with gallery lighting to showcase the thousands of dollars' worth of artwork on display. Dealers and artists inspected and debated the placement of each masterpiece before the guests arrived.

Erin was once again in the kitchen, but she'd changed into a formfitting gray dress. Rhett helped himself to a glass of water, feeling slightly claustrophobic around so many changes to his home.

"How's it going?" he asked, surveying all the scribbled notes on Erin's clipboard.

She smiled up at him. "We're right on schedule. The guests should start arriving in a few minutes, and the harpist is about to begin. You should eat something now, before you're monopolized for the rest of the night."

He glanced at the chaffing dishes lined along the counter. Sirloin, prime rib, and hickory smoked ham steamed from carving stations about to be wheeled out, but all he wanted was one of Skylar's PB and J sandwiches.

He wished she would have reconsidered attending the party. While it might be a silly fundraiser, the art was interesting and a portion of the proceeds went to the art program at the community college where she'd earned her associate's. He hoped she might attend simply because she was an alumna.

Even in her absence, she remained on his mind. Every time he took in a beautiful work of art, he questioned if it would be something she'd like.

She once made a comment that the house needed more personal touches. Perhaps he would buy something from the auction, but he wanted to pick something she'd like.

When the guests arrived, he was cornered, just as Erin predicted. He'd learned long ago to simply go with the flow at these events. He smiled and nodded and laughed at all the right places, but the charade struck him as especially artificial and hollow tonight.

He'd been so full of laughter recently, he often found himself staring into space and smiling, simply remembering something funny Addison had done or something sweet Skylar had said. Nothing anyone said to him tonight seemed to reach or register in his heart. He missed his girls.

One of the artists had the last name McCullough, and that caught his eye. His work was charcoal realism and it was incredibly lifelike.

"What do you think?" a man with jet black hair and startling blue eyes asked, joining Rhett as he stared at the portrait of an older woman cradling a baby.

"Are you the artist?"

"I'm the messenger. The art comes to me, and I put it to paper, but I never take credit for the design."

Rhett grinned, liking his explanation. "I think it's strikingly realistic. Who is she?"

"My mother. She's holding my newest nephew."

If this man was one of Skylar's uncles, that would make the woman her grandmother. From everything she said about her and the many times she and Addison visited, he knew they were very close.

The portrait showed time in the most delicate fashion, evident in the space between generations. He could feel the woman's affection for the child in her arms. He wondered what it might feel like to receive such unconditional love, wondered if anyone ever held him in such a way.

"How much is it?"

"Fourteen hundred or highest offer."

Rhett went to the ballot and filled out a slip of paper for three thousand dollars. He folded his bid and dropped it into the secret box.

He wanted the work of art because he thought Skylar might appreciate it, but he also wanted it because the subject matter was riveting. Unconditional love always fascinated him, as it was something he'd never experienced firsthand.

But that was exactly what the portrait conveyed. And when he stared at the woman holding the baby, he felt her unreserved affection somehow.

Constituents kept him locked in conversations for most of the night, and Erin kept him hydrated. The musicians played classic cocktail music and, despite the confusion with the venue, the house seemed to be working out just fine.

They were at the halfway point of the evening when a commotion caught his attention at the front door. Erin squared off with a dark-haired man dressed in street clothes, demanding entry.

"Excuse me," Rhett said, slipping out of a conversation to investigate.

Several heads turned as the situation and the man's voice escalated.

"Sir, you'll have to step outside," Erin said. "This is a private event."

"I'm not leaving until I see the mayor!" the man barked.

Rhett rushed over, as did the McCullough artist he'd been speaking with earlier. He would not allow anyone to disrespect his staff in such a way. "What's going on?"

"You," the man growled.

"Ant, what are you doing here?" the McCullough artist asked, apparently familiar with the crazed intruder.

The best option, with so many watching, seemed to be to

diffuse the situation and move them outside. Rhett kept his voice calm and placed a casual hand on the man's shoulder. "Let's take this outside so we're not disrupting others."

The man flung his hand away. "Don't touch me."

Rhett paused and scowled, sure he hadn't seen this man before in his life. "Do I know you?" There was something familiar about him, but he couldn't place his face.

"I'm Anthony Marcelli."

Understanding registered and Rhett lowered his head. "Ah. Nice to meet you, Mr. Marcelli. How about we go to my study where we can speak privately?"

"You're all about keeping things private, aren't you?" The man's fists locked at his side and his neck pulsed with thick veins. "Afraid people might actually learn who you really are?"

"All right, that's enough," Erin interjected, but the man stepped forward and spoke over her.

"Did you touch her?"

The room silenced, and Rhett drew in a slow breath. "This is the last time I'm offering you a choice. You're welcome to speak privately in my study, or you can leave."

The McCullough artist was now scowling as well. "Who did he touch?"

"I didn't touch anyone!" Rhett snapped, but that wasn't necessarily true.

"Skylar!" Marcelli barked. "You took advantage of her! What kind of man does that?"

"What?" The McCullough man turned and scowled like a crazed, blue-eyed devil. "You put your hands on my little niece?"

Rhett held up his hands. "Hold on. I didn't take advantage of—"

"She's half your age!" Skylar's father glared like a homicidal man on a mission.

Rhett's jaw locked. Now they were just throwing out lies.

Eavesdroppers gasped and crowded closer. Sweat gathered beneath Rhett's collar. Even Erin was glaring at him. He felt cornered and unfairly judged.

"This is neither the time nor the place—"

"How about you answer the fucking question?" the artist snapped. "Or I can let my brother-in-law beat it out of you."

This was insane. These men were acting like Neanderthals. This was a formal event, not a truck pull. "Gentlemen, I'm afraid my patience has run out, and it's time for you to leave. Both of you."

"She's a kid!" Marcelli snapped, bearing his teeth.

Rhett balked, unable to let that one go. "She's twenty-one—"

The right hook came out of nowhere, and white light exploded behind his eyes, momentarily blinding him. Voices erupted as he staggered back, falling into the crowd, only to be pushed back toward the man who just hit him.

Several other men raced forward and absolute mayhem broke out. Shoulders were shoved, voices raised, accusations were hurled, and reputations were burned to ash, all due to a father's irrational and misplaced concern.

"Enough!" Rhett barked and the room silenced. A swipe of his thumb over his throbbing lip revealed a smear of blood. "This is insane!"

Anthony Marcelli charged forward, but another guest caught his shoulder. He squared off with Rhett, until his glare lifted to something beyond the crowd.

Rhett turned, following his gaze to the top of the stairs and his heart sank when he saw Skylar standing there in her pajamas, a look of confused horror on her face.

"Daddy?"

She looked like a little girl, her hair parted in pigtails and her body dressed in pajamas with snowflakes on them. Jesus, this looked terrible.

The guests followed the drama like a tennis match and

gaped at her. He wanted to race up the steps and cover her from their view, protect her from their judgement. Who were they to look at her? They didn't know her. They didn't know him.

"Christ," her uncle cursed.

"Skylar, get in the car. We're going home," her father ordered.

She frowned. "What are you doing here? What's going on?"

"We can discuss it later—"

"Tell me now." Her confused stare fell on him. "Rhett?"

He hated agreeing with a man who just burst into his home and attacked him, but in this situation, he had no choice. Constituents stared at him with cold accusation in their narrowing eyes.

Short of showing them her birth certificate and driver's license, there would be no way out of this unscathed. He could physically feel his ratings dropping, but his greatest concern was protecting Skylar. She didn't deserve this sort of exploitation.

The fastest way to protect her from their unfair judgement was to get her out of there and someplace safe. He looked up at her, doing his best to help her read the apology in his eyes. "I think it's best if you go with your father for now, sweetheart." Several guests gasped at the endearment and he snapped. "For the love of God, she's an adult woman!" He turned to Erin and snapped, "Party's over. See that everyone finds their way out."

He marched up the stairs, only to pause when he reached the step where Skylar waited. He looked at her, tears of humiliation welling in her eyes and regret spilling from his heart.

"You're welcome to stay, but I think it's best if you go."

She glanced at her father, still detained by the door. Her humiliation was palpable, and he felt responsible.

He knew it was only a matter of time before she left him. And yet, he still foolishly hoped their time might last.

"I'm sorry, Skylar. Go with him." He continued to his room and slammed the door.

18

ONE WEEK until Christmas

"When's Skylar coming back?" Addison asked, the same bored expression on her face that had been there since the day after the party.

"I don't know."

"I miss her."

Rhett pushed out a breath that did nothing to ease the tension in his shoulders. "So do I."

It had been three days, and she hadn't returned a single one of his texts or calls. All her belongings were still at the house, and he assumed she'd have to come back for at least her laptop, as her final was this week, but she hadn't been by.

The mansion had been put back to rights, but everything felt wrong. The tree no longer appeared decorated with amateur hands, the rooms smelled of disinfectant and chemical furniture polish instead of fresh baked goods, and everything was quiet—no Christmas carols, no laughter, no silly songs about cleaning up or washing hands. And where the hell were Addison's paper snowflakes and craft projects. The walls were once again naked.

He'd been trapped in the house, hiding from the rumor mill, and nursing a nasty black eye and swollen lip. Seriously, who punched people at this age?

He glanced at his daughter and had his answer—fathers trying to protect their little girls.

He wasn't sure how anyone found out about him and Skylar, but what irked him more was the fact that he hadn't consciously meant to keep their relationship a secret for any reason other than his desire for privacy. Yes, she was younger, but she was of legal age and an adult. He'd done nothing wrong!

But the more he thought back over their time together, the more things came into view. He recalled their first night together and all the things he didn't want to see. The way her body felt. The innocent way she looked at him. Her notable shyness.

The longer he thought about her inexperience, the more he felt like an absolute monster.

Her father was right to hit him.

He hated thinking he'd caused her any kind of pain. As someone in the public eye, he was emotionally prepared for the backlash of gossip. No one was universally accepted by all. But he never wanted the criticism he faced on a daily basis to touch those he cared about.

He could handle it. They shouldn't have to.

Growing up as he had, an outcast amongst so many kids who hardly realized how privileged they were, he'd formed a thick skin. He never had the clothes other kids had or the popular toys. Hell, he was lucky if he even had food.

But it was never his envy for their material possessions that kept him up crying at night as a boy. It was the sight of their parents picking them up at the end of the day, the sound of moms and dads asking how their days were and if they had fun at school.

Most evenings, Rhett wandered home alone. The days he didn't were the days he hid in the school and slept overnight. For years, his mom didn't notice him missing from his bed, but when she eventually did, she beat him black and blue. That was when the questions started.

They said their meddling was out of concern, but their questions only made things worse. The closer the teachers and principal examined his home life, the more his world seemed put on display. The few friends he had started to notice all the ways he was different and then they didn't want to be his friend anymore.

When he found his mom dead, a needle still in her arm, his first thought was how much she'd spent on the stuff that stole her life. People said children were expensive, but Rhett now knew they didn't have to be. His mother never spent on him what she put into her addiction.

She never held him or claimed to love him, but he still cried over her body that night. She was all he knew, and the unknown loomed with terrifying possibilities he couldn't face.

The days after her death were a blur. He remembered the blue car that picked him up and drove him to a brown building where he waited for his new foster parents to arrive. The foolish hope that these foster parents might act like the other parents at school, gave him the courage to go with the strange family.

But in a matter of days, it became clear that he would never be viewed the same as their other children. He would never be theirs. Always an outsider. Always different.

He became withdrawn, preferring to watch television or read rather than interact with people. Addicted to old TV shows where a mom and dad lived together with a family in a happy house tucked away in a safe little town, he lost interest in reality. Reality was ugly.

The idea that such a picture-perfect life could exist captivated him. It was nothing like the life he had with his mom or the one he claimed with his foster family, but it became everything he wanted.

Then things changed again, and his foster parents started fighting more than usual. They said they couldn't keep him and he had to go back to the brown building. Their rejection hurt, because no matter how much they fought, they wouldn't give up any of their real kids, the kids they loved.

Rhett spent a lot of time in that brown building. Over the years, the interior had changed, but the outside always looked the same and the outcomes never brought lasting relief.

No matter where he went, the people didn't love him. They loved their other children, but never him.

When he was seventeen, on his way back to the brown building again, he'd finally admitted that he might be unlovable. Rather than suffer another family's rejection, he ran.

He took odd jobs and stayed at boarding houses, until he crossed paths with a dairy farmer who offered him a job with free room and board. For nine years he worked on that farm, saving almost every penny he earned. He read a lot and bought a cell phone, which gave him access to the internet. He'd spent hours searching properties and dreaming of a day he might own his own home, perhaps even have a wife.

It had been years since anyone had taken interest in him, so when Adel showed up at the country fair one year with her pretty blonde hair and flirty eyes, he didn't think it was anything personal. She said she needed a friend, someone who wasn't tied down and could travel with her to singing gigs.

Her voice was pure gold and when she sang, he thought she might be an angel. But there was nothing pure about Adel, and the first time she touched him, she introduced him to a world of sin.

He should have known she was dangerous. Everything she did was fast. He quit the dairy farm and followed her down the coast where she'd spend the days sleeping wherever he managed to book a room, and the nights singing and partying with strangers.

He didn't like when she came home smelling of other men, but he didn't know who he was without her. She started dabbling with drugs, reminding him a lot of his mother, and he couldn't be her friend anymore.

Finally, Rhett left and found a job working for a broker who taught him how to buy and sell stocks. He ran into Adel again, several years later, and she was no longer singing. Her body was skin and bones and she pleaded in desperation, begging him to help her get well.

She was the only true friend he ever had, so he couldn't turn his back on her. If she died, he'd have no friends at all.

Rhett had secured a nice apartment and let her stay for a few months. She slowly nursed herself back to health, but she never fully recovered to the girl she once was. The claws of addiction had a permanent hold on her, and she'd often cry for an exorcism that didn't exist. She could be so warm and feminine and then in the next moment out of her mind irrational.

He cared about her and wanted to see her get well. He arranged for her to see a doctor and speak to a professional. They told her she suffered from bipolar disorder, which explained why it sometimes felt like he was living with two people. He knew then, no matter how much part of her cared for him, she'd never fully love him, because another part of her would always love drugs more.

He told her it was best if she found her own place, and he'd help her any way he could. In a moment of weakness, when she was soft and weeping over the fact that she couldn't be enough for him, he allowed her to get close again. Nine months later, Addison was born.

Rhett stared at the fireplace, taking in the grand hearth and expensive moldings. His life now unrecognizable from what it had once been.

After Addy was born, he made a promise to her and to himself. She would never want for anything. He knew how ugly the world could be, and he wanted to take her someplace safe and removed from crime and danger, a place like the towns he saw on television.

When he found Jasper Falls, he knew he found the perfect town. He just had to figure out how to make a home. Finding a place to live was easy. He had money from buying and selling stocks. But he had no idea what made a house a home, and he desperately wanted a warm, happy home for his daughter.

No one knew him there. They didn't know his background or his upbringing. They only knew what he showed them. And while the small town was worlds away from the rough city he escaped, it was a far cry from perfect.

He wanted to give his daughter perfection. He wanted to create a place that mimicked the life he only saw on television shows and movies. He wanted to raise her somewhere safe, where people waved and left their doors unlocked. He wanted her to feel surrounded by love, always.

When the prior mayor announced he was retiring, Rhett saw an opportunity. He sold an idea to the townsfolk, with a promise that they could be more.

Jasper Falls needed work. It needed an economic boom, and without change, that wouldn't happen. He campaigned hard and painted a picture the locals could see and feel. Vincenzo Marcelli, Skylar's grandfather, had run against him, but Rhett had won in a landslide.

The thing about selling an entire population a fictional ideal, was that beneath all the antiquated charm, real secrets still hid. Families had dirty laundry, married people had affairs, and even their police station required a jail cell from time to time. Hell, there was a reason the line at the confessional was as long as the line at Dairy Queen some days.

But despite everyone else's flaws, they expected him to be perfect. He wasn't even close.

One would think that being a single father might have tipped them off, but no. They believed what they wanted to believe, and the other night had ripped away the illusion of perfection, exposing him as a flawed human who didn't have all the answers, and now they were angry.

They felt tricked and deceived. Betrayed. He should have cared, but the only one who had truly been cheated, was Skylar.

He tried calling her again but the call dumped into voicemail. "It's me. Please call me back. I'm worried about you."

Was she worried about him? Probably not. She had every right to be angry. If not for him, she wouldn't be the focal point of the town's gossip. People could be so heartless.

He needed to do something. Would she be at her parents'? No, he couldn't go there. That would be disastrous. But he couldn't just sit by and wait for something to happen. He had to get the facts straight and clear things up if he ever wanted to fix this.

No clue what to do or how to repair the damage, he felt helpless. He needed to get out of this house and do *something*. Anything was better than sitting in his den sulking.

"Addison, get your coat. We're going into town."

They drove around and he looked for any sign of Skylar's car but found nothing. He wound up parked outside of Vincenzo's. What would happen if he went inside?

He glanced in the mirror and his daughter smiled at the reflection of his eyes. "Are we getting pizza, Daddy?"

"Yes." He shut off the car.

They entered the restaurant where Sinatra played from hidden speakers. Pots and pans clattered in the back and voices chattered from the dining room. A crowd was good. It meant less possibility of a scene.

"Can I help you?" A woman with black hair came out, her eyes shifting down as she tied her apron. She looked up and stilled. "Oh crap. You're not supposed to be here."

As the mayor, there was no hiding who he was. He saw the resemblance to Skylar in the woman's nose and realized this was another relative, perhaps one of Vincenzo's daughters, which would make her the sister of the man who punched him.

"Do you know where she is?"

The woman glanced back at the kitchen, then dashed around the counter. Her voice was rushed and low as she ushered him toward the front door. "Seriously, it's not wise for you to come in here."

"Nicolette, who's at the counter?" Vincenzo emerged from the kitchen and let out a string of Italian words that could only have negative meanings. "*You*," he growled.

"Mr. Marcelli, I've been meaning to stop by—"

"You're not welcome here. Get out of my store."

"Sir, if you'd just let me explain."

Vincenzo reached behind him and lifted a cleaver off the counter. "Let's hear it."

Rhett paused, unsure if this man was really as crazy as he wanted everyone to believe.

"Can I have a fritta?" His daughter's little voice interrupted, and Rhett panicked when she was no longer standing by his side.

The tension in the room shifted, and Vincenzo glanced down at Addison who was tugging on his apron. Vincenzo's bushy eyebrows bunched and he put down the cleaver.

Rhett watched the transformation with stunned disbelief as the man selected a warm piece of knotted dough from the display and sprinkled it with sugar from a sifter, then handed it to Addison. "Here you are, *bellezza*."

"Thank you, Mr. 'cenzo." She took a big bite and smiled up at him.

"Good?"

She nodded, white crystals of sugar clinging to her lips.

"And have you been behaving? Santi-clause is watching, you know."

"I know. I've been good."

The man grinned and pinched her cheek. Then he turned his eyes back to Rhett and glared. "You, in the back. Nicolette, watch the little one."

Rhett followed the man through the kitchen where his wife and two other daughters were cooking. It was like walking to the gallows—and he feared it might be one-way.

Vincenzo led him out the back door, which was propped open so the cold air could come in. The man dropped to sit on an upside-down bucket, careless of the cold even though his shoulders were bare.

He popped a half-smoked cigar into his mouth and lit it, puckering his lips around the chewed off tip until the other end glowed cherry red. He blew a ring of smoke in Rhett's direction. "You tell me your side. I already know my son's."

Rhett frowned. "Your son has nothing to do with this."

"My son has everything to do with this. Skylar is his daughter."

"With all due respect, Skylar is a grown woman."

"She's just a girl."

"You're wrong. She's independent and smart and completely capable of taking care of herself. She hasn't been *just a girl* for a long time."

Vincenzo waved away his words. "Are you saying, if you were in Anthony's shoes, you would have behaved differently? Think of that little *bellezza* out there."

"I would have acted a little more civilized. Your son stormed into my home during a formal event, made a scene, and attacked me."

Vincenzo folded his arms over his meagerly clothed, hairy chest. Unconcerned by the savage behavior of his son. Rhett wasn't getting through to him.

"Mr. Marcelli, your son might have come with the impression that he was protecting your granddaughter, but he humiliated her. I'd never do anything to hurt Skylar the way he did."

"My son's been under a lot of stress with work."

"That's not an excuse. She didn't deserve to be embarrassed in front of a room full of strangers."

"You disgraced her."

"I did no such thing. I respect her."

"If you respect her, you wait."

"Did any of you consider that she might not have wanted that? She's her own person, capable of making her own decisions. We're still figuring this out, but I know for certain that I never took advantage of her the way your family assumes."

Finally, the man nodded. "And what is *this*? I know how men act around pretty girls. They think with the wrong head."

He couldn't debate that fact, but Skylar was more than just a pretty girl to him. "I care about your granddaughter very much."

"Love?"

"I...don't know." Aside from Addison, he had no experience with love. What he felt for Skylar was different, darker, and more layered. "I'm trying to be completely transparent here."

"You're a politician. Your kind's as muddy as gravy." He snuffed out his cigar on the side of the bucket and stood. "Here's what I want." His hand gripped Rhett's shoulder in an unbreakable hold and steered him around the corner of the building. "You see the street there, where all the cars are parked?"

Rhett squinted through the alley. "Yes."

"I want a parking spot for my driver. Every time there's a delivery, we lose time looking for parking. You get me that, and I'll talk to my son."

He was freaking bribing him? What the hell was this, *Good Fellas*? Still, Rhett was desperate to make things right with Skylar. "I'll see what I can do."

Vincenzo turned and smacked him twice on the cheek. "If you really care about her, you'll find a way."

19

"Try to eat something, love."

Skylar picked at her breakfast, but she didn't have an appetite.

"If you don't start eating, you're going to give me a complex about my cooking." Gran refilled her coffee, nudging it closer to Skylar's fingertips. "At least have another cup of coffee. You're wilting away."

She'd been staying at the big house since the night she left Rhett's, unable to face her parents after her father caused such a scene, nor willing to make excuses for her actions. Gran's had always been a sanctuary, so she disappeared to the one place she'd always be welcomed and accepted, no matter what the circumstances were.

Despite how much her grandmother loved to gossip, she would never stand for one of her grandchildren being the center of unwanted attention. Skylar had given her a brief explanation, but Gran didn't push. Pop watched her with concern, but never said anything on the subject. He simply gave her a passing cuddle and a kiss on the head, like good grandfathers are meant to do.

"You know, dear, your parents will come around. I mean,

they'll have to. They made their fair share of senseless mistakes. Glass stones and such. You know how the saying goes."

But she hadn't done something senseless. She always overthought her actions and choices. It offended her that everyone assumed they knew what was best for her and that they somehow believed they might know her better than herself.

"I never saw him behave like that before. It was...humiliating." As if their family didn't already have enough of a reputation for being the crazy people up on the mountain.

"Oh, he's just being a dad. Hell, your grandfather once tried to leave your father for dead in the woods. Men do all kinds of stupid things when it comes to protecting their daughters."

"He treats me like a kid."

"That's because you're his first. It pisses them off, seeing their little girls turn into women. You've grown into a beautiful young lady, Skylar. Imagine how terrified that must make him. Plus, it reminds him he's gettin' old. Their fragile egos can't handle aging." She glanced at the hall as Pop shuffled by, picking at his ear hair as a fart squeaked out. Gran shut her eyes and solemnly shook her head. "And forget about any of them trying to age gracefully."

Her phone buzzed, and both she and Gran read Rhett's name on the display. Skylar silenced it. "I'm not ready to talk to him."

Then came another text from her father. She flipped the phone over so she wouldn't be distracted by the screen.

"You're quite popular."

Skylar gave a humorless grin. "Why should Dad care what I do? He's never even around anymore."

Her grandmother clicked her tongue with disapproval. "Hush now. Your father's working very hard for your family. You have younger siblings he still needs to support. They're getting older, and he has to plan for their futures. He's not absent because he wants to be. He's absent so that he can be around later, for the important things."

Important things like Hannah's graduation or Vinny, Ciera, and James's older years. Every time he showed up at one of Frankie's games, Skylar shoved down more envy, making excuses for the events in her life he'd been unable to attend.

She had always been the most accommodating of all their siblings, always trying to make things easier for others and put their needs first. This was the first time she acted for herself, doing something purely self-indulgent, and everyone lost their shit.

There was no excuse. "He just burst in there and started screaming. Everyone was staring at him. And then he punched Rhett!"

"Your father has a temper."

"Uncle Kelly was standing right there, and he didn't do anything to help matters!"

"Oh, well, Kelly probably didn't know what was going on. Don't be upset with your uncle."

Her jaw locked as she thought of Colin. "None of them treat me with the respect I deserve. This wouldn't have happened if Uncle Colin didn't go running his mouth. He's the biggest hypocrite of them all—acting so self-righteous, as if he never did anything wrong in his life."

Gran burst out laughing. "My Colin? Oh, please! You can dress a man up in robes, and teach him whatever prayers you like, but it's all just slapping lipstick on a pig at the end of the day. Colin's no better than the rest of them, and he should know that."

"You should have seen Uncle Colin's face when I told him about me and Rhett. He looked at me like some sort of victim."

"He's just protective of you." She sipped her coffee. "You

and Frankie were the first grandbabies. I've had enough children to know that they all grow up eventually, but your aunts and uncles are still learning that. They'll see. Colin's scared because his Tallulah isn't far behind you, and soon she'll be going off to college, falling in love with boys, and making decisions on her own. And he'll have no choice but to let her go."

Maybe that was it. She never experienced that overprotective side of her uncle before. The shift from his usual supportive, encouraging position felt like a betrayal.

She thought he was her friend and confidante, someone she could go to with anything. Things were even more frustrating, because at a time like this when she found herself in a family dispute and needing guidance, she would typically go to him, but he was the one who started the drama.

She missed her friends, the ones who seemed to take her side without bias—even if their advice wasn't always the most experienced or logical. But after high school, everyone scattered in different directions. Some went away to college, others joined the military, and a few, like her, stuck around Jasper Falls to work.

Within a few months, daily calls turned to random texts, until Skylar hardly heard from her old friends at all. She still thought of them and hung out with them occasionally when they were home for summer, but time created space and, the sense that she was now out-of-the-loop, left her feeling disconnected and alone, even when in their presence.

Her family never took a break or spent more than a few days apart, so there was never a sense of disconnect. Until now.

It seemed like the strangest oxymoron that a family as obsessed with each other as hers could somehow make her feel like an outsider. She trusted the elasticity of their connection to eventually snap them back into normal but, currently, she felt stretched thin.

Gran scooted closer and ran a hand over her back. "You know, judgement only bothers us when it's a judgement we've already started to believe ourselves. If you're sensitive about the age gap, it might not be because of what happened but because of worries you already harbored. Perhaps you should ask yourself, how much does it really matter to you? Don't worry about what others think. Just try to figure out what you feel in your heart."

She'd always been aware of Rhett's seniority, but her concern was less about his age and more about his position as her boss. She knew it was reckless, giving in to her lust and sleeping with him, but their chemistry was too strong to resist and she was weak against the temptation.

There had been a dozen other opportunities to run off with friends and do something stupid with some forgettable guy. She had no regrets that it had been Rhett, and she counted herself lucky that he'd made it so intimate and pleasurable for her after some of the nightmares her friends had shared about their first times.

The dangerous thing about Rhett, the one thing she'd been most cautious of the entire time, was how easily she could fall in love with him. She knew him well enough to understand that such sentiments made him uncomfortable.

She couldn't deny her feelings, but she could do her best to manage them. But sometimes, when he looked at her, her heart fell into a gallop and her chest filled with a warm, fizzing sensation. Butterflies tickled her stomach, and inexplicable smiles teased her lips.

Only because she'd been so aware of his maturity, had she tried to quell those elated emotions, fearful any giddy display might be seen as a juvenile red flag and scare him away. Then her father showed up and threw a temper tantrum in front of all of Jasper Falls' high society.

No wonder Rhett wanted her to leave. Her father literally punched him in the face. As a teacher, and a civilized human being, it had been drilled in her head that there was no excuse to hit others.

None of it made sense. Her father couldn't even harm a spider. He wasn't the violent type.

Her shoulders drooped and she wrapped her cold fingers around the still warm porcelain of her coffee mug. "I just don't get it."

"Sometimes men just feel the need to act like jackasses, dear. You'll only hurt yourself trying to rationalize their asinine behavior."

She had no energy to fuel her anger, because deep down she was more hurt than anything else. Her mind kept replaying the look of mortification on Rhett's face. He left her there. Told her to leave.

As much as she found it unacceptable that her father had burst into the mansion, fists swinging and ready to fight, she found it equally unacceptable that Rhett hadn't fought harder for her. Now, she supposed he was fighting—texting and begging for a chance to talk—but she believed actions spoke louder than words and she couldn't get over the look on his face when he left her standing on the steps facing everyone alone.

She couldn't deal with a man who would run from confrontation or sticky emotions. Love was bound to get messy. If he couldn't handle that...

She swallowed, afraid to admit that Rhett might never open up to her the way she wanted. The love she dreamed of... It should be boundless, obsessive, and intrusive in every way. The McCullough in her demanded such a love and she wasn't sure she could settle for less.

She hadn't been there for the fight, only the aftermath. But then, when she heard the commotion and rushed to the stairs to see what was the matter, Rhett just stared at her and gave up. Defeated.

The stares of all the guests burned into her. Her father behaved like an out-of-hand mob goon in a bad movie. And Rhett left her there.

She was used to her family acting nuts, but accustomed to their antics taking place in private. She'd never been so embarrassed in all her life.

She suddenly broke into tears. "Everything's falling apart."

"No, honey, this is just the mess God makes before a masterpiece. Gotta break some eggs to bake a cake. Things will get better. You have to be patient." Gran pulled her into a hug and cocooned her in warm, maternal support.

"It's not just what Daddy did or everything with Rhett. It's school." She sniffled and wiped her nose on the back of her hand, careless of her appearance at this point.

"What about school? Are you struggling?"

"I wasn't. I did all the work and never missed a deadline. But somehow, I overlooked a page of an exam and flunked a test. The professor emailed me with a chance to retake it, but I missed the email and lost my chance. There's nothing I can do at this point. Even if I got straight A's in everything else, it wouldn't be enough to bring up my grade. I'm going to have to take a withdraw-fail from the course or it will seriously damage my GPA."

"Oh, honey." She kissed her head and stroked a calming hand down her hair. "Accidents happen."

"I'm always so on top of everything. I don't understand how I got here."

"Sometimes, dear, life just kicks us in the balls for no reason."

She laughed, wiping her nose when snot came out. "I don't have balls."

"And it's a good thing, too. Who wants to walk around

with all that nonsense?" Gran handed her a napkin. "Blow your nose, love. You're dripping."

Skylar mopped up her face and drew in a calming breath. Gran went to the cabinet under the sink and returned with a bottle of whiskey. She topped off Skylar's coffee and gave her a commanding nod to take a sip. Skylar didn't argue and brought the mug to her mouth.

"Do you want my advice?"

She nodded, her coffee slipping down with a calming burn.

"I think your heart's a little bruised over this man, which makes sense, since he's the first you've ever given your heart to. They're all clumsy, and I'm afraid it never gets easier, no matter how many times they screw up and we try to teach them better. But, if you care for this man and actually want to make things work with him, you have to talk to him. Good relationships come from good communication. Believe me. I know. Don't hold parts of yourself back, Skylar. Show him the good, the bad, and the ugly. You have to be real with each other if you want a real love. And, trust me, you're too genuine for an artificial relationship. So what if he screwed up the other night? You'll make mistakes too. We all fumble. Luckily, the heart's a difficult thing to fully break."

Skylar tried to think over the past month with honest appraisal. Rhett didn't like discussing his past, but had she truly expressed her desire to know him deeper? Her need to please others often made her too agreeable.

Confrontation was difficult. Her family thrived on chaos and drama. There was so much of it in her life, she learned to avoid additional conflict whenever possible. But some confrontation could be healthy. Like her grandmother had said, good relationships come from good communication.

She didn't have to meddle in Rhett's personal life to the degree Gran liked to meddle, but if they wanted to grow as a couple, Rhett would have to share something more personal than his appreciation for a North Carolina sky.

Maybe Skylar could explain why she needed that and, if they truly were meant to be, he'd understand that openness was a must with her.

The terrifying possibility that he might not be able to open up, however, left her shaken. No matter how bad things were at the moment, she wasn't ready to lose him. She wanted them to figure this out.

She smiled up at her grandmother through glassy eyes. "Thank you."

Gran pointed to her chest. "You should see the shape of my heart. It's been through hell and back. But it still beats strong, and no matter how many times I want to strangle your grandfather, our love remains the realest thing I know, and that gets us through whatever shitstorm comes our way."

Skylar sniffed. "What about my class?"

Gran shrugged. "You made a mistake. You're human. I'd bet a million dollars you won't make that same mistake twice. Learn from it, forgive yourself, and move on. Tomorrow's another day."

20

It took Skylar a while to face reality. Even after hiding away at her grandparents', surrounded by love and blind acceptance, Skylar still wasn't fully convinced she could handle what might come next, but she was certain she needed to.

There were only two days before Christmas Eve, and then her world would be overrun by relatives and festivities. She still wasn't sure how she would handle facing her dad and uncle.

Despite her doubts and insecurities, she got up, fixed her hair, put on her makeup, and went to clean up the mess she was in. She still had some gifts to get, so she had no choice but to face the music and head into town.

Unable to recall specific guests from the party, Skylar only remembered a blur of scrutinizing eyes judging her. When she got into town, however, she felt those same eyes ogling her again.

The problem with living in a small town was that everyone knew everything about everyone, down to what color underwear people put on in the morning. And since she was related to half the town, she often felt even more exposed.

The hair on the back of her neck rose as she passed people on the sidewalks and they stared. It was impossible to tell who had been at the art gala or heard the rumors, but they all seemed to know.

While waiting in line for a hot cocoa, two women looked at her and one covered her mouth and whispered something in her friend's ear. Were they whispering about Skylar, talking about how she'd slept with the mayor and caused a scene at the gala?

Her stomach soured and she no longer wanted her hot cocoa, but the barista had already begun fixing it. Skylar steeled her nerves and forced herself to wait.

The women finally left, but through the front window of the café Skylar caught them staring at her as they walked away. In a town the size of Jasper Falls, there was no escaping the backlash of a good scandal. But this was the first time Skylar had been the focus of town gossip.

She wished there was time to finish her shopping online. Being so exposed drained her on an emotional level she never experienced before. But, no matter how much it pained her ego, she kept her chin high and finished shopping.

The cashier at McGinty's, a girl she recognized from Hannah's class, studied her as she rung up her order and chewed a mouthful of watermelon-scented bubblegum.

"You're Skylar Marcelli, right?"

Unease snaked through her veins. "Yes."

The girl smiled and leaned closer. "Are you really having an affair with the mayor?"

Her jaw locked. She sliced her credit card through the swiper and punched out the commands to finish the transaction.

"Thanks a lot." She snatched her bags.

"You forgot your receipt!"

The lump in her throat prevented her from responding.

When she reached her car, her hands were shaking—and not from the cold. Everyone knew her personal business. And she hated—*hated*—that the cashier girl called it an *affair*, as if her and Rhett's relationship was something tawdry or immoral.

They were two consenting adults! If her father hadn't reacted the way he had, no one would have ever twisted things into some sort of taboo *affair*!

Rushing inside the car and locking the doors, she tried to catch her breath. This was her first real relationship. It was personal. Private. Her eyes glazed and stung with unshed tears as her privacy once again felt violated.

She was helpless to stop the rumors and exaggerations of the truth, knowing full well people assumed he'd somehow taken advantage of her when no such thing had happened. But people were going to spin her life whatever way made it the juiciest gossip.

She hit her steering wheel and cursed. Her stare turned toward Town Hall and she glared at the building. She wasn't mad at Rhett. But he hurt her. He left her there, standing alone on the staircase, facing those vultures and her dad.

She considered how many times Rhett must have felt this way. As the mayor, he stood in a constant spotlight. It was no wonder that he liked to keep his private life private. Perhaps she'd been wrong to pry into his secrets.

Tipping her head back, she stared at the roof of her car until a tear slipped past her lashes. She was so confused.

He came off as this protective man and she trusted that sense of security. Had that just been another stupid mistake she could chalk up to her younger age and inexperience? She'd always assumed she'd be safe with Rhett. Maybe that was what hurt most—her misjudgment.

She took about fourteen unnecessary turns to get to the mansion, taking the longest way possible. But, in a town the size of Jasper Falls, there were only so many detours a girl could take.

When she pulled up, she didn't see his SUV. She did, however, see Erin's car, which might have been worse.

Reluctantly, she went to the front door and used her key to let herself in. This time, she had the novel experience of being the one to catch Erin off guard.

"Skylar!" Addison yelled and rushed over to give her a hug.

"Hey, cutie! I missed you." And she truly had. The familiar weight of Addison in her arms and the soft scent of her curls sent her emotions spiking in every which direction, and Skylar had to put her down so she didn't start crying again.

She pouted and popped two chubby fists on her hips. "Where have you been?"

"I…" She didn't want to lie to Addison, but this was one of those tricky situations that kids shouldn't have to understand. "I was helping my grandmother."

"Miss Maureen?"

"Yes." She ran a hand over Addison's hair, finding it matted in the back and knotted. "How come you're still in your PJs?" Her shirt was stained with something purple and her feet were bare and dirty.

Erin approached, arms crossed over her chest as she observed Skylar with a cold stare. "You know, you shouldn't just let yourself into someone else's home, especially now that you no longer work here."

Skylar narrowed her eyes. She'd never know for sure, but she was almost certain Erin had been the one to delete the message from her professor. When she looked back, it arrived on the same day the PA showed her the toy Addison wanted online.

"I just came to get my stuff."

"You're leaving?" Addison gasped. "No, I want you to stay!"

She crouched down and looked her in the eye. "Just for a little while. After the holidays I'll come back for a visit."

Addison's brown eyes magnified under a wall of tears and she flung her arms around Skylar's shoulders, squeezing tight. "I don't want you to go."

In that moment, she considered that her heart may be able to survive men, but she wasn't sure she could survive this. Blinking back tears, she hugged Addison's little body, then forced herself to let go.

"Is your daddy around?"

Addison shook her head. "He won't be back for a few days."

Confused by her answer, she frowned. "Where is he?"

"Go get a soda, Addison."

Skylar met Erin's icy stare and the woman practically sneered as Addison disappeared toward the kitchen. "You didn't honestly believe you were the only woman in his life, did you?"

Skylar wasn't going to be bated or play her games. "Where is he?"

"That's private information. All I can say is that he isn't here."

"Not with me," Skylar stated, helpfully pointing out what Erin so eagerly wanted to make clear. Then she cocked her head with unmistakable pity and said, "And not with *you*."

Erin drew back with a quick show of artificial confusion and scoffed. But she didn't deny Skylar's accusation and all it implied.

She was done letting this woman make her feel bad. "As a matter of fact, Erin, he's never been with you or taken any interest in you on a personal level whatsoever. You're just someone on his payroll. And no matter how much you try to abuse me or make me believe I'm unwanted, it won't make a difference, because *he* tells me I am. When he holds me and stares into my eyes, he whispers things you can only dream of him saying to you. So, I'm not going to let your insecure, passive aggressive comments bother me anymore. As a matter of fact, I'm not even going to think about you. And when I have the unfortunate displeasure of seeing you, the only thing I'll feel is pity. And that's more than you deserve, because you've spent your life bullying others and showing everyone you're just a mean, bitter woman."

Her face darkened and she snarled, "Get out of this house before I call the police and have you removed!"

"I'm not leaving without my things."

She withdrew her phone from her pocket with a shaky hand. "I'm calling the cops."

The kitchen door opened and Addison appeared, soda spilled down her front and soaking her pajama top. "I spilled."

Erin snapped. "Goddamn it! I told you not to shake the cans!" The woman marched angrily toward Addison, and Skylar bolted ahead of her, blocking her path.

"Just who do you think you're talking to?" Skylar's entire presence seemed to swell to the size of a momma bear, claws extended and ready to protect her cub. "You don't speak to children like that. And if you were watching her, she wouldn't have had an accident."

"Get out of this house! You're fired!"

"Back off!" Skylar jutted her body forward, causing the woman to stagger back.

Erin looked unstable and ready to strike Addison —or her.

Skylar's jaw hardened and she scowled right into the other woman's eyes. "You can't fire me. And there's no need for the cops. I'll leave. But I'm taking Addison with me.

When Rhett comes back, tell him he can find us at my grandparents' house on the mountain."

"You can't take her! I'm calling the police."

"Go ahead. Let them get involved. The first call they make will be to her father, and whose side do you think he'll take?"

Forgetting her personal belongings upstairs, Skylar hoisted Addison onto her hip and grabbed her coat off the hook in the foyer. As she opened the door, she turned back and said, "And if I were you, I'd start looking for a new job."

"You can't fire me," Erin snapped, throwing her words back at her.

Skylar looked at her with absolute pity. "I won't have to." She shut the door.

21

RHETT SIGNED the last of the paperwork and listened to the familiar spiel about the care Adel would be given and the programs she'd endure. He'd been on this ride several times before. It would work for a while, but eventually, she'd be on her own again.

Like before, she'd pick up new friends from rehab, friends with similar problems and familiar demons. They'd keep each other strong for a while but, soon, those old habits would return.

She'd either find the strength to cut ties, stick to the meds and behavioral therapy the doctor recommended, or she'd go down with the rest of them. But only she could decide her future.

It didn't matter how many friends Adel watched die or how many times she brushed shoulders with death herself. She'd sell her body, her dignity, and her soul to the devil himself, if she wanted to get high bad enough.

And the heartbreaking truth of who she'd become would be inescapable when she came back to herself again, sick with regret, hysterical and suicidal. That's how she sounded when she called him, begging for Rhett to come save her and put her somewhere safe.

He'd spent years trying to do right by her. Not because he loved her. He never had. But because she was Addison's mother and, despite not knowing her, one day Addison may want to meet the woman who gave birth to her.

He'd do everything he could to keep her alive until then, but sometimes survival was ugly, especially when a person's demons overtook a life so completely it hardly resembled living anymore. He wished he could kill the beast that haunted her, but as with his mother, he was as powerless against her addictions as she was. Addiction distorted love, twisting it into something unrecognizable and broken.

If he could get her help, and if she stuck with a program, she might actually have a fighting chance. The bipolar disorder was manageable, but only when she was clean because only then did she love herself enough to do the work.

He didn't have much faith that this time would end any differently than the last. Erin told him to stop bailing her out of trouble. She swore that was the only way people like Adel would learn. But Adel was Addison's mother and he couldn't give up on her.

Adel wasn't like his mother. In rare moments of clear-headed sobriety, she asked about Addison and thanked him for taking care of their daughter. Beyond her gratitude hid a world of remorse. Adel wanted to be a decent mom, but she continuously fell short. She'd once told him the best thing she did for their child was give him sole custody.

Adel asked about Addison, where his mother only ever acknowledged him with cold indifference. He thought of Skylar and how good she was with children, how selfless and considerate she could be of others. So often, people who grew up in nurturing homes forgot that love and affection were not always a given. Skylar didn't realize the gifts she had, or how lucky he considered himself and Addy that they were able to reap her endless affection for a short time.

But was it endless? Everyone had a limit and he feared he might have pushed Skylar to hers.

"Your card will get billed on the third of each month. After her three-month-stay is complete, your deposit gets refunded, as long as there are no damages."

Rhett took the folder the woman offered. It looked like all the rest. "And she can't sign herself out?"

"Not without your knowledge."

"Thank you."

Thoughts of his childhood and Addison's preoccupied his mind the whole ride home. Every time he considered his daughter's future and Adel's role in her life, he was comforted by the idea that Skylar would be there to help with the things Addison might need a woman's assistance with.

Then he wondered if that was true. What if Skylar didn't come back? His first thought should be about Addison's care, which it usually was. But, this time, his worries were more selfish. What if *he* lost Skylar?

An ache formed in his chest and he rubbed it as he drove. He didn't like imagining a future without her.

Not bothering with the radio or paying attention to the exit signs, he drove on autopilot and somehow made it back to his house late that night. The house was dark and quiet when he let himself inside. Since Skylar left, it hadn't felt much like a home, just a house made up of walls and furniture.

"Erin?" He set his keys on the table by the door. "Addy?"

The living room was clean, not a single thing out of order. Something didn't feel right.

He went upstairs only to find Addy's bed empty. "Erin? Hello?"

He pulled out his phone and called his PA, his stare

falling on the door at the end of the hall, despising that no light shined from within.

"Hello?"

Shoving away his longing for the girl he'd become so accustomed to, he focused on locating his daughter. "Erin, where are you guys?"

"I'm home."

He frowned. "Where's Addison?"

She hesitated and the tension in his shoulders tightened. "Addison's with Skylar. She picked her up this morning."

His worry subsided, overrun by something unnamable. Hope? Fear? No, not fear. He trusted Skylar. But what did this mean?

"Where are they?"

"At the big house on the mountain. Her grandparents'."

"Thanks." He ended the call.

Ten minutes later, he was navigating the dark roads of what was known as McCullough Mountain and trying to find what her family called *the big house*. The place was literally like a compound with various homes tucked on cleared acres, secreted away and ensconced in the wilderness, blending beautifully with the wide-open mountainside.

None of the homes tucked in the slopes of rock and pine were what he would consider small. When he approached the sprawling log cabin with its wrap around porch and pointed dormer windows, he knew he'd found the place he was looking for.

He pulled the SUV beside an old Jeep Cherokee, and the front door of the house opened. Skylar stepped out, wrapped in a fleece blanket, and waited at the top step of the porch. She must have been expecting him.

He exited the car and approached slowly, fighting the urge to take her in his arms and apologize for the way he handled things. They needed to discuss everything that happened, but he wasn't sure if now was the time.

He paused at the foot of the steps. "Erin told me you were here."

She nodded. "Addison's sleeping. I don't mind keeping her until morning."

He read the exhaustion in her eyes. Somehow, she was still the most beautiful woman he'd ever known.

She shivered and he wanted to wrap her in his hold and kiss her until her body warmed. The distance weighed him down like an anvil anchored to his neck. It was all he could feel, but he didn't want to pressure her.

She was here because she obviously wanted space and needed time. He wanted to give her that, especially if it would help fix things. But she had to know this was killing him.

"She misses you," he said, wanting to convince her to come home.

"Don't."

His eyes pleaded with her, confessing what he lacked the courage to say. *I miss you...*

Casting her gaze aside, she looked so sad, and he understood the repercussions of the other night had outlasted the party for her. He regretted that any sort of public criticism might have reached her.

"I'm sorry this happened, Skylar."

"Which part?"

Unsure where they stood or if she was through with him, he hesitated. Did she regret everything?

He'd felt this terrible doubt before, usually the day before he returned to that brown building where he waited inside the plain brown walls for someone new to come collect the unwanted boy. He would never go back to that place, but tonight it felt like he might.

He didn't want her rejection. He needed her acceptance. What if he had spoiled everything?

"I never meant to put our relationship on display. You have to realize that."

"I didn't realize I was a secret."

"You weren't."

He wasn't ashamed of her. How could he be? They were still in the beginning stages. His need for privacy had been the result of simply wanting her all to himself and wanting to protect her from gossip, as well as protect Addison from jumping to conclusions.

Aside from sheltering Addison, they'd obviously failed in all other areas. He hadn't protected her. "The gossip will fade and your dad will come around."

"They're calling it an affair like you're married or something, like we did something dirty and wrong."

"We didn't do anything wrong."

"I know. But to hear them sum it up that way... It takes something personal and strips away all the emotion, leaving nothing but a sexual act." Her voice cut off as if she wanted to say more but decided not to.

He wanted to shake her and convince her what they shared was more than just sex. If only she knew all the ways he...

He swallowed hard, trespassing into uncharted territory. The fear of losing her was so strong, he gave up trying to play it cool. He knew he should give her time, but he couldn't bear the thought of her rejection, he couldn't stomach the fear that she might never come back.

"Come home." The words spilled out in an honest plea, and he winced at the desperation in his voice. So much for not pressuring her. "You belong there, with us, with me."

She shook her head. "I can't come home with you, Rhett."

"Why?"

"Because I need time to figure things out."

"How much time?" This was torture. It was worse than waiting for new parents to take him, worse than fearing none would show up. He wanted her, but what if she didn't want him?

"I don't know. I just need time."

He scowled at the muddy ground. "I hate this."

"Do you think I'm enjoying it?"

There had to be a way to move this along. She belonged with him. He had to make her see that. "Have you heard from your father? Has he said anything to you?"

Her grandfather promised to speak to him. Rhett got him the damn parking space. When would Vincenzo take care of his part of the bargain and knock some sense into his thick-headed son?

"I haven't been home. I've been avoiding everyone."

He put his foot on the first step and she paced backwards a step, telling him she preferred the distance.

"I...regret abandoning you at the party. I should have protected you better."

He didn't know how to make this right. His greatest fear was that she'd take herself and all her affection away, without ever explaining it to him. And he would once again prove unlovable.

"I don't want to lose you, Skylar. I want everything to go back to the way it was."

"I don't know if things can go back to the way they were. People know about us. It isn't right for me to live with you and work for you."

"Who cares what people know? It's none of their business."

"I don't want to be the town scandal."

"You're not. There's nothing wrong with us being together. They're just a bunch of bored gossips making noise. It doesn't mean anything."

"It does to me." She looked down and smiled sadly. "Did you know, the night of the ball was my first time?"

Shame burned through him. "I…suspected."

"I had plenty of chances before, but I never cared about anyone enough, until I met you. I don't know how people do this and keep it casual, Rhett." Her hand rubbed over her chest. "This doesn't feel casual. Casual doesn't hurt."

He ached, too. "It's not casual."

Secrets and unshed tears danced in her eyes as she looked at him. "I'm terrified you'll suspect the thoughts in my head and the feelings in my heart and run away screaming."

His greatest fears were his own inadequacies. He worried he wouldn't be able to match her affection because no one ever showed him how. But he was willing to try. "I won't run."

"Are you sure?" She looked at him with sad acceptance. "You never even tell Addison you love her, and she's your daughter. I need to feel loved, Rhett. I want someone who isn't afraid to tell me."

A lump formed in his throat. "That isn't fair."

"Why isn't it? This is what I want, what I need."

And he wanted to give it to her, but he didn't know how. He didn't know how to care without the fear that he would eventually be cast aside and crushed all over again. Every experience he had with others proved nothing was permanent. Even Addison would one day leave him to make a life of her own, he just prayed he was a good enough father to her that she still came back to visit from time to time.

He did his best to take care of his child and show her what a decent man should do. He didn't have a father, so he had no personal experiences to draw from, but he remembered the families he watched on television and tried to do his best by her.

"Just because I don't say certain words, doesn't mean I

don't feel something for those I care about. I *love* my daughter."

Why did that word feel so unsafe to say? He despised the sense of vulnerability and fear it stirred.

Her mouth formed a weak smile. "You should tell her that."

"Isn't it more important that I show her?" He showed Addy affection every day by taking care of her and taking interest in her. "Why does everyone always want so much more than I can give?" *So much more than I was ever given?* "I'm doing my best."

"Do you love me?"

Her question shot through him like cannon fire, leaving an aching void too wide to close. Pain slipped from the hole left by her words, exposing all the empty secrets he hid. How could he measure something he'd never felt before?

"I..."

Her head lowered and twin tears rushed down her cheeks.

"Damn it, Skylar, why do we have to label it? Why can't we just be happy with what it is?"

Did she love him? Why did he have to say it first? What if he loved her and then she lost interest in him? How would he survive that?

She lifted her head, and blinked away anymore tears. "I'll go get Addison."

He grit his teeth. "I thought you said she could stay."

"I think it might be better, now, if you take her home. Tomorrow's the day before Christmas Eve. I'm sure you two have things to do."

She disappeared into the house and returned a few minutes later with Addison bundled in her arms. He climbed the steps and collected his daughter, her weight in his arms an instant comfort to his soul.

He carried her to the car and Skylar followed but kept

her distance. His daughter only slightly stirred when he buckled her inside, but then quickly fell back to sleep.

He started the car with a click of a button and faced Skylar. "When will I see you again? What do I tell her?"

"Tell her I love her."

What about me, he wanted to shout. When would he finally hear those words from someone who mattered?

He caught her hand and brought her fingers to his lips. "You're freezing."

He shrugged off his coat and draped it over her shoulders, pulling the lapels together as he looked into her eyes. Sure enough, tracks of tears showed on her skin. He couldn't help himself. He hugged her.

Her arms bunched between them, providing a modicum of distance, but he held her tight anyway. Was this ache in his chest love? How could something so sought-after hurt so much?

"I'll fix this. I'll show you." He kissed her head and stepped back, afraid to let her go. "I'll call you tomorrow. Please answer the phone."

She nodded and he released her, stepping to the driver's side door.

"Rhett?"

Hope rose in his chest and he pivoted. "Yes?"

"Don't let Erin watch Addison anymore. Call me if you need someone to sit with her."

He had questions but lacked the strength. His mind wasn't on work so he didn't waste much thought on her request. But he did realize this meant she still intended to see Addy, which meant she'd also see him.

He trusted her without needing to hear her reasons. "Okay."

She pulled off his coat and placed it on the passenger seat, quietly shutting the door. "Drive safely."

22

"SKYLAR, move your *culi*! This order's gettin' cold and we've got three more in the hopper!"

Despite how sweaty she was from working in the kitchen, she put her wool hat on her head and bundled back up for another delivery.

It was the day before Christmas Eve, which meant the takeout orders were running nonstop, on top of the catering orders they still had to prepare for tomorrow's customers. Half the dining room was covered with trays of manicotti while the other half was draped with homemade pasta airing out to dry.

Thanks to her family, families all over Jasper Falls could have a nice home-cooked meal from someone else's kitchen on Christmas Eve.

"Skylar!"

"I'm going!" She took the box and plucked the receipt off the front, holding it between her teeth as she used her butt to push open the front door of the restaurant.

The blustery cold cut right through her coat. This was how people got sick. She was sweating and freezing at the same time. Luckily, her grandfather had somehow managed a permanent parking spot for deliveries, so she didn't have far to trek by foot.

She punched the address into her GPS only to recognize it at the last second. Rolling her eyes, she headed toward her cousin, Ryan's, house.

She appreciated when her family ordered from the restaurant, especially around the holidays, because they always tipped generously. However, the deliveries took twice as long because relatives always wanted updates on any family gossip. Being that she was the recent gossip, she didn't have much to say.

"Stay for a beer," Ryan begged, already a little tuned up himself.

"I can't. I'm driving."

"Oh, right."

His wife Maggie plated out two slices. "Leave her alone, Ryan. She has other deliveries to make."

"Fine." He took his plate and shoveled half the slice into his mouth, taking an enormous bite. "Well, I guess we'll see you on Christmas."

"I'll be there."

He slid her a few extra dollars. "Have fun at your fish feast."

"I will, thanks. Merry Christmas!" She rushed out the door and dove into the heat of her car.

Christmas Eve belonged to her Italian relatives. They had the usual Feast of the Seven Fishes, and yes, it was absolute insanity with everyone screaming over each other, bickering about how much salt should be used to brine the *bacalao*, drinking way too much red wine before midnight mass, and then staying up until Christmas morning playing cards. It was one of her favorite holidays of the year, but this year she was dreading it.

She hadn't been home or spoken to her father, but there

would be no avoiding him tomorrow. Her mother had called a few times, but Skylar let it go to voicemail.

She knew how they worked. Her dad likely already convinced her mom of his side, and that's all she'd see. Sometimes the two of them were more like teenagers and inseparable best friends rather than rational thinking adults. Skylar didn't feel like dealing with their opinions.

The next delivery was to a house on the west side of town then it was back to the restaurant to pick up three more orders. They were in the final stretch, and stores were preparing to close so the holiday could officially begin, but, for her family, there was still a ton of work to do.

Come Christmas day, after a long day of cooking and celebrating on Christmas Eve, they would open presents then head over to the big house where Gran and the great-aunts would be cooking up a storm. No matter what the temperature was each year, the heat stayed off and all the windows remained open, and it was still a sauna inside. That's what happened when a hundred big mouths and a hundred pounds of hot food filled every inch of free space in the big house.

Christmas was one freakishly chaotic meal, but no amount of mayhem could save her from the unwanted confrontations that waited. She knew, without a doubt, her Uncle Colin would make a point to talk to her, and she dreaded the thought.

She stopped by Rhett's house earlier. He and Addison were gone and the house was empty.

She packed her personal belongings but couldn't fit everything in one trip. Once she had her laptop, she contacted her professor and apologized for dropping out of the course without notice.

She explained the situation, and that there was no possible way to bring up her F, so it was what it was. She'd never actually failed a class before, and it didn't feel good.

But it also didn't feel quite as terrible as she imagined. Maybe she was disassociating.

She was on the road most of the night making deliveries, which gave her plenty of time with her thoughts. She'd talked to Rhett a few times on the phone after swinging by his house, but their calls were quiet and subdued, except when Addison took the phone to say hello. She still needed time to think, so there wasn't much she could say.

She'd laid her feelings on the line the other night and told him what she needed. She knew he wanted her back, but she needed to move forward with open eyes. She didn't want to pressure him, but she also couldn't ignore what her heart wanted. She was falling in love with him and couldn't bear the idea of falling for someone who wouldn't love her back.

If anything, this whole experience taught her that she was not a casual kind of girl. She wanted monogamy and she wanted substance. She needed to be honest with him, and honest with herself.

The truth was, she wanted a love as open and accepting as the love her grandparents shared. She wanted the friendship her parents had. Those things couldn't exist without open communication, and right now, Rhett seemed incapable of expressing how he felt.

But a relationship was two sided. She hadn't been clear about expressing her needs until he stopped by her grandmothers the other day. Only then did she have the courage to tell him she needed a man capable of love. Since then, she'd been sick to her stomach, fearing she might have asked for too much.

Her heart broke at the thought that this might actually be their end. She had to stay true to herself. Not only did she need a man capable of loving her, but she wanted a wild and riotous love. She needed a man capable of expressing his affection through more than physical touch.

If Rhett couldn't give her those things...

If he couldn't speak such words...

Deep down, she believed he felt them, but he refused to let her in. She didn't want to date someone who locked his emotions behind walls.

She didn't want to let him go. She wanted them to work this out and grow closer. But this might just be all he could offer and she would have to accept his limits. And, if she truly wanted an open and honest love, she would have to make the difficult choice to put herself first and walk away from any man who refused to open his heart—even if leaving him meant breaking hers.

Yes, he claimed to want her back, but she wasn't sure how much that had to do with Addison and how much had to do with their relationship. And was it a relationship, or was it merely sex for him? She still wasn't sure, and her lack of experience made her extra cautious.

It had been so much more than sex for her. The way he looked at her and took an interest in her thoughts and opinions, those weren't sexual things. Intimate things, yes, but not sexual.

She took the same interest in him, but the deeper she dug the harder he worked to hide parts of his past. Didn't he realize she only wanted to know him. She would never judge him unfairly or use his secrets to hurt him. She only wanted to take care of him.

It didn't help that she had no one, aside from her grandmother at the moment, to speak to about everything she was feeling. Many of her friends were home for the holidays, but only for a short time. Everyone was busy with family and she wasn't speaking to much of hers.

When the deliveries ended for the night, she returned to the restaurant. The dining room was closed so her aunts turned up the stereo. Frank Sinatra sang "Have Yourself a

Merry Little Christmas" as Skylar and her aunts layered lasagna and stuffed pasta shells with ricotta.

She watched her dad's sisters work, wondering why they never got married. They were each beautiful and nurturing in their own crazy way.

Nonna brought out a plate of cannoli and the work stopped so they could sample the batch.

"Delicious, Ma," Angela said.

"What is this, happy hour?" Her grandfather came out of the kitchen, catching them all gathered around the cannoli tray. "We have work to do!"

"Shush, Vinnie. Here. Eat a cannoli." Nonna stuffed the cheese filled shell in his mouth and he laughed, pretending to smoke it like a cigar.

The music shifted to Frank's, "I'll Be Home for Christmas," and her grandfather pulled Nonna into his arms, nuzzling her shoulder and twirling her into a spin. The aunts got back to work, but Skylar watched her grandparents dance.

The steam on the window was a perfect winter backdrop against the snow. The air smelled of tomato and basil and all her favorite things.

"Sky, you done with this tray?" Aunt Nicky asked.

Skylar couldn't pull her stare away from the happy dancing couple. "Look at them. Have you ever seen a couple more in love?"

"You're drunk. All they do is fight."

Skylar smiled. "Maybe that's how they say I love you."

She wondered if it was hypocritical of her to think love could only be expressed in a four letter word. As she watched her grandparents dance and smile into each other's eyes, so evidently in love, she wondered if she'd ever actually heard them say *I love you* to each other.

Perhaps people communicated love in many different

languages. Was she too focused on her own love language to hear Rhett's?

As Sinatra crooned out the last line *if only in my dreams* her grandfather dipped Nonna and kissed her cheek.

Skylar didn't get back to the big house until well after midnight. She expected to find the house dark, but Gran and Pop were curled up on the couch watching *It's a Wonderful Life.*

"Did you eat, Skylar?" Gran asked as soon as she took off her coat.

"Yes, at the restaurant." For once, her grandfather wasn't in his recliner, so Skylar sat in the old, battered chair.

Her grandparents leaned into each other on the sofa, Gran's lap full of yarn and knitting needles while Pop held a big empty bowl that had been filled with some sort of snack.

"How often do you two say I love you?" Skylar asked, stealing their attention from Jimmy Stewart and Donna Reed.

"Every day," her grandmother declared. "But I have to wait about a decade to hear it back."

Pop looked at her as if she were crazy. "I tell you every time I hang up the phone or leave the house, woman. Maybe if you ever stopped talking and actually listened to what other people around you said, you'd hear me more often."

She grinned. Even if Pop didn't say it as often, there had never been a man who loved a woman as completely as he loved his wife.

"Why do you ask?" Gran wondered.

She shrugged. "Some people aren't as affectionate as us. I'm trying to understand why."

"Some people don't know how."

Skylar frowned. "What's to know?"

Her grandmother glanced at her grandfather. "Some men can't express their emotions, and they don't much like feeling them either, especially when their life experiences haven't taught them much about the nice ones. Sometimes they fear loving others because they worry it will open them up to more pain."

Skylar's frown deepened. Did Rhett have a painful past? Had someone hurt him? Broken his heart? Perhaps Addison's mother had wronged him and that was why they weren't together. There was only one way to find out.

That night, as she lie awake in bed, Skylar thought of all the ways Rhett made her feel loved. Sometimes it was a gesture, other times it was a look or touch. His actions gave away his feelings more than his words.

So, why did she need those words? Maybe love was about trusting a person's intensions based on the proof shown through behavior.

In the end, she admitted that growing up with such an overwhelming family she'd become sheltered. She took love and affection for granted and overlooked that not every child grew up the same way.

As a teacher, she'd always been aware of that fact and sure to look for any symptoms of neglect. It was a part of her training, to not just educate, but fill any voids where nurture and care seemed low. How had she been so naive to think that such problems belonged only to children.

Everyone in Jasper Falls adored the mayor, but they didn't truly know him. She saw the real Rhett Buchanan, and recognized how lonely he'd actually been before she'd come into his life. Maybe she could be the braver person and tell him he didn't have to be alone any more.

In that moment, she admitted she loved him enough to wait for his heart to thaw.

23

Christmas Eve

Skylar slept as late as she physically could, wishing for any excuse to avoid facing her parents. She was still angry with her father and unsure what she would say to him when forced to confront him tonight.

She needed coffee before making any difficult decisions. Shuffling into the bathroom and then lurching into the kitchen of the big house, she sensed something was off the moment she reached for the coffee pot. The hairs on her arms rose and she twisted, finding Gran and her parents waiting at the dining room table—each one watching her expectantly.

"What's going on?" A strange sense that she was being ambushed crept over her, and she regretted being too foggy headed to run.

"Get your coffee, dear, then we'll talk," Gran said with her usual cheer.

A vision of a wild gazelle tumbling to the earth flashed

in her mind, ripped from the pack and taken out by an unexpected predator.

She got a little dramatic when cornered first thing in the morning before she had her coffee.

Her eyes narrowed and her mouth pursed. She hadn't expected to start the day this way. Taking her time, she filled a mug and took an extra minute to stir in the cream with extra slow swirls of a spoon with perfectly spherical strokes.

She debated taking her coffee and walking right out the back door, but it was cold and she was only wearing slippers, so she carried her mug into the dining room. Her mom's expression was unreadable and her dad was scowling.

"Have a seat," Gran said invitingly, like this could somehow pass as normal and unthreatening.

Skylar obeyed, only because her grandmother had been so kind to her and she didn't want to disrespect her in her own house.

The mood at the table was icy, and she suspected this meeting wasn't at her parents' request.

"I asked your mother and father here because I think there are some things we need to get straight. First, I want to set some ground rules. This is my house and it's a holiday. I won't tolerate yelling and it's bad luck to fight on Christmas Eve."

"Mom—"

"Don't interrupt me, Katherine. Second, *everyone* at this table is an adult and should be respected as such. We aren't here to hurl insults or hurt each other. We're here to fix things. Anthony, maybe you should start. Do you have something to say to your daughter?"

"How could you let this happen?" His words cut off as Gran smacked him in the back of the head.

"Mom!"

Skylar's mom gaped at Gran, but Gran only snapped, "I meant an apology."

Her father crossed his arms over his chest. "I'm not apologizing for pulling her out of that house."

"You didn't pull me out," Skylar reminded. "I walked out. *You* humiliated me in front of half the town."

"You were embarrassed for your own actions. I didn't raise you to behave like that. Christ, Skylar, he's more than a decade older than you!"

She jumped to her feet. "So what? Pop's older than Gran, and Uncle Alec is way older than Aunt Sheilagh. Age is just a number."

"Well, you're behaving like a child—"

"That's enough!" Gran shrilled. "I don't understand why you two can't speak to each other with more respect. This is nonsense. Anthony, she's a grown woman. If she wants to sample every man in town, your overprotective opinions can't stop her. You have to accept that she's grown up. You would never treat Frankie the way you're treating her. And while that sort of double standard might fly with your Marcelli side of the family, it doesn't fly with ours." She turned her stare to Skylar's mother. "Katherine, you've been awfully quiet."

Her mom looked at Skylar and it wasn't quite disappointment in her eyes but something else. "I think you're too young to get tied down in a relationship right now. You have so much ahead of you, Skylar. This man—"

"Rhett."

"Fine. *Rhett* has a child. You're young. You need your freedom."

She scoffed at the irony. "Mom, what freedom did I have? I'm always taking care of James or Ciera. I couldn't even go away to school because of Dad's work schedule. I have never had the autonomy Frankie or even Hannah has."

"I think you should go away to school and finish your degree."

Skylar gaped, her hands spreading wide. "With what money?"

"You could get loans."

It was a pipe dream. She heard her parents arguing about finances. They had remortgaged the house to help cover her dad's research expenses while he waited for the grant to come in. They weren't poor, but there were eight of them. It was a lot.

Her grandmother folded her hands and looked at her. "What do you want to do, Skylar?"

"I...don't know." She liked watching Addison, but she didn't know if she could go back there. No matter what she chose, the governess gig would only be until Addison started kindergarten, so it wasn't a permanent solution.

"Here's what's going to happen." Gran reached into her bra and pulled out a folded piece of paper. "I have here, a check for ten thousand dollars. It's made out to Skylar." Both her parents gawked at the amount, but Gran ignored them. "I'm going to leave it up to Skylar, how she spends it."

"What?" Her brain still wasn't caffeinated enough. It sounded like... "I'm sorry. Did you say ten *thousand* dollars?"

Gran smiled. "You can either use it for tuition or invest it in property somewhere or use it to start a business. It's your decision."

"Mom, she can't accept that—"

"It's not your decision, Katherine. This is a gift between me and my granddaughter."

"Maureen, how can you do that?" Her father's disapproving scowl hit like another betrayal. "It's not fair to the other grandchildren."

"You let me worry about them, Anthony. Focus on your own problems for now." She unfolded the check and slid it across the table. "It's yours, Skylar. Use it wisely."

Skylar stared down at the check, afraid to accept such a sum. "I could pay you back—"

"It's not a loan. It's a gift. Nonrefundable, I'm afraid. As it turns out, we're only allowed to give a little over that amount each year. I spoke to the accountant and he says we can claim it on our taxes as a gift." She grinned. "This year, you're the lucky grandchild. Merry Christmas."

Skylar's eyes flooded with tears. She could do so much with that money. "I don't know what to say."

"Thank you will work."

Her voice lodged behind a lump in her throat. "Thank you."

"Then I think we're finished here."

Her parents pushed up from the table, seeming more irritated than they had been when this started, and her dad walked out of the house. If gratitude was a balloon, his disapproval just punctured it, and Skylar's heart sank to the ground.

She stood and followed him. She had some things to say that might break her grandmother's rules, so it was best if she said her words outside.

She let the screen door slam behind her. "I'm not sorry for what I did." The statement burst from her, and she shook in the wake of such truth.

Her father pivoted, already in the driveway, and scowled at her. "Skylar, go back inside."

"No." She marched down the stairs, stalking him. "Why do the men in your family think they always know what's best for the women? This is why your sisters never got married. Grandpa was so overbearing and controlling, he never let anyone get close to his girls. Well, I want to be close to people, Dad. I like having someone pay attention to me."

"Then find someone your age."

"What does age have to do with anything? If Rhett and I

share a connection, you should be happy for me! Don't you want me to be happy?"

"Of course, I want that, but I know a thing or two about men and—"

"So do I!"

That shut him up.

Softening her voice, she said, "I have more uncles than shoes. I grew up watching them and all my cousins. Do you think I'm so naive that I don't know how men are and what they think about? I could have had a ton of empty relationships by now if that was all I wanted. But I want more. Rhett gives me something I need. It's more than sex."

The word hit him like a slap and he squeezed his temples. "Skylar, I can't discuss this with you."

"Why? You talk about this stuff with Frankie. Why not me, Dad?"

"Because you're my baby girl!"

Her eyes flushed with tears and she blinked. "I'll always be that."

He glanced at the car as if he wished he could run away. "You grew up so fast. It feels like I missed a part."

She understood his position, but that was a personal issue he had to work through. She wouldn't guilt him for working overtime or being preoccupied with his research. None of that could be undone now. This was where they were.

"Your behavior the other night..." She shook her head, still shocked he'd acted so crazy. "You hurt me."

He looked at her with genuine regret in his eyes. "I was trying to protect you."

"Then you should have talked to me. You could have asked what was going on and I would have told you."

"I doubt that—"

"This is what I mean, Dad. You might not be able to accept that I'm a grown woman with adult relationships, but

I'm living it. It's not weird for me. If you had come to me, I would have told you Rhett and I were together. I would have told you how he makes me feel important and special, how he values my input and when I speak, he listens. When he looks at me, he truly sees me. That's what I mean when I say he meets my needs, Dad. I *need* to feel like someone sees me."

He studied her for a long moment. "We *see* you, Skylar."

"When? If Frankie has a game, you're there. If Hannah has a dance, you make it for the pictures. You go to Vinny's school concerts and have tea with Ciera and watch cartoons with James, but you don't do any of those things with me."

His stare wavered. "I did all those things with you, too."

"But you stopped. You got busy and you never have time anymore."

"I always have time for you, pumpkin. Maybe I've been preoccupied. I know I've been absent a lot because of work, but you guys are always on my mind. You're my entire world." He frowned and looked down. "You've always been so reliable. I guess I just figured you could handle more than the others and maybe that's why I pulled back, but it's not because I love you any less or think of you any less."

She wiped her eyes. "I love him, Dad. And I want to fix this with him, with or without your blessing."

He exhaled and turned away. "Why him? You're still so young and, now, with Gran's gift, you could—"

"You've been with Mommy since you were kids. Do you think we can't do math? You two had Frankie when she was barely eighteen."

"Your mom's situation was different. If you ask her, she'll tell you all about the plans she had and the things she sacrificed to be a young mom. She and I don't want to see you make those sacrifices."

"That's not your choice." And being with Rhett didn't feel like a sacrifice. It felt like a privilege.

She scuffed her slipper over the dusty driveway and pushed her hands into the pockets of her robe. "You asked why him."

His gaze met hers and she understood that this was him finally hearing her out, that he truly wanted to understand the appeal of Rhett Buchanan.

"Because he's who I fell in love with. He's decent and kind, and when I'm with him, I know I matter."

"He's a politician. They're inherently untrustworthy."

"You see the mayor side of him. You don't see the side I get when we're alone. I know the real him. He's a good father. He's humble and considerate." She didn't think it would help her argument to share how handsome she found Rhett, so she skipped that part. "He's kind to me."

"Kindness should be a given, Sky."

"I let him get close to me, because we have chemistry, Dad. I know you don't want to hear that, but we make sense together. He appreciates who I am, and that sort of kindness isn't the same as simple manners. It's deeper. I haven't found that in many surface relationships."

He sighed, huffing out a breath that turned into cold vapor. "It's going to take me some time to accept this."

She shrugged. "I don't know if we can repair the damage done or deal with being the center of what everyone has made into some ridiculous scandal. Our family is always on display. We're everywhere and everyone knows us. This was something private, Daddy. Not because we were hiding or ashamed, but because a relationship is personal. The way you acted that night—"

"I shouldn't have done that. Your uncle came to me and I overreacted."

"Ya think?" She shook her head. "You acted like a maniac. And you embarrassed me."

His head lowered. "I'm sorry."

Skylar swallowed, accepting his apology as genuine. "I

want to try to make it work with him, and I want you to support my decision."

He sighed. "When did you get so grown up?"

"I probably just look mature, because you're still running around punching people."

"Not my best moment."

She rolled her eyes. "No kidding."

"Okay," he finally agreed. "I'll back off and let you figure this out, but if I catch wind of this guy doing anything disrespectful to you, I'm coming for him. That's not an age thing. That's a father thing. I reserve the right to vet any man my daughters date. And you won't find a single relative who disagrees with me on that."

She grinned. "Thank you."

24

Christmas Day

"Have you decided how you want to spend your money?" Gran asked as Skylar helped her set out the desserts.

The majority of the family was exchanging the white elephant gifts in the den, so they had the kitchen to themselves for a brief moment.

"I, um, I'm going to invest it."

"Oh, good. On what, dear?"

She laughed, because no matter how much her grandmother wanted to show unbiased support, her nature was to micromanage. But she was showing excellent restraint.

"There's a room in the rec center that can be rented long-term. It's nothing fancy, but the price is good and it has a sink and a closet and two bathrooms. I want to make it a pre-K classroom."

She smiled, the expression full of sincere joy. "Well, I think that's a lovely idea."

It was a plan she'd always harbored, and one she'd

researched some time ago. A pipe dream that needed a lot of seed money, which she now had.

She believed through all their little talks about nothing, her grandmother was actually listening and heard the dream in Skylar's heart. And *that* was more meaningful to Skylar than the actual ten thousand dollars.

She smiled at the woman who, no matter how busy and overrun by family her life had become, still made time to talk with each grandchild. And also, because Skylar stuck with the suspicion that she might be a favorite.

"I don't know how successful it will be," she explained. "But I'm legally allowed to have five students—ten if I have an assistant. And if I can manage that, I can bring in enough tuition to afford the curriculum supplies and possibly finance my future education."

"It sounds like you've thought of everything."

She thought so. The only drawback was that this meant she wouldn't be returning to Rhett's. But she believed if she opened a school, Addison would be among the first enrolled.

Gran set out serving spoons with the desserts. "And who knows? Maybe down the line you'll have an entire faculty working for you and you'll need a bigger building—a whole preschool."

Skylar grinned. "That's the goal."

"Well, I think it's a lovely dream to have."

They announced the desserts were ready and a stampede of children raced through the house. The parents paused from the white elephant exchange to refill coffee and cocktails.

Skylar stepped outside for some air and that was when he found her. "Mind if I join you?"

She glanced over her shoulder at her Uncle Colin, but kept her expression blank. "It's a free country."

He approached the porch railing and rested his elbows beside hers. "I guess you're pretty mad at me."

"Do you blame me?"

"I was trying to protect you, Skylar. I didn't think your dad would storm the mayor's mansion and lay him out."

She gave him a skeptical look.

"Okay, I guess I figured it was a possibility, but I was hoping for a more civilized reaction."

"Since when does anyone in this family behave civilly?"

"I should have stayed out of it."

"Yes, you should have."

He was silent for several minutes. "I don't want you to ever think you can't come to me if you need something, Skylar. It was a mistake for me to go to your parents. I should have trusted you and waited to see how things progressed."

"And what if he broke my heart, Colin? What then?"

His jaw twitched. "You know we're a protective bunch."

She shook her head. "You know, I see other girls with normal families and I often wonder *what that's like*."

"I hear it's boring."

She scoffed. "Again, I wonder what that's like."

He turned to her. "I'm really sorry, Sky. I hate feeling this distance between us."

"That's the thing." Her lips pursed and her brow pinched. "This past week has been really awful. I needed a friend and I couldn't come to you."

"You can always come to me."

"Not if I can't trust you."

He drew in a long breath. "I want your trust."

"Trust is a two-way street. I can only trust you if you trust me. That means you have faith in my ability to make my own decisions and know I'll ask for help when I need it."

"Deal." They returned to leaning their elbows on the

railing and staring out at the sea of clustered vehicles. "Are we okay?"

"Yeah. But next time—"

"No next time," he interrupted. "I promise that anything you tell me from now on will be kept in confidence." Her gaze shifted to a car approaching in the distance, the wheels slowly crunching over the snow.

Her heart lifted at the sight of the familiar, black Escalade pulling up the driveway.

"Is that him?"

What was he doing there? "I thought he was smarter than this."

"He realizes your whole family's here, right?"

"He's driving right into the belly of the beast." They were going to eat him alive.

Uncle Colin patted her back. "Good luck." He returned to the house.

She walked down the steps and waited as Rhett parked at the end of the long line of cars and trucks. He helped Addison out of her seat and set her on the snowy ground.

"Skylar!" She raced toward her, catapulted off the ground and into Skylar's arms. "Look what Santa brought me!"

She stared at what should be a chinchilla and frowned. This was why people should never shop online from the dark market of the internet. The toy was half the size as advertised, *not* computerized, and definitely more of a red than a yellow. She glanced at Rhett and he shrugged.

"It's beautiful. What's its name?"

"Her name's Marigold, like the flower."

"Why don't you go show her to Michael and the other kids? They're all inside." Skylar set her down.

"Okay!" Addison raced into the house and Rhett closed the distance between them.

"Merry Christmas." He pressed a kiss to her cheek.

"Merry Christmas." She shifted her weight. "So, is that the one I ordered?"

He laughed then paused. "Wait, *you* ordered it?"

"Yeah. I swear all the stats claimed it was authentic. You didn't know I… Ah, Erin told you she did all the shopping."

He frowned. "Why would she lie?"

"I think we need to have a long talk about your assistant, but let's save it for another day." She definitely didn't feel like discussing Erin on Christmas. "Did Addy like all her other gifts?"

"Yes, but I think that red mouse thing is her favorite. To her, it's as good as a real chinchilla."

Skylar smiled, loving that Addison was such an easy child. "She's a sweet girl."

He nodded. "How's your Christmas going?"

"Okay. It's a little nutty but that's normal. How about you?"

He shrugged. "This is it. We did the presents, and now we're just waiting for it to end."

"God, you make it sound so bleak."

"I don't really get all the hype. We didn't do holidays when I was young."

She considered what her grandmother had said about some people not being shown much love and, therefore, never learning how to show it. Rising on her toes, she brushed a kiss over his lips.

He blinked in surprise. "What was that for?"

"For Christmas. I wanted to give you something special." She smiled. "That's only half of it, though."

"When do I get the other half?"

"Now, come here." She crooked a finger and he leaned down. She angled her mouth close to his ear and whispered, "I love you, Rhett Buchanan."

He drew back and stared at her, a look of shock in his eyes.

"You don't have to say it back. I don't need anything in return. I just wanted to tell you that."

His lips parted as if he wanted to say something, but he frowned and glanced away. His hand rubbed over his chest and the crease in his brow deepened.

"Is it supposed to hurt?"

"What? No." She laughed, nervously.

It was the first time she'd said those words to someone not related to her. She didn't do it to hurt him.

He continued to rub his chest. "Then why does it hurt here?"

She didn't have a clue but now felt a little foolish. "I'm sorry?"

His frown carved deeper as he paced, still rubbing his chest. "There's this weight... Like something's sitting on my chest... I feel like I can't breathe."

Real concern raced through her. "Do you need to go to the hospital?"

"I don't know. It's crushing me."

"Oh, my God. Hold on. I'll get my cousin. He's a doctor." She raced into the house and yelled, "Patrick, come quick!"

Her cousin, Pat, followed her out to the front yard, where Rhett was doubled over with his hands braced on his knees. Of course, her entire family followed.

"What's going on?"

"Who's that man?"

"Should someone call 9-1-1?"

Addison raced forward. "Daddy?"

Pat held up a hand and approached Rhett. "Everyone just give him some space." He calmly took his pulse and asked several questions. Then he suggested he take a seat on the steps.

A hoard of McCulloughs and in-laws gathered on the porch, nosily waiting for Pat's verdict.

Skylar worried her hands and Addison came to her side. "What's wrong with Daddy?"

"I'm sure he's fine. Patrick's a doctor. He's just checking him out."

Despite the reassurance in her voice, Skylar felt anything but comforted, so she pulled Addison into her harms for support.

Pat removed a doctor's bag from his car and instructed Rhett to open his coat and shirt. Then he started attaching wires to Rhett's chest that plugged directly into his phone.

"What is that?" Skylar asked, worried.

"A mobile EKG that reads through an app on my phone." He looked at the screen. "Try to relax, Rhett."

A few minutes later, Pat disconnected the wires and put his phone away. "Your heart rhythm appears normal and your vitals seem fine. No elevated blood pressure and your chest sounds good. I think you're safe," Pat finally said. "Chances are you just had a mild panic attack."

The family slowly disbursed, and Aunt Sammy took Addison back inside with Michael. Skylar listened as Pat explained the differences between an actual heart attack and a panic attack.

Rhett appeared instantly relieved and Skylar felt the same. "Thank you, Patrick."

"Any time. Call me if any symptoms return." Pat handed him a business card and packed up his bag.

Once they were alone again, she looked at Rhett. "Well, that'll make a girl think twice about her words. First time I tell a man I love him, it nearly kills him. Just one more tick in the old self-esteem column."

Still sitting on the step, he looked up at her with his collar open and laughed. "It's not you—*believe me*."

"Then why do you think you reacted like that?"

He glanced away and the energy around him chilled. "No one's ever said those words to me before."

Startled by his confession, she said, "That can't be true."

"Unfortunately, it is. I didn't grow up with a family, Skylar. It's always just been me watching other families. So, when you ask why I have a hard time expressing myself, it's because I've never had to. Those words aren't easy for me. I've never heard them and I've never said them." He held her stare. "But I feel them."

She sat beside him on the step. "You do?"

"Yes. First time I held Addison, I knew it could only be love. And then you came along, and I felt something similar, but different. It's...hotter and sharper."

She smiled. "Passionate."

"Yes."

Hooking her arm around his, she rested her head on his shoulder and let his nearness soothe her. "Rhett, I can't come back to work for you."

He drew back so he could see her. "Why?"

"Because I'm opening my own preschool after the New Year. I think you should enroll Addison."

"Here in Jasper Falls?"

"Of course. Where else would I go? I'm in love with the mayor."

He laughed. "I like how that sounds. Love."

She grinned up at him. "I love you."

He held her stare and nervousness danced in his eyes. "I love you, too, Skylar. I'm sorry it took me some time to put a name to it, but now that I have, there's no denying the feelings in my heart. I feel like I've waited a lifetime to find you. You're so special to me, I was terrified I'd do or say the wrong thing and lose you. I almost did."

"I don't have all the answers, Rhett. I think it's normal to be nervous when you feel so much for someone. It shows how much we care."

He pressed a kiss to her hair and smiled. "I like saying it. I love you."

He had no idea how much she loved hearing those words. "Over the past week I've done a lot of thinking. As much as I appreciate the words of affirmation, I realized you show your love in other ways, too, and that's okay." Her lips brushed his. "I've missed you."

"Ditto."

She pressed her lips to his and kissed him slowly. The tattered edges of her heart seemed to sew back together. "Merry Christmas."

He cleared his throat and something uncertain flashed in his eyes. "I'm still learning how all this Christmas stuff works. I might have bought you something a little extreme for Christmas."

"I hope it's a dejected chinchilla from China."

"Close. It's a diamond."

Her head drew back and legs went numb. "No, you didn't."

He reached into his jacket and removed a small velvet box. "Is now a good time to discuss your plans for the New Year?"

That was not the box of a necklace. "Rhett..."

"I know it's fast. And I literally bought it knowing that you would likely say no. But I need to explain something to you, Skylar."

She felt like she needed to sit down but she was already sitting. "Okay."

His gaze shot to the side as he seemed to gather his words. "I love this town. I've always had a thing for small town charm. Everyone's been very welcoming of us and they never made me feel like an outcast of any sort—until the night of the gala."

"Why would they treat you like an outcast?"

His lips pressed into a thin line. "Because that's what I've always been." He took her hands, and she realized how much this confession cost him as his fingers tremored in her grip. "I didn't have a father growing up, and my mom saw me as more of a burden than a son."

Her heart suddenly felt bruised. "I had no idea."

A sad smile curved his mouth but quickly disappeared. "I didn't want anyone to know."

She never saw him so vulnerable and open. "We don't have to talk about your childhood if it upsets you. It's Christmas. We can just enjoy the holiday and discuss this stuff another time."

"I spent a week without you, and that was too long. I don't want to wait to tell you the truth about who I am."

"Okay."

He drew in a steady breath. "My mom died of a drug overdose when I was ten. She was never nice to me, but it devastated me. She was still my mother and all I knew. I cried for days, unsure what my life would become. Eventually, the state took custody of me, and I went into the system."

She hadn't known or suspected any of this. "You're so...*together* now. They must have put you with a good family."

The bleak look in his eyes told her she was wrong. "They put me with a dozen families, none of them kept in touch through the years."

"Oh, Rhett, I'm sorry. I had no idea."

"It's okay. I worked for a while, landed some good jobs and got my life together—actually saved some money. Then I met Addison's mom."

Her mind returned to the day she'd snooped in his bedroom and spied the ledger on his desk with all the medical expenses recorded. She prepared for a complication, certain the woman who gave birth to Addison was still alive.

"Adel is a good person with a troubled heart. She has a

lot of mental health issues, and like my mother, she's an addict."

Understanding dawned. "That's where you were this week."

He nodded. "I take care of her for Addison's sake, but also because I can afford to. My daughter is my whole world. She gives me a purpose, and I never want her to feel the emptiness I felt growing up. I know Adel will never be a normal mom, but it's important for me to make sure Addison never feels abandoned."

"Of course."

"She sends her cards on birthdays and holidays, and when Addy's old enough she'll realize who Adel is to her but, for now, we've agreed that distance is best."

"Does she fight you for custody?"

"Not when she's sober. And when she's not… No judge would even hear her out in that condition."

"And you've been dealing with this on your own, keeping it to yourself all these years?"

"My staff knows, because I occasionally have to leave town to deal with problems when Adel has a bad episode, like this week. But they understand my personal life isn't open for discussion."

She considered what Erin said about Skylar assuming she was the only woman in his life. "Are you and Adel still… Do you ever…?"

"Are we intimate? No." He looked her in the eye and the confidence she was used to finding in his stare returned. "Skylar, I've been with others, but it's never compared to what I experienced with you."

"Really?"

He pulled her hand to his lips and kissed her fingertips. "I know you don't have a lot to compare it to, but what we shared… It was life changing."

Her finger brushed over the satin box and his gaze

followed the motion. "This is a big deal, Rhett. Marriage is a lifetime commitment in my family."

"Remember how I told you I was greedy?"

She smirked. "Yes."

"Well, this week gave me a lot of time to think. I want you, Skylar. Not just as my daughter's nanny or as a lover in my bed, I want you in my life—every day. At first, I wasn't sure what this obsession was. I'd never felt anything like it before. The only thing close to comparing to the feelings I have for you is the devotion and affection I hold for Addy. I...love my daughter, but I'm duty bound to do right by her."

"Call it whatever you want, Rhett, but you're a good father because you're a good man. Duty has very little to do with how well you treat her."

"But it's how I managed to figure out fatherhood having never had a father of my own."

She could understand that.

"Skylar, I'm more than obsessed with you. I'm addicted to your presence. When you're around, I feel centered and balanced. I hang on your every word and find you one of the most captivating women I've ever met. And then I see the way you are with my daughter and my heart actually aches, physically hurts because it's never known such contentment. You make me feel full and right. And when you're not there...I feel empty. I don't want to spend another day without you."

She exhaled, utterly speechless. No one had ever said such sweet words to her. "I don't know what to say."

"You don't have to say anything. But please don't tell me no. At least think on it. I can wait as long as it takes. Wear the ring or don't. I've waited a lifetime to find you, I can wait another to make you fully mine. But I can't walk away from us."

Was it crazy that she was actually considering telling him yes? Like, without a doubt in her heart, fully invested, do a cartwheel in the front yard, plan the big wedding and go for the happily-ever-after storybook life in the cute little town with all of her crazy relatives buried deep in their business, yes?

"You do know I come with a hundred crazy Irish relatives and a bunch of Italian nut jobs. I mean, my grandfather's basically your nemesis."

He smiled. "Vincenzo and I have recently come to an understanding."

She frowned. "How?"

"Let's just say I lobbied for his vote and pulled a few strings."

She thought of what he could have possibly used for leverage. "The parking space?"

He laughed and quickly explained, "Your grandfather's a very intimidating man, and I'd already been beaten up once this week!"

"Well, it's good to know what I'm worth."

He nudged her with his shoulder and teased. "It's on Main Street."

She nestled close to him, stealing a bit of his body warmth. "Can I see the ring?"

His eyes turned serious and he studied her for a long moment. It was her last chance to think without partiality or foolish romantical whims influencing her decision.

Did she want to marry Rhett?

She loved him and didn't want to spend another day without him. No one had ever made her feel the things he made her feel. Could it really be this simple?

He lowered to one knee and popped open the lid, revealing a stunning princess cut diamond ring. Oh yeah, it was that simple.

"I love you, Skylar. I've never willingly entrusted my heart to another person the way I've entrusted it to you. Will you marry me?"

Her jaw unhinged. "I can't believe this."

Twenty minutes ago, she'd been worried for his life, and now he was asking her to tie her life to his. Forever.

"Is that a yes?"

It didn't matter that others wouldn't understand her haste. She'd never wanted another person as deeply as she wanted him. "Yes, it's a yes!"

She kissed him, nearly knocking him to the ground. He caught her weight in his strong arms and rose to his feet, hugging her tight.

He slipped the ring onto her trembling finger, and she admired it through the tears in her eyes. "It's so pretty."

"So are you, my future *wife*."

"Oh, my God, I'm going to be a wife—wife of the mayor! First wife! First lady? What's my title?"

He chuckled. "I believe it's mayoress."

"So, fancy!" And Addison! Addison would be her step-daughter! This was the best Christmas ever! "We have to celebrate!"

Eyes hungry, he tucked a hair behind her ear and softly kissed her neck. "We can celebrate tonight—when you come *home*."

Home. Their home.

She smiled at him, a thousand dark promises passing between their eyes. She cuddled closer, looping her arms around his neck and dragging her lips along the hard edge of his jaw. "I've missed sleeping in your bed."

He groaned then nipped her ear. "We won't be sleeping."

Her body softened. She didn't want to wait. She wanted the future to start right now. "Promise me something," she whispered, brushing her lips softly over his.

"Anything."

"When we're old, promise you'll cuddle on the couch with me, and we'll slow dance in the kitchen for no special reason except that you love me."

He smiled. "We don't have to wait for those things." He hugged her close and pressed a kiss to her temple. "I've waited a lifetime to find you. Let's not waste another minute waiting to show our love."

For a man who struggled to vocalize his feelings, he sure had no issue being romantic now that the gates were open. "I love you, Rhett."

Pure sincerity showed in his eyes. "I love you, too, Skylar. I'm not sure there's a limit to what I would do for you."

She laughed. "Good. Then you can break the news to my family."

EPILOGUE

One Day until Thanksgiving

"Don't forget your folders!"

The kids emptied their cubbies and buttoned their coats. "Miss Skylar, can you help me?"

Skylar crouched down to help Samuel fix his zipper then righted his turkey hat. Gran handled the other students.

"Michael, take your finger out of your nose before you hit brain. And Ciera, stop chewing on your hair. Lennon, hold Aiden's hand. Addison, are you coming with us or going home with your mother?"

"I wanna go with my cousins."

"Then let's go. Coats on." Like a small battalion, Gran's little pre-K soldiers fell into line.

Skylar smiled at the beautiful chaos.

After Christmas, her grandmother announced that she was retiring as the family's free childcare provider. Gran told the family that if they wanted her services, they could find her at the new pre-K class, where she would be assisting as a volunteer. That left their family desperate for coverage, and by January first, Skylar's roster was full.

Almost a year later, and things were going better than great. She was finishing her degree, happily married, and Rhett had won the recent election. It wouldn't be long before he was running for a larger office, like state representative.

Once the kids cleared out, the classroom was blissfully silent. Skylar wiped down the tables and straightened up the bins. By four o'clock, all the work stations were tidy and she was ready to go home.

She left the rec center and walked to Town Hall, smiling at the first signs of Christmas approaching. Holly wreaths and twinkle lights were already showing on some front doors, and storefront windows were switching over their holiday displays for the shopping rush that would begin that weekend.

The door to the hardware store opened and a woman rushed out, nearly colliding with Skylar on the walkway. "Oh, sorry—" Her words cut off as she recognized the familiar scowl. "Erin."

The woman glared at her as if she were a bug in her morning coffee. She didn't bother with a greeting, but scoffed. That huffy little breath said everything about her feelings toward Skylar.

Skylar pitied her.

She had said it a year ago as a nasty threat, but her premonition had come true. Looking at Erin now, noting the creases around her eyes and the brittle energy surrounding her so tightly it kept others at bay, Skylar sensed this woman's misery stemmed from something lonesome and broken inside.

Sympathy crowded Skylar's heart, pushing away any lingering resentment. "Happy Thanksgiving, Erin. I hope you have a nice weekend with family and friends."

A cold look stole over the other woman's eyes as if Skylar's well wishes somehow offended her.

Did she have family? Skylar didn't know. If things hadn't ended so badly, she might have welcomed the woman to their table, but Erin made that impossible.

When Rhett fired her, she'd screamed and lied, and accused Skylar of things that simply weren't true. Rhett refused to forgive such a betrayal from someone he'd trusted. But Skylar wasn't so severe.

Erin pushed past her and Skylar caught her arm. She didn't flinch when her glare cut through her. "Erin, I know we didn't have a great start, but if you ever need a friend, you know where to find me."

She yanked her arm away. "We're not friends."

"We could be."

Something trembled in her gaze, then any sign of vulnerability was shut away behind another glare. "I don't need your charity."

Skylar watched as she stormed off, wondering what could make a woman so cold. She believed there was a story there and she hoped, one day, Erin might find the right person to listen to her story and possibly heal some of the pain that made her that way.

Closing her coat against the November wind, she continued to walk toward Town Hall. The liaisons and office staff were used to her coming by at the end of each school day. If she didn't collect her husband, he'd lose track of time and wind up working late.

He was always thinking of new ways to improve their town, and he did his best to meet everyone's needs. Skylar made it her job to see that he met his own. She helped.

"Hey, Mrs. Buchanan," the new PA greeted with a friendly smile as she entered the office.

"Hi, Jason. How is he today?"

"Stressed, as usual, but I think he'll make it. By the way,

another gift basket came for you guys. Should I send it to the house?"

"Yes, thank you." She had no idea that so many people spoiled the mayor rotten, each one trying to influence his decision on one matter or another. She was amazed that he remained diplomatic in most of his decisions—except for that one incident with that unwarranted parking space.

She admired the gift basket, spotting one of her favorite gourmet jams and some expensive cheeses. No wonder he liked the job. "And Jason, please help yourself to anything inside."

She tapped on her husband's office door. "Knock-knock."

He was on a call and waved her inside. She quietly pressed a kiss to his lips.

"Sounds good, Kevin. Yeah, my wife just walked in. I'll be sure to call you after the holiday. Happy Thanksgiving."

She sat on the edge of his desk as he hung up the phone. "Kevin Connors?"

"Yep. He's still after that traffic light."

She rolled her eyes. "I don't know where you find the patience."

He shut off his computer and stood. Once he gathered his belongings, he paused for another kiss, cradling the little bump under her shirt with a gentle hand.

"How are you feeling today?"

"Okay. A little nauseous this morning, but I'll live."

"Addison go home with your grandmother?"

"Yes. My mom's picking her up when she gets Ciera. She said she'll drop her off after dinner tonight."

"Ah, so I get you to myself for the next two hours?"

"Sorry. My dad's at the house. He's installing one of those surveillance cameras out back."

He made a playful scowl. "He's doing that so he can keep an eye on us when he's not there."

It went unsaid that since her father finally finished his research and got the grant, he was visiting a lot more often. A little too much for newlyweds, Rhett frequently mumbled under his breath.

"Be glad he's accepted you."

"Is that what you call it, acceptance? All this time I've been calling it cock blocking."

"Well, he must not be doing that good of a job if you managed to get me pregnant."

"I'm a man on a mission." He nibbled at her neck until she yelped with laughter.

He shut off the lights and followed her out. By five o'clock, the office was closed. Some days were more hectic than others, and there were always unexpected events that popped up from time to time, but for the most part, their life was pretty predictable.

Rhett said he dreamed of their life when he was a little boy. And when he found her, he knew she was the one. He claimed falling for her was as simple as PB and J.

She had made him the one sandwich he'd envied for years and, from then on, she owned his heart.

At the time, she thought that was just about the nicest thing anyone could say to her, especially from a man who once struggled to tell others how he felt. But, now, he said sweet things like that to her every day. It would be impossible to pick a favorite. Every word out of his mouth made her fall more and more in love.

Rhett didn't struggle with expressing himself anymore. He claimed, for the first time in his life, he believed he found a true home, one where he would always be accepted and loved. And the house no longer felt cold or empty. Love radiated from every room.

They were currently renovating the bedroom between the master bedroom and Addy's room for a baby nursery. They hadn't settled on a theme, yet, but Skylar loved the rocking chair they bought from the antique shop in town, especially because it sat across from one of her Uncle Kelly's pieces, a portrait of Gran holding her youngest cousin.

Rhett said, he bought it because it was a drawing of true, unconditional love and it reminded him of her.

He never missed an opportunity to show her or Addy how much they meant to him, and they never missed the chance to do the same, which was exactly how it should be.

Their love was exactly the kind of love she'd always wanted—wild and riotous and free—the kind of love she needed.

THE END

BONUS MATERIAL

Keep reading for a bonus recipe for Gran's Irish Cream

❄

Don't miss the next book in the Jasper Falls Series, *MY FUNNY VALENTINE!*

Don't want to leave Jasper Falls?
Escape to some of the other books in the series:

Wake My Heart
The Best Man
Love Me Nots
Pining For You
My Funny Valentine

AND DON'T FORGET TO VISIT MCCULLOUGH MOUNTAIN!

Almost Priest

Book #1 is currently FREE!

Beautiful Distraction

Irish Rogue

British Professor

Broken Man

Controlled Chaos

Hard Fix

Intentional Risk

OTHER BOOKS BY LYDIA MICHAELS

www.LydiaMichaelsBooks.com

Follow Lydia Michaels on Instagram and Facebook!

Don't stop here!

Grab your free books and keep reading...

What to Read Next?

FREE Books

(Some offers may have expired)

Almost Priest | Calamity Rayne | Sacrifice of the Pawn | Blind | Forfeit | First Comes Love

Billionaire Romance

Falling In | Sacrifice of the Pawn | Calamity Rayne

Small Town Romance

Wake My Heart | The Best Man | Love Me Nots | Pining For You | Almost Priest

Emotional & Heartwarming Romance

La Vie en Rose | Simple Man | Wake My Heart | Sacrifice of the Pawn | Forfeit

Romantic Comedy

Calamity Rayne

Erotic Romance

Breaking Perfect | Protégé | Falling In | Sugar

Dark Psychological Romance

Hurt

First Books in Binge Worthy Trilogies and Series

Almost Priest | Falling In | Wake My Heart | Forfeit | Original Sin

Paranormal Vampire Romance

Original Sin

LGBTQ+ & Menage Romance

Broken Man (MM) | Breaking Perfect (MMF) | Forfeit (MMF) | Hurt (Non-Consensual) | Protege

Sexy Nerds

Blind | Untied

Teacher Student, Workplace, and Age-Gap Love Affairs...

British Professor | Pining For You | Breaking Perfect | Falling In | Sacrifice of the Pawn

Single Dads or Teen Moms

Simple Man | Pining For You | First Comes Love | Intentional Risk

Non-Fiction Books for Writers

Write 10K in a Day: Avoid Burnout

Other Titles by Lydia Michaels

Wake My Heart

The Best Man

Love Me Nots

Pining For You

Falling In: Surrender Trilogy 1

Breaking Out: Surrender Trilogy 2

Coming Home: Surrender Trilogy 3

FREE! - Sacrifice of the Pawn: Billionaire Romance

Queen of the Knight: Billionaire Romance

Original Sin

Dark Exodus

FREE! - Calamity Rayne: Gets a Life

Calamity Rayne: Back Again

La Vie en Rose

Breaking Perfect

FREE! - Blind

Untied

FREE! - Almost Priest

Beautiful Distraction

Irish Rogue

British Professor

Broken Man

Controlled Chaos

Hard Fix

Intentional Risk

Hurt

Sugar

Simple Man

Protégé

FREE! - Forfeit

Lost Together

Atonement

FREE! - First Comes Love

If I Fall

Something Borrowed

About the Author

Lydia Michaels is the award winning and bestselling author of over forty titles. She is the consecutive winner of the 2018 & 2019 *Author of the Year Award* from *Happenings Media,* as well as the recipient of the 2014 *Best Author Award* from the *Courier Times.* She has been featured in *USA Today, Romantic Times Magazine, Love & Lace*, and more. As the host and founder of the *East Coast Author Convention*, the *Behind the Keys Author Retreat*, and *Read Between the Wines*, she continues to celebrate her growing love for readers and romance novels around the world.

In 2021, Michaels released the groundbreaking, non-fiction series, ***Write 10K in a Day,*** to commemorate her career in the publishing industry. She looks forward to many more years of exploring both fiction and non-fiction writing, teaching about the craft, and learning from the others in the author community.

Lydia is happily married to her childhood sweetheart. Some of her favorite things include the scent of paperback books, listening to her husband play piano, escaping to her coastal home at the Jersey Shore, cheap wine, *Game of Thrones*, coffee, and kilts. She hopes to meet you soon at one of her many upcoming events.

You can follow Lydia at www.Facebook.com/LydiaMichaels or on Instagram @lydia_michaels_books

KEEP IN TOUCH!

Join Lydia's Reader Group,

READ BETWEEN THE WINES!

https://www.facebook.com/
groups/ReadBetweenTheWinesStreetTeam

GRAN'S IRISH CREAM

This recipe originally belonged to Joann, one of the many women who inspired the character of Maureen McCullough. It was later passed down to my mother, who greatly influenced Maureen's maternal side. In our family we call it Nonna's Irish Cream, *and I love that, through Gran, I am able to share the recipe with all of you!*

Christmas has always been a big deal in our family, and the women do an extraordinary job of filling the season with extra magic. While Christmas remains one of the most commercialized holidays, we still value gifts from the heart and quality time together above all else.

Every year, my mom makes several bottles of Irish Cream and we drink it throughout the holiday. I hope this recipes adds some sweetness to your table and warms your heart.

Season's Greetings to All!

Lydia Michaels

(Recipe on next page...)

INGREDIENTS

GRAN'S IRISH CREAM

1 pint light cream
1 can sweetened condensed milk
1 tablespoon chocolate syrup
1 tablespoon instant coffee powder
1cup Irish Whiskey
(Tullamore Dew if you're a McCullough,
Jameson if you're an O'Malley)

Mix in blender. Chill and serve.
Keep refrigerated.
Enjoy!

ABOUT THE AUTHOR

Lydia Michaels is the award winning and bestselling author of over forty titles. She is the consecutive winner of the 2018 & 2019 *Author of the Year Award* from *Happenings Media,* as well as the recipient of the 2014 *Best Author Award* from the *Courier Times*. She has been featured in *USA Today, Romantic Times Magazine*, *Love & Lace*, and more. As the host and founder of the *East Coast Author Convention*, the *Behind the Keys Author Retreat*, and *Read Between the Wines*, she continues to celebrate her growing love for readers and romance novels around the world.

In 2021, Michaels released the groundbreaking, non-fiction series, ***Write 10K in a Day,*** to commemorate her career in the publishing industry. She looks forward to many more years of exploring both fiction and non-fiction writing, teaching about the craft, and learning from the others in the author community.

Lydia is happily married to her childhood sweetheart. Some of her favorite things include the scent of paperback books, listening to her husband play piano, escaping to her coastal home at the Jersey Shore, cheap wine, *Game of Thrones*, coffee, and kilts. She hopes to meet you soon at one of her many upcoming events.

You can follow Lydia at www.Facebook.com/LydiaMichaels or on Instagram @lydia_michaels_books